TRY RIGHT

JILL BRASHEAR

Momentum Press

This book is dedicated to my ten-year-old self who practiced giving interviews in the bathtub because she thought she was going to be famous someday.

Contents

The Surfing Lesson

Honolulu, Hawaii
June 1962

Claudia

CLAUDIA WAS in the middle of a surfing lesson with a man who looked like a Hawaiian god when the weather ruined her day. One minute, the sky was as placid as a lake. The next it ripped open like the seam on a too-tight pair of pants.

It didn't just rain. It poured.

The rain fell in sheets. It fell sideways. She'd been clinging to the surfboard, praying she wouldn't make a fool of herself in front of her surf instructor—who was a dish if she'd ever seen one—then suddenly she was fearing for her life.

Hawaiian rain was unlike anything she'd ever seen. Claudia remembered she was floating on top of a thin strip of wood in the middle of the ocean and panic seized her.

She gripped the board tighter, her fingers slipping. When she tried to take a calming breath to ease her fear like she'd learned in drama class, a wave sloshed forward and filled her mouth with seawater.

She choked and sputtered, squinting through the rain toward shore. The beach had been crowded with tourists when she and her cousin had ventured out of their hotel in search of something fun to do. When they'd seen the two Hawaiian surfers offering lessons, they'd made a beeline for them.

After nearly an hour of waiting, it had finally been their turn for a lesson. Mary had shimmied right up to the big guy with impressive muscles, leaving Claudia with the instructor who closely resembled a Hawaiian warrior.

She couldn't see a thing through the heavy rain. Was there anyone still on the beach? What had happened to Mary?

Fear paralyzed Claudia. She knew she had a tendency to be dramatic, but she had a terrible feeling that she was going to die in these foreign waters.

She blamed her cousin Mary for talking her into coming to Hawaii for their graduation trip. Claudia's vote had been Paris, where she'd hoped to get a glimpse of her idol, Brigitte Bardot. But Mary had shown her a postcard of Waikiki Beach, and Claudia changed her mind. She'd never seen sands so sparkling or water so clear. Paris could wait.

Or so she'd thought.

Now, she realized she was going to die without ever setting foot on the most famous shopping streets in the world. She was going to die without the world knowing her name.

Something heavy slammed into Claudia's back. She flopped facedown on the hard surfboard, her chest flattened to the slick surface.

"Hang on!"

It was *him.* The warrior surf instructor. How he'd swum so far so quickly was incomprehensible to Claudia. He'd been standing on the shore shading his eyes to look at her a moment before the sky split open, and now he was on top of her, his big body protecting her from the rain.

He was crushing her, but his weight was a comfort that eased her mind. She wasn't going to die.

Claudia swore right then and there under the shield of her instructor's broad back that when she got home, she was going straight to Minneapolis to catch the first bus to Hollywood.

She was done with pushing aside her dreams of becoming an international movie star. Destiny was calling Claudia's name, spelling it out in neon lights.

"Almost there." His mouth was near her ear, his voice filling her with a sense of calm while his body shielded her from the rain.

He couldn't be much older than her, but he was hardly a boy. The command in his voice told her he'd done this before.

The fear gripping her body notched down to a tolerable level as Claudia realized she was in the capable hands of a hero. He was big and warm, and she could breathe under the protection of his body.

A tingle of awareness shot down her spine. Being rescued by her very attractive surfing instructor was the most exciting thing that had ever happened to Claudia. The wet slide of his skin against hers awakened a shiver deep inside her. Anticipation eclipsed her fear as his arm brushed the side of her breast. Each stroke brought them closer to the safety of the shore, but Claudia did not want this ride to end.

His heart thudded with his efforts, stirring a primal desire Claudia had never felt before.

She turned her face to breathe him in. He smelled strongly of the ocean, salt and sea and waterman. So different from the boys back home who smelled like sweat, smoke, and feet.

He tilted his chin downward and their eyes met and locked. "You awright?"

She felt a little dizzy, but it had more to do with his hips pinning hers to the surfboard than her near-death experience.

"I'm okay."

They reached shore too soon. Claudia's instructor hopped

off the board, then reached for her. He plucked Claudia off her feet and tucked her under one arm; the board went under his other arm. The thick rain made it impossible to see, but he seemed to know where he was going. The sand under her feet gave way to earth as they ducked under the cover of a grove of palms. A dozen others had had the same idea, and they huddled together under the thin shelter of the leaves as rain streamed from the sky.

Relief flooded Claudia when she spotted her cousin Mary and the other surf instructor who looked like he'd been hewn from a bronze mountain. She waved at Mary, sending her a silent thank-you for choosing the beefcake surfer. Mary lifted her arm and waved back, beaming. The girls had gotten more of an adventure than they'd bargained for, but Claudia wasn't complaining.

Her surf instructor leaned his board against a tree trunk and gazed out at the pouring rain.

"It stay clear in one second, yeah?" Rain plastered his dark hair to his forehead and dripped down his cheeks. "My grandma would say this is a sign or some shit li'dat."

"What?" Claudia squinted up at him, trying to decode what he said. Her Mid-west twang seemed clumsy compared to the music of his words.

He glanced sideways and down at her. "We can resume the lesson in just one minute," he said enunciating in overly perfect English. "The rain won't last long."

"Oh." A blush crept over her cheeks as she shifted closer to him to make room for a few others dashing out of the rain.

"I'm sorry I'm so horrible at surfing."

"Nah." He waved his hand at her, blessing her with a rare small smile. "You'll get the hang of it."

So far, he'd been stingy with his smiles, probably because Claudia was indeed horrible at surfing. She'd been hoping to impress him before the rain had sprung up out of nowhere, but she had the feeling he didn't impress easily.

She got the feeling he didn't enjoy giving lessons. Unlike his buddy, who'd been full of white-toothed smiles for Mary, Claudia's instructor had been all business. He hadn't even allowed her to touch his board for the first twenty minutes of the lesson. He'd insisted she lay flat on the sand and learn to paddle first. It had been humiliating. She'd felt like a sea turtle, flapping useless legs in the sand.

When he'd finally given her permission to wade into the water with his board, she'd flipped it over while trying to get on. He'd spared her a glance filled with barely concealed contempt and told her not to try so hard.

"You can not control everything, yeah?" he'd said cryptically.

That prophecy had fulfilled itself when the rain came. Claudia studied the surfer's stoic profile as he watched the ocean.

"Do you enjoy giving lessons?"

His mouth twisted, and he gave a terse shake of his head.

"Then why do it?"

"I make more in one surf lesson than I do in an entire day at the marina."

"Your friend seems to like it." Claudia nodded at the gigantic man and Mary.

"Yeah," he agreed, glancing at the duo who were sharing a laugh a dozen yards away.

It was the friendliest her instructor had been since they'd started the surf session. She shuffled closer. Pushed her luck. "I bet you're a better surfer than him."

He shrugged slightly. "Nah."

"Don't be humble." She shifted another inch closer when someone bumped her from behind. "I can tell by the way you took your time teaching me to paddle that you know what you're doing."

His shoulders lifted an inch, then dropped. His gaze flicked to her. "He ain't so bad."

"But you're better."

"Surfing is in our blood." His smile flashed. "Where you stay at?" he asked.

He wanted to know where she was staying? The tingle racing through her became a full-fledged roar. "I'm at a place called The SurfRider."

His brown eyes narrowed, and he gave her a glare similar to the one he'd flashed earlier when she couldn't stay afloat on the surfboard.

"I meant where are you from? On the mainland? Eh?" His tone was clipped. Definitely annoyed.

Her skin heated. "Minnesota."

He made a noise in his throat that sounded like disapproval.

"You ever been there?"

He shook his head. "Nah."

"It's a drag." She looked out at the beach, which was barely visible in the downpour. "It's much nicer here, even with the rain."

"It never rains at Waikiki," he said.

Claudia laughed at the perplexed expression on his gorgeous face. "It can't be perfect all the time. Not even in Hawaii."

He cocked his head at her, giving her his full attention. Her knees weakened, and she felt like she'd been stealing sips from her dad's stash of liquor.

"Lucky we live in Hawaii," he said.

"I'm not so lucky, but I'll take a week."

He laughed, and the low rumble zigzagged straight to her heart. His friendliness made her bold. His energy invaded her senses.

"Since you hate giving lessons, and I'm hopeless at surfing, let's forget about it." She pressed closer. "Why don't we do something else?" He crossed his arms over his chest, his muscles bulging. "Like what?"

"Anything." She let her voice go breathless, very Marilyn Monroe. "Everything."

His eyes flicked toward her mouth, and Claudia felt the tug of attraction stretch taut between them like an elastic band about to snap. She licked her lips and his eyes flashed up to hers and held. Tension crackled in the air between them.

Desire spread through her belly and licked lower. Her heart hammered, and her knees turned to jelly. None of the boys back home had made her feel this aware of her body.

His very nearness made her nipples harden to tight pebbles.

Claudia shifted closer, brushing her breast against his bicep. A spark ignited in his dark eyes.

"I have a week," she said. "Show me everything."

A loud cheer went up from the grove of palm trees, and Claudia realized the rain had stopped as suddenly as it had started. Everyone ran back to the beach. Except them. They didn't move.

"What's your name again?" His eyes were back on hers. Warm velvet brown.

"Claudia." She wet her dry lips with the tip of her tongue. "And yours?"

"Keoni." His eyes drifted down her body, scalding hot. "I don't like tourists."

"Ain't that a bite." Her voice was husky. She gathered her courage and reached up to brush a hank of wet hair from his forehead. "Because I really like you."

Keoni caught her wrist, sending a throb of anticipation from the pads of his fingers straight to her core.

Claudia swallowed roughly and channeled Marilyn, Brigitte, and Jayne. She stretched up on her toes and pressed a kiss to Keoni's mouth. He froze. His mouth was firm against hers, resistant. His muscles tense and tight.

She moved her lips across his, tasting him, breathing him in. It was like kissing a statue. She'd never been so bold in her life, and his rejection cut deeply.

Disappointment swept through her as she ended the kiss.

She settled back on her heels just as his hand curved around her arm and he yanked her behind a big tree.

"You're trouble," he said.

He pinned her against the tree, and his mouth crashed down on hers. Sparks exploded inside her as he took her mouth with a passion she'd never dreamed existed. Bold and confident, his kiss erased all memories of the fumbling exchanges she'd had back home. He kissed like a man; the others had been nothing but boys.

Keoni was the one who was trouble.

The very best kind.

Home-wrecker

Los Angeles, California
January 1968

Claudia

"I HAVE some good news and some bad news. Which one do you want first?"

Claudia didn't like the sound of that. Her agent's definition of good was sometimes questionable, like the time he'd booked a commercial for Camel Shoe Emporium, which featured Claudia riding an actual camel. And there'd been the embarrassing audition for *Bye Bye Birdie*, when he knew full well Claudia couldn't sing. Despite these missteps, Ari Goldberg had been responsible for securing Claudia's lead role in *Jezebel*, the 1966 hit that had launched her career.

If there was any man she could trust in the industry, it was Ari.

"Hit me with the bad news first," Claudia said, cradling the phone against her ear and shoulder as she lit a cigarette.

There was a pause and then Ari asked, "Are you sitting down?"

Claudia stretched the phone cord across the kitchen counter, her heart officially in her throat as she perched on a barstool. "I am now."

"It looks like Rick is going to get the nomination."

Her heart dropped from her throat to her stomach, and she felt like she was going to throw up. She gripped the counter to stop the dizzy spell, glad Ari had told her to sit down before spilling that nugget of nastiness.

"Of course he did," she said, taking a long drag off her Kool.

Claudia Montgomery's name was well known for two things: her role as Sissy Saxon in *Jezebel*, and her scandal with California's golden boy politician, Richard Dunlap. Claudia's relationship with the charming, handsome, and very married assistant district attorney had been the biggest mistake of her life.

While she was paying the price by being blacklisted from every decent role in Hollywood, Rick had somehow come off as even more desirable. Now it looked like he was going to be California's democratic candidate for senate.

It didn't seem fair that their brief affair had tanked her star and inflated his. Rick was a mischievous rogue, and she was a home-wrecker.

"The good news better not be another shoe commercial," she warned. Her heart couldn't take that kind of good news.

Ari chuckled. "Nothing involving live animals, well… possibly a horse."

"Ari!"

"Probably not a horse."

"Ari."

"Have you heard of *A Long Road Home?* It's the one with the private detective who gets sent back in time a hundred years to the Wild West."

Claudia sighed heavily. "I don't know that one, but it sounds fascinating."

"I'm glad you think so," Ari said.

"That was sarcasm, Ari." Claudia blew out a stream of smoke. "It sounds horrid."

"It's top notch, I assure you. Stan Beatty plays the lead, and Benji Donahue is the director."

That did sound promising. Stan Beatty was all the rage, and Benji was a respected director. "What's the part?" she asked, as if she had a choice in turning it down. This was the first role that had come her way since the scandal with Rick broke nearly six months ago. She'd been scraping by on voice-overs. She was desperate.

"It's a generous offer. All expenses paid, your own two-roomer, and Megan as your assistant."

"What's the role?" Claudia asked, her teeth gnashing together.

"Wait until you see the costumes! They are gorgeous recreations from the eighteen sixties."

Claudia pictured corsets and bustles and cringed. "The role? What's my role?"

"And I didn't tell you the best part of all!" Ari steamrolled on, ignoring Claudia's question. "It's shot on location in Hawaii."

A tingle raced down Claudia's spine. The role wasn't important anymore. For the moment, she didn't even care about her slimeball ex-lover, or the potential career-ending role in a dead-end series with a crazy plotline that she'd never heard of.

Ari continued to talk, but Claudia stopped listening.

Hawaii was a magical place. She'd gone on a trip after high school, and it was the last time she'd been truly happy, truly free. She'd fallen in love with the island of O'ahu and a man who lived there. Claudia always dreamed of going back, of finding the joy she'd experienced there and reconnecting with the man who'd shown her how to love.

She tuned Ari out and started a list in her mind of all the things she wanted to do in Hawaii.

Resurrect pre-Rick Claudia.

Try something new.

Do something wild.

Find joy.

Reunite with Keoni Makai.

FIVE DAYS LATER, at a hotel on Waikiki Beach, Claudia wished she'd have paid a little closer attention to Ari's instructions. Megan zipped up the gown Ari had arranged for her to wear to her first appearance while Claudia skimmed over her lines for her first rehearsal. She was playing the role of Melanie, a time-hopping witch whose unreliable magic had landed her in sticky situations. The actress who'd originally booked the role had taken another offer at the last minute, and Claudia suspected it had something to do with the poorly written script, or maybe the costumes.

Claudia handed Megan the script and bent over to adjust her breasts in the low-cut bodice of the gown. Once they were properly fluffed, she stood upright and grabbed her tube of lipstick. "Who's my date tonight?" she asked, applying a coat of Paint the Town Pink to her lips.

Megan's cheeks turned pink, and she fanned herself. "Declan Bishop," she said in a breathless voice. "What a fox."

"Declan Bishop," Claudia said, her nose wrinkling. This would be her second appearance with the champion surfer. Their agents were friends and thought the couple looked good together. Tall, tan, and blonde, Declan was the perfect Ken to Claudia's Barbie. It was too bad Declan was a stick in the mud. He didn't drink, didn't dance, didn't even smile unless it was for the cameras. "It's going to be a long night," Claudia said.

"Some of us are meeting up at a bar later. You should meet us."

"You already made friends? I'm not even over my jet lag yet."

Megan laughed. "I told you I knew some of the cigarette girls working for sponsors. A few of them are my old roomies. They're here for the contest."

Claudia really should have listened better to Ari, but all she'd been able to focus on was finding Keoni. "That little surfing contest, right?"

Megan's mouth dropped open. "Claudia, get with the program. It's the biggest surfing contest in the history of surfing contests. All three networks are showing it live. And Declan Bishop, the favorite to win, is your date tonight." Megan's tone started out annoyed but ended envious. "You're supposed to be surprising him tonight. You have to greet him with a kiss. Sounds like a fun evening, Janice." Megan winked.

Janice Steele was the name Ari always used to book her rooms. Claudia didn't think it fooled anyone. Most of America knew who she was, either from her hit movie or her scandal with Rick.

"What's this about a kiss?" Claudia had definitely missed that message.

"Ari said you were okay with it. Are you not okay with it?"

Claudia rolled her eyes. She didn't care if she had to kiss Declan Bishop or any other man. She was an actress. A kiss didn't bother her. "Of course I'm okay with it. I just forgot. I've had my mind on other stuff." Important stuff like how to find Keoni when he wasn't listed in the phone book.

"Oh, right?" Megan's smile faltered. "That was a bummer about Richard Dunlap."

"Yeah." Claudia had forgotten all about Rick since hearing about Hawaii. "It was pretty heavy."

"Don't worry, I'd never vote for a pig like him. No modern woman would."

"He's charming. People vote for charming."

"Not me, and not any of my friends." Megan lifted her chin

and squared her shoulders. Her chin-length bob brushed her jaw, and the gleam in her eyes said she was ready to take on every two-timing charmer in the world.

Claudia laughed. "Maybe you should run for office," she said.

Megan's grin beamed as if she'd swallowed a lightbulb. "Maybe I will."

Claudia left her room and headed downstairs toward the lobby. The likelihood of Megan winning a seat in the senate was about the same as Claudia's chances of having fun tonight at another boring banquet: not very likely at all.

The First Fight

Henry

HENRY LONGCHAMP WAS A SUCKER.

His life would be a lot easier if he learned how to say no. He was too good-natured, too go-with-the-flow, too good-time Charley. Not that he was too soft. Nope. Henry Longchamp was as rough and tumble as they came. He jumped out of helicopters and crashed cars for a living, but on the inside, he was a marshmallow. And he couldn't say no to a woman. Ever.

"Hey, Champ?" Debi raised her voice over the loud buzz of conversation. "Can you be a sweetie and grab another keg for the beer bar?"

"Already?" He'd just delivered one a few minutes ago, and his lower back still ached.

"Already. These surfers drink hard."

"They brag harder," Henry said. "I surfed a wave *this* big." He raised his hand over his head and said in his best Australian twang, "Oy suhfed a wave thiies big."

Debi giggled. "The waves get bigger with every beer."

Debi was the reason Henry was hefting kegs of beer from

the hotel kitchen to the banquet hall after a long day at work. Well, technically the favor was for Margie, Debi's mother and the makeup artist at the studio. Margie was sweet. She treated everyone on set as if they were her kids, even Henry, who was only about five years younger than her.

All Margie had to do was mention to Henry that Debi needed help getting her new business started, and he volunteered to lend his big strong muscles. His muscles, already sore and tired from a long day of training with the horses, weren't happy with him at the moment, but it was worth the pain and suffering to help Debi.

She was a chip off Margie's block, a cute girl with straight black hair that hung all the way to her tight little way-too-young-for-him butt. Debi wasn't more than nineteen, ten years younger than him. Just a baby. Henry could appreciate the view, even if he wasn't interested in climbing the mountain. And Debi's idea to get a few of her friends together to form a union of "Cigarette Girls" for hire at parties was brilliant.

The SurfRider was booked five days a week for parties that could use a service just like hers. The girl was onto a gold mine, and who was Henry not to volunteer when Debi's usual muscle was laid up with a broken leg? Anything to help a young female entrepreneur. He was all for women's lib. No bra? No problem. And all that equal rights jazz too.

At least the party wasn't boring. Not like that last one he'd helped out with. Those stuffy politicians who tried to impress each other with their high morals were a snore.

This party was at least entertaining. The drunken surfers were fun to watch, and the women were out of sight. There was a women's exhibition show featuring the best female surfers in the world, and every one of them was a looker. Unlike most of their male counterparts, the female surfers were not drunk. They were more interested in sizing each other up than getting wasted. Competitive glares shot across the room with deadly accuracy. Henry watched from behind the bar, keeping an eye on all Debi's girls, making sure none of them were getting harassed or caught in an unpleasant situation.

"Who do you bet on for the first fight?"

It was a game Henry played with Debi and her coworkers. At these parties, people were bound to throw punches. It was fun to guess who'd be the first.

Henry swept his gaze around the hall, eyeing the drunken crowd. Most of them hadn't ever surfed a wave like what they were going to see at the contest in the morning. Forty-eight of the best male and female surfers in the world were packed into one room. It was a tight fit for all the swollen egos, and only a matter of time before someone started swinging.

Henry spotted a few men he knew. Bobby Carter was a long-time resident of Hawaii from California. He was one of the favorites to win because he knew the waves. Then there was Declan Bishop, a native Hawaiian who Henry knew from the days when he'd been fresh off the boat from the mainland. Back then, Declan had been out of control, the wildest one in a wild crowd. The last time Henry had seen Declan was the night he ended up wrapping his Corvette around a light pole out at Hale'iwa.

Henry had heard Declan put his life back together since then. He'd gone to some hippie commune out in Malibu and gotten straight. Declan looked outwardly calm, but Henry could tell by the set of his shoulders that he was on edge. Having a target on your back could do that to a man.

He took a five-dollar bill out of his wallet. "My money's on Declan Bishop," he said. He stuffed the five into the glass Debi held out for him. There were already several bills in there, and Henry liked his chances.

Amy added her money to the glass. "I'm betting on one cat fight," she said, nodding at a group of women near the stage. "These women hate each other. And they aren't afraid to scratch. I'm taking those two by the stage." She pointed at two female surfers who currently had their arms around each other's shoulders.

Henry chuckled. "I wouldn't mind seeing that."

"My money's on her," Debi said, indicating a gorgeous blonde bombshell in a tight dress.

She looked familiar, but gorgeous blondes were a dime a dozen in Hawaii. She was tall, with a body. Plenty of boobs. Lots of hips. And that face? Out of this world. Dark eyes, button nose, lush mouth. She was the prettiest thing he'd ever seen.

Debi jabbed him in the stomach. "You're lettin' flies in, Champ."

He closed his mouth but couldn't tear his eyes away. There wasn't a man in the room who wasn't staring at her, but she was headed straight for Declan Bishop, the lucky asshole. She sauntered toward Declan and threw herself right into his arms. The kiss she laid on Declan made Henry's heart race in his chest like a car speeding toward a crash. Cameras flashed as Declan's arms came around her waist.

Henry blinked against the bright lights, and by the time he cleared his vision, all hell had broken loose. Declan pushed the woman away—was he out of his mind?—marched toward a man in a fancy suit and decked him.

More cameras flashed, and Henry lost sight of the gorgeous blonde. She seemed to have disappeared into the crowd, which should have been impossible for a girl who looked like her.

He spent the rest of the night looking for her with no luck. When the speeches were finally over and all the drunken surfers had been escorted back to their rooms at The Royal Hawaiian Hotel, Henry was still thinking about the mysterious blonde.

Debi gave him the money from the bet jar plus a fat joint of the good *Hawaiian kine* bud for payment. Henry stuck the joint in his pocket and kissed Debi on the check.

"Tell my mom hi when you see her," Debi said. "And thanks! You're one in a million."

Henry arched his sore back. He'd tweaked something sliding under that car today on the shoot. Damn getting old.

Even though he was beat, Henry didn't want to go home tonight. His cousin and her friend were crashing at his place, and they'd taken over his tiny house. Their stuff was everywhere, and Henry wasn't looking forward to another night on his lumpy sofa. Two more days and the girls would be gone, taking all their shit with them. Why women needed so much stuff was beyond his understanding.

Henry had five sisters, and he wouldn't dare to claim he understood women. His sisters hadn't let him be since he'd moved to Hawaii. One of them was always visiting, claiming she missed her brother when what she really wanted was a free place to stay on vacation. Between the Longchamp siblings and his multitude of female cousins, it seemed there was always a woman occupying his bed. Meanwhile, Henry got the lumpy sofa.

It was a second-hand thing with threadbare upholstery. He should really think about getting a new one. Or maybe he should get a woman in his bed who wasn't on his family tree.

He blamed work for his lackluster social life. He barely got a day off, and when he did, he was too tired to enjoy it.

Yeah, getting old was a real bummer.

4

Pretty Harmless

Henry

THE SURFRIDER WASN'T JUST the oldest and most prestigious hotel on the beach; it had an excellent bar and the best bartender.

Dave made a martini so cold and crisp, Henry could imagine ice-skating on the surface.

When Henry got to the bar, he was surprised to see it was deserted. The radio was still on; the lights blazed, and the door was unlocked, but no one was there.

"Hello?" he called. "Anyone around?"

Dave poked his head out from the kitchen. "Hey, Champ! We're closing up early tonight for the contest tomorrow. I'm just finishing up back here."

"That's all right," Henry said, leaning against the bar. "Got time for one last round?"

Dave waved at him and ducked back into the kitchen. "Help yourself. It's on the house, buddy."

Henry stepped behind the bar and grabbed the vodka. He was in the mood for an ice-cold martini. His mixing skills weren't quite up to Dave's gold standard, so he added a little extra vodka to compensate for what it lacked in flavor. He was giving the tumbler a good shake when the woman of his dreams walked in.

She'd changed out of her gown and heels, but she was no less sexy in a sky-blue dress that showed off her legs. He'd thought her tits were her best feature, but that was because he hadn't yet seen her legs. He dragged his gaze up her long, tanned stems and eventually landed on her face.

The tumbler almost slipped from his hand as he lost control of his fine motor skills.

She'd scrubbed her face free of makeup, and she was even prettier without it than she'd been all dolled up. Henry's heart stuttered and then leaped into his throat, preventing any words from coming out of his mouth.

"Is it too late to get a drink around here?" she asked, leaning her elbows on the bar.

Henry forced himself to move, to act naturally. His heart was beating so fast and hard and was trapped so high in his throat that his voice came out in an unnatural squeak. "What's your poison?"

She slid onto the stool and plucked a cigarette from a silver case. "Don Julio shaken not stirred, with a lemon not a lime."

Henry's instincts kicked in, and he reached for a book of matches before she could grab them. He struck a light and offered it to her, cupping his hand over hers as she leaned forward.

"Brown Eyed Girl" came on over the radio, and their eyes met over the cigarette. Hers were big and brown, like drops of melted chocolate against her creamy skin. Even though the song had been saturating the airwaves for months, Henry couldn't help but think it was a sign. Here he was alone with the prettiest brown-eyed girl in the world. Just the two of them in one of the most popular bars on the strip. Luck was on his side tonight.

He grinned and shook out the match, then put on a little

show as he fixed her drink. He filled the tumbler with ice and a generous shot of tequila, capped it and shook it dramatically. He even flipped it a few times, like he'd seen Dave do. Luck was still on his side as he caught the tumbler and poured the contents into a glass with a flourish. His luck ran out when he realized there were no lemons. Dave must have put them up already.

"No lemons, sorry."

She frowned a little, her bottom lip forming the perfect pout. "It's all right. Put it on my room. Janice Steele."

"I'd be glad to, Janice." He grabbed his own drink and walked around the bar. "But the thing is, I don't actually work here." He grinned and tapped his glass to hers.

Her eyebrows rose. "You don't?"

"Nope, and I think we should probably get out of here before we get busted for stealing." He started toward the door and gestured for her to follow him.

"But—"

Henry tugged her off her barstool. "Come on, I don't want to get arrested."

She grabbed her purse and fell into step beside him. "I think you're stretching it a bit," she said. "We won't get arrested over a drink. Besides, I'm a hotel guest."

"I don't want to find out. Pretty boys like me don't do well in the slammer." He made a silly face, crossing his eyes as he looked at her.

She rewarded him with a warm laugh as they stepped outside into the balmy night. The beach was quiet so close to midnight. The only sound was her melodic laugh and the crash of the waves.

"I'm Henry," he said, offering his hand.

"Hello, Henry," she said. "Thanks for the stolen drink." She rolled her eyes and took a long drag off her cigarette, then exhaled a cloud of minty-smelling smoke. "It's been quite a night so far."

He couldn't get enough of looking at her. "You look familiar."

"I get that a lot." She raised her glass and drank.

Henry thought maybe she did. Men probably said whatever they could think of to talk to her. He was feeling a bit of that now. He wanted desperately to keep her talking, keep her standing next to him. He'd propelled her outside on a whim, but he liked that she'd been up for an adventure and followed him.

"Were you at the surfing banquet earlier?" he asked.

She eyed him curiously. "I was. Were you?"

"Yeah. That was quite a scene you caused."

She shrugged. "Can you keep a secret?"

His heart raced at the gleam in her eyes. "Sure," he said.

"It was all a setup, staged for the cameras."

"Thanks," Henry said, sipping his drink.

"What?"

"You won me a lot of money tonight."

She narrowed her eyes at him. "How's that?"

"I bet on who would be the first to start a fight. You made me win."

She flicked her cigarette ashes into the air. "Seems a stupid thing to bet on."

He shrugged. "It passed the time." He kicked off his shoes and stepped into the soft sand. "Want to walk a bit with our stolen drinks?"

She paused, considering. Henry forced himself to keep calm while she deliberated, looking down at her shoes.

"These cost a hundred dollars," she said finally, pointing at her sandals.

Henry couldn't keep his smile at bay. She was worried about her shoes, not him. He took it as another sign. "That's a lot of money, but I promise, they won't get stolen. If they disappear, I'll buy you a new pair with the winnings you got me."

"Big spender," Janice teased, crushing her cigarette before reaching for the buckle on her flowered sandals.

"This way, if you please." Henry attempted an upper-crust English accent, but it fell short. Janice laughed anyway, and Henry's chest swelled. "You going to the contest tomorrow?" he asked. "To watch your boyfriend, Declan?"

She grimaced. "I told you that was all a setup. I had to chase Declan down and apologize after I left. Apparently his agent didn't tell him the plan, and that kiss almost ruined things with his actual girlfriend."

Henry's brows came together. "His agent the one he punched out?"

"Sure was." They walked closer to the shore, and she dragged her toe through the water. "I won't be at the contest tomorrow," she said. "I'm probably the only one on the island who isn't going."

She sounded more disappointed than she should be for missing a contest. "You must really love surfing," he said.

She shook her head. "Not really. I'm meeting someone and he's supposed to be there tomorrow."

A flare of jealousy sparked to life in Henry's chest. The man she was meeting was one lucky son of a bitch. "You're not the only one missing it. I'm not going either. I've got to work."

"What kind of work do you do?"

"This and that," he said. He didn't like to tell people he just met that he worked in television. They incorrectly assumed he must be famous. And if they found out he worked on *A Long Road Home*, they wanted an introduction to Stan Beatty, the star of the show.

"What kind of this and that?" she asked.

"I work with heavy equipment. Help out with the animals. Fix things that no one else wants to mess with." Henry listed the mundane tasks of his job, intentionally leaving out the more exciting parts.

"You work on a farm?" Janice asked, wading ankle-deep into the water. "My uncle has an apple farm in Minnesota."

Henry took a long look at her. "I didn't take you for a farm girl."

Her gaze drifted down the beach. "It was a long time ago."

Henry remembered the joint in his pocket, courtesy of Debi. He pulled it out and waved it in the air. "You smoke?"

She eyed the joint, deliberating. "Sometimes."

"You want to smoke this with me? Otherwise I'll have to get very stoned by myself." He made a serious face. "They wen grow da pakololo strong out here, yeah?"

Janice burst out laughing. "That was the worst impression of a Hawaiian accent I've ever heard."

"You laughed." He took the pack of matches from his pocket and fired up the joint.

"I didn't say I'd smoke that with you."

"You don't have to. But just keep an eye on me, will you? I don't smoke much grass. I might do something stupid."

She grabbed the joint from him and took a long drag. Coughing a little, she passed it back to him. "I can't miss out on Hawaiian grass. It's on my list of things I want to do out here."

"What else is on the list? All the tourist shit?" He covered a cough as he passed her the joint. "I mean stuff. Tourist stuff."

She laughed again, and the sound was like music to his ears. "Some of it is tourist shit. Some of it, not so much," she said mysteriously.

They reached the section of the beach where the strip of hotels ended, then walked a little farther until the beach ended abruptly at a rocky ledge.

"Just around those rocks is a great secret beach. There's an old cave they say is haunted by selkies, and a natural tidal pool that is as calm as a warm bath."

She giggled. "I thought selkies were Irish."

Henry leveled her with a mock-serious stare. "I'm not making this shit up. It's real Hawaii stuff. I've been here four years, I'm a local now."

"Bull," she said, peeking around the corner of the huge rock.

"We can check it out," he said. "Maybe we can sneak up on one of them."

She peeked around the ledge again, curiosity naked on her face. "Maybe we can."

Henry held back a smile. Janice was cool. In his experience, the prettier the face, the greater the bitch. But not in Janice's case. She was fun and beautiful.

Henry put their glasses on top of the rock. "We'll grab these on the way back," he said. "Grab my hand. I'll show you where to put your feet. It isn't hard."

It was low tide, and Henry knew just where to step on the rocks to get around the side of the ledge. They ended up on a secluded stretch of sand just big enough to stretch out on. The sparkling sands of Waikiki Beach unfolded to their left, and the yachts moored at the marina bobbed to their right. Sure enough, the cave at their back yawned open in the darkness.

"Shh," Henry said when Janice giggled. "They'll hear us." He cupped his hand to his ear and crept closer to the mouth of the cave.

Janice followed closely behind and bumped into him when he stopped suddenly. She suppressed another giggle. Henry shook his head and took a book of matches from his front pocket. He lit one and peered into the dark cave.

"See anything?" She pressed close to his back, her hand still tucked in his.

Henry let the match burn down to his fingers. "Nothing," he said. "Looks like the selkies are out for the evening."

Janice made a sound of disappointment. They walked back to the little beach where the water was calm between the natural barriers of the rocks.

"Hmm," Janice said, transferring her gaze from the tidal pool to Henry. The twinkle in her eye made Henry's blood heat.

"What?"

"You know that list I was mentioning?" she asked.

"Sure."

She could hardly contain the sparkle in her eyes. "Don't take this the wrong way, but you seem pretty harmless."

His eyebrows pulled together. "I am."

"You don't seem like the kind of guy who'd get the wrong idea if a girl proposed skinny-dipping."

Henry's eyes went wide. His heart skipped a beat. "What?"

"Forget it," she said. "I'm stoned." Her laugh danced on the air. "This is the perfect spot though. Don't tell me you've never done it."

Henry swallowed roughly. "I've done it. But never with a girl I just met ten minutes ago." And never one who looked like Janice.

She shrugged. "It's been more like half an hour at this point."

"You're stoned."

"I am." She reached for his shirt and tugged it up over his ribs.

Her eyes sparked with appreciation as she glanced at his flat stomach. Henry had never been so thankful for his strict fitness routine. His job as a stuntman was physically demanding. He ran or hit the weight bench six days a week, and his reward was washboard abs and thickly muscled torso.

"Come on." She teased his shirt a little higher, shamelessly checking him out. "I dare you."

Henry's brow arched. She'd gone and done it now. He'd never been one to walk away from a dare.

5

It's a Small Island

Claudia

CLAUDIA REACHED for the hem of her dress. "Turn around," she said.

"I shared a bathroom with five sisters," Henry said. "I've seen it all. Trust me."

She frowned. "I don't trust anyone. Turn around."

"Fine." He gave her his back. "But I promise I'm harmless."

Claudia pulled her dress over her head and slipped out of her underwear. Securing her hair into a knot on top of her head, she snuck a peek at Henry and saw his back was still to her. A thrill ran along her spine. This was exactly what she'd been searching for when she'd come to Hawaii— freedom, excitement, feeling alive… She'd been dead for too long, hiding from scandal and bottled up by other people's opinions.

She'd been right to trust Henry; he hadn't even peeked once. She waded neck deep into the water and called, "You can turn around now."

Henry peeled off his shirt, and Claudia couldn't look away. At first glance, Henry didn't seem like her type. His bright russet hair, fair skin, and freckles weren't exactly leading man attributes. Then again, she'd always been partial to redheads. Her first kiss had been with a boy with a headful of soft, strawberry-blond curls. She'd only been in kindergarten, but she'd never forget locking lips with Rodney. He'd been so sweet and generous with his crayons.

Then Henry slid off his pants and Claudia forgot all about her kindergarten kiss.

He wasn't wearing any underwear.

Claudia had not been prepared for that scenario. It was impossible not to stare as Henry shucked off his pants. His pale body shimmered in the darkness, his bright hair shining like spun copper under the moonlight. The hard lines and rounded muscles of his lean body were sculpted to perfection.

Claudia dragged her gaze over him as he tossed the pants and turned around. He'd promised not to look at her, but she hadn't done the same. She stared openly, not caring if he saw. Men ogled her every day, but it was a rare chance when she got the chance to do the same.

And the view was more enjoyable than she'd imagined. Her eyes roamed over the mounds of his shoulders and down to his defined pectoral muscles sprinkled with russet hair. She followed the trail of hair down his flat belly.

Lower.

Lower.

Lower.

"You're lookin'," he said.

"I never said I wouldn't."

He chuckled and dove through the water, cutting short her visual exploration. She'd seen enough to know he was impressive. Most notable was his confidence. He hadn't minded that she'd been looking. Not a bit. There was something sexy about that.

Claudia floated in the water, surprised at herself. Henry had made her forget all about her disappointment at not finding

Keoni already. Henry had made her laugh, joined her in an adventure, and seemed content to pretend he didn't know who she was. He'd acted as if she were just a regular Janice instead of a celebrity. It had been years since Claudia had felt like a regular girl. Years since she felt so free. Not since her first time in Hawaii.

Henry sliced through the waves, swimming with an efficient stroke until he popped up next to her.

"Like what you saw?" he teased.

She laughed and splashed him. "I've seen worse."

"The water is a little chilly," he said, ducking and splashing her back.

She shrieked and dodged him. "Don't get my hair wet."

"Are you gonna melt like a sugar cube?" Henry ducked under the water and emerged a foot away from Claudia. "How long are you here for?"

Her contract was for five episodes, but she'd never worked with the director before. It could be five weeks. It could be ten. "Not sure."

She did a few easy breaststrokes, letting the ocean water soothe her muscles. Her arms and legs felt weightless in the gently rocking waves.

"I can show you around," Henry offered.

Claudia felt a tug of regret. If she'd been Janice, she might have liked that. But she was Claudia, and she had an agenda: find Keoni.

"I have someone for that," she said. "We are meeting up in a few days."

"Of course," he said good-naturedly. "Can't blame a guy for tryin'. I hope he shows you the best of the island. You don't want to miss Diamond Head, or the Pali Highway, or…" He trailed off, laughing at himself. "There's so much you don't want to miss."

Henry was different from most men. Although he flirted, he never made her feel like he was coming on to her. And while he wasn't quite as harmless as he claimed to be, at least he was easy to be around.

The gentle waves pushed them closer together. His arm brushed hers, and she felt the charge of his energy.

"It's amazing, isn't it?" he asked.

Had he felt it too? That jolt of awareness when they touched?

"What?" Her voice was tight with tension.

"How big the ocean is," he said, his voice a quiet whisper over the waves. "How small we are."

Claudia studied Henry's profile as he stared out at the waves. He wasn't what she'd call handsome. He was a little rough around the edges, but he had a nice smile. His mouth was his best feature. Wide and generous with a smile. He was interesting. And electric. She could feel his energy buzzing between them. She guessed he was older than her by five years or so, but he didn't act it. He was one of those boys who never really grew up, Claudia could tell after five minutes with him.

He was full of smiles and jokes, but she had a feeling there was more to Henry than met the eye.

"We should get back," Henry said. "Don't want anyone to take your shoes."

Claudia felt a pinch of anxiety. "You don't think—"

"I'm kidding."

Claudia watched as he turned and stroked through the water. She was surprised to realize she wasn't ready to go. Despite her earlier disappointment about Keoni, she'd had fun tonight.

"You can go first," Henry said. "I'll wait in the water until you're dressed."

She swam to shore and ran to her pile of clothes. The water had been warmer than the night air, and she shivered as she pulled on her panties and shimmied into her dress. She called to Henry and turned her back so he could dress.

"Wish I would have brought a towel," he said, grinning.

"But I had no idea I was going skinny-dipping tonight. Here." He draped his shirt over her shoulders for an extra layer of warmth.

His fingers brushed her neck as he fixed the collar. Their eyes met, and from the way Henry's widened, she knew he'd felt the sizzle of electricity between them that time. He brushed back a strand of hair from her cheek. Her skin flushed as a bolt of desire shot through her.

"Next time I'll bring a towel," he teased, tucking her hand in his as he led her around the jutting rocks toward the long stretch of beach.

"Next time?" Claudia's voice was a little rushed and breathless. Her heart rate was out of control. She blamed the grass. The tequila. The treacherous rocks. "Who says there will be a next time? We probably won't ever see each other again." And she'd ticked an item off her list. Maybe two.

Henry picked up the glasses they'd left in the sand, and they walked the rest of the way back to Waikiki in silence. Their shoes were right where they'd left them.

Henry bent down to get his shoes. "I'm sure we'll run into each other again," he said. "It's a small island."

The idea might have been intriguing if Claudia wasn't hell-bent on finding the love of her life. Henry was a blast, but she was in Hawaii for one man: Keoni Makai.

6

One Chance

Henry

THE NEXT MORNING while everyone on the island of O'ahu was on the North Shore watching the most prestigious surfing contest in the world, Henry was driving a Pontiac GTO along the winding Hawaiian highway, preparing to crash. He jerked the steering wheel and slammed his foot on the gas. The car took off, its back tires squealing and smoke billowing out of the back end. He shifted gears and reached up to adjust his helmet. Somebody had made a mistake when they'd cut the eyeholes. They were too high, and it reduced his range of vision to two small slits.

He'd be going into a high-speed car chase half blind. Fortunately, Henry was meticulous. He never entered a stunt without leaving a back door open. He didn't need to rely on his vision to get him through the shoot safely. He knew these roads like he knew the cowlicks in his hair. There was a bend up ahead that would give him a hard time, just like that stubborn cowlick at the back of his head. If he cut his hair too short, those hairs would stick up, giving everyone the chance to rib him for looking like Howdy Doody. If he took the corner too slow, it wouldn't make for good TV, but if he took it too fast, he would turn the car over. If he turned the car over, the cannon mounted under the back end could go off too early and it would ruin the shot.

The car would catch on fire, but that was the least of Henry's worries. He couldn't wreck the car. Not before it was time. He had to do everything right, and he only had one chance.

Henry wasn't known as one of the most reliable stuntmen in the industry for nothing. His reputation depended on his success in the craziest situations. He'd jumped out of helicopters, crashed through windows on a motorcycle, and been in so many fight scenes he'd lost count.

Car chases were his favorite.

Even though he could hardly see out of his helmet as he flew over the hills of the curving highway, he was having a hell of a time. He let out a whoop of excitement as he careened around the dangerous bend in the road. The GTO hung in the air for a full three seconds before slamming back to the pavement. All the air whooshed out of Henry's lungs as his body shook with the impact. He gritted his teeth against the pain that rocketed through his leg. His broken shin wasn't completely healed from an injury he'd sustained three months ago, and when he stood up on the gas, the blast of agony in his right leg nearly gutted him.

The sweet spike of adrenaline coursed through his body, and the pain receded to a dull throb. He yanked the steering wheel with all his strength and flew around the corner toward the set.

Up ahead, Henry spotted his final destination: a silver Buick Skylark parked in front of the fake police station. A remote-control explosive device was planted under the hood of the Skylark as a backup, just in case the cannon in the back of the GTO didn't explode on impact.

Henry flew toward the Buick at breakneck speed. He was

going too fast, but if he hit the brakes now, he would ruin the shot. He was meant to be flying out of control, but this was beyond dangerous. In a last-ditch effort to reduce speed without leaving a telltale burn of rubber on the road, Henry jerked the wheel and clipped a Volkswagen Beetle parked on the side of the street.

The GTO bounced off the Volkswagen and fishtailed wildly to the other side of the street. The screech of scraping metal filled the set. Extras walking along the sidewalk dove for safety, and the ground crew scrambled to film every angle. Henry righted the GTO and sped toward the Buick with steely determination. He relaxed his muscles as he prepared for impact. Doubt flickered through his mind, but he banished it before it could take root.

He didn't have time for fear or doubt. It was too late to change course. All he could do was try to remain calm as he T-boned the Skylark. At the moment of impact, Henry's life flashed before his eyes.

He smiled. It had been a damned good life. If he died now, he had no regrets. A tickle of uncertainty clogged his throat, and he swallowed it down. Okay, he had one regret, a really big one, but he wouldn't think about it now. It might derail him. Instead, Henry thought about the places he'd lived, the friendships he'd forged, and the thrills he'd experienced.

He'd spent the weekend at a surf competition, skinny-dipped with a blonde bombshell, and sailed to Maui for a coral dive. The dive hadn't gone as planned, but Henry couldn't afford to dwell on that, not when he was about to crash full speed into a parked car. He thought instead of Janice, picturing the sexy pout of her lips and wondering what it would feel like to kiss her. A vision of Janice filled his mind as he sped toward disaster. He wished he would have pushed it further with her. He regretted not charming her a little more, persuading her to meet up with him again.

Janice's face was the last thing on his mind as the crash

jarred him from head to toe. His stomach dropped, and his heart threatened to beat out of his chest. A thrill raced down his spine when he heard the boom of the cannon at the GTO's rear. It had worked! He let out a cry of joy, ecstatic that the design he'd come up with had worked. The director wouldn't be able to ignore this achievement. Maybe now he would give Henry a chance to direct a stunt scene. He'd earned it.

Henry took a moment to revel in his success before he started his countdown. Flames engulfed the side of the car, and smoke leaked in from a side window. Henry had to time everything perfectly. He had two minutes to get out of the car before the bomb in the Skylark detonated, but if he exited too soon, it would ruin the shot.

A minute ticked by slowly as the car filled with smoke. He couldn't see a damn thing with his helmet on. He still had thirty seconds to go when a second boom pierced the air.

"Well, shit," Henry mumbled, realizing what had happened.

Some dumbass had pushed the button too soon, detonating the bomb in the Skylark. The GTO burst into flames, trapping Henry inside. Smoke stung his eyes as he reached for the door handle. Fire licked into the car from the driver's window, and Henry scrambled away into the passenger seat. The fire suit protected his body, but the heat was unbearable. He couldn't breathe from all the smoke.

The passenger door wouldn't budge, so he slammed his elbow through the window. He tumbled out with the broken glass and landed in a heap on the pavement. Crew members dragged him away from the wreckage and hosed him down.

Albert Skidmore, the stunt director for *A Long Road Home*, pushed his way through the crowd around Henry, shouting obscenities at everyone in his way. "You okay, Champ?"

Henry coughed, gagging on the smoke that filled his throat. "I've been better."

Albert narrowed his eyes at Henry, assessing him. "You up for another take?"

Henry's heart sank. Another take might kill him. And where were they gonna get another car as pretty as the GTO? He blinked slowly to clear his head. His eyes burned, and his skin felt too tight, as if the fire had gotten inside him.

"I got another take in me, Boss." Henry had a reputation to uphold. There were plenty of young guns who wanted his job. He couldn't afford to let anyone think he couldn't handle a stunt. He pulled off his helmet. "I'm gonna need a better helmet though. This one almost killed me."

Albert laughed. "I'm just pulling your leg, Champ." He clapped Henry on the back. "That was one helluva stunt! I thought you were a goner."

It hadn't been perfect, but it could have been worse. He could have had to do the take over again.

7

Island Time

Claudia

THE SOUND of screams and cheers drew Claudia from her trailer. She rushed onto the set with her costume half buttoned, in time to see a low-slung muscle car barreling around the corner toward the fake police station.

"Wait!" Megan ran after her. "Let me finish with those hooks."

Claudia's wardrobe was comprised of dresses that were impossible to get in and out of on her own. The corsets had dozens of hooks she couldn't reach, no matter how she contorted her arms.

She sucked in a sharp breath as Megan secured the last hook. Claudia was glad Ari had insisted she take Megan with her as her assistant. Not only was Megan good for helping with her costumes, she also had the inside scoop on all the cast and crew of *A Long Road Home*. She'd come out a few days early to make sure Claudia's trailer was satisfactory, and she'd already made friends with everyone on set.

Megan clutched Claudia's arm as the car skidded around

the corner, losing a hubcap. "He's not slowing down!" She clapped a hand over her eyes. "I can't look! Tell me if he makes it out alive!"

The car sped past Camera Two, clipping a Volkswagen Beetle on the turn. A chill ran down Claudia's spine as the speeding car slammed into a parked car. Metal screeched, and a deafening boom split the air. Claudia covered her ears, gasping as flames burst to life around the collision site.

Megan screamed when another boom sounded. Flames leaped higher, and smoke billowed into the sky. The crew burst to life, running from every direction toward the scene of the accident.

Claudia's heart pounded against her ribs in a furious rhythm. She'd never filmed an action scene before. Her acting roles had been limited to drama or comedy. She'd never seen stunts performed.

Adrenaline rushed through her as she watched the crew race onto the set. She'd never known how much excitement she'd been missing, not filming action scenes.

Megan buried her face in Claudia's shoulder as another boom sounded from the crash site. Flames danced into the cloudless blue sky. Smoke billowed, creating thick plumes that turned the air around the crash site into a hazardous zone.

"Get him out!" The stunt director scurried past the cameras, ripping off his headset as he raced to the crash site. "Get him out now!"

Crew members dressed in fire gear swarmed the set. Claudia's heart pounded furiously as the seconds ticked by. Everything was happening too slowly and too rapidly at the same time. The driver was trapped inside, possibly knocked unconscious from the horrible crash.

"Don't worry," Megan whispered. "He told me it's all illusion. He's fine."

"Then why aren't you looking?" Claudia asked.

Megan peeked out from behind her fingers and grimaced as she took in the disaster. "There he is!" she cried.

The passenger window shattered and a man in a fire suit crawled out of the car. Flames licked the lower half of his body as he rolled on the ground. Two crew members grabbed the stuntman under the arms and dragged him to safety. A moment later, the stuntman raised his arms in victory, and the crew erupted in cheers.

"He's such a fox," Megan said, her voice breathless. "I bet he's incredible in bed. A man like that? It turns me on just to be in the same room as him. Those jeans he wears ought to be illegal."

Claudia laughed. "I haven't met him yet," she said.

"Champ is out of sight."

Claudia's thoughts came to an abrupt halt as the stuntman ripped off his helmet, revealing a headful of bright russet hair.

"Everyone calls him Champ," Megan said. "I don't even remember his actual name."

A quick shiver raced down Claudia's spine as she watched the stuntman unzip his fire suit to reveal a perfectly ordinary pair of gray sweatpants and white T-shirt. She'd seen him in much less, and she'd recognize him anywhere. "I'm pretty sure his name is Henry."

"I wish those jogging pants would have burned up in the fire," Megan said, craning her neck for a better look.

Embarrassment heated Claudia's cheeks, and she ducked behind Megan when Henry swept his gaze across the set.

"What are you hiding for?"

Claudia pressed her hand to her fluttering stomach. The thought of seeing Henry again made her feel queasy. She hadn't been able to get him out of her mind since their naked swim session. Even her memories of Keoni Makai paled in comparison to Henry stripping under the moonlight.

He'd lied about working on a farm, and he'd also lied when

he'd said he was harmless. She wished she could tell that to the butterflies in her stomach.

Claudia tore her eyes away from the redheaded liar. "I've got to get to that meeting," she said. "I'm already late."

"Claudia!" Megan called after her. "What's the hurry? No one will be there yet. This is Hawaii." She spread her arms wide as if Claudia hadn't noticed the tropical paradise around them. "Everyone operates on Island Time."

Claudia dismissed Megan and hurried around the craft table, where a variety of unrecognizable food was laid out for the day. She opened the door to the warehouse where they filmed the indoor scenes and skirted around the set designers who were busy dressing the library for her first scene. A bubble of excitement lodged in her throat. She always felt jazzed up her first day on set. That must be why she felt dizzy and weak in the knees.

Every nerve in her body felt more sensitive than usual. Her senses jumped to life. The flood lights burned her eyes, and the smell of stale cigarettes assaulted her nose. Noises from the busy crew followed Claudia as her shoes clicked down the hall, but the only sound she could hear was the thudding of her heart.

She pulled in a hasty breath, hoping the conference room was empty as Megan had promised.

And it was. Claudia sagged against the door and dragged in another breath. Her skin tingled all over, and she felt like she might faint.

Henry didn't work on a farm; he was a stuntman. On *her* television show.

Claudia needed a smoke. She grabbed a cigarette from the carousel on the conference table. They weren't her usual brand, but she didn't care. She lit one and sank into an empty chair, then tilted her head back as she exhaled. A strange hum buzzed through her veins that had nothing to do with the cigarette.

The door opened, and the rest of the cast filed into the room. Claudia stood to greet them. She'd already met most of the cast, including her co-star Stan Beatty, who was currently topping the list of most teenage girls' fantasies. He was just as handsome in person as he was in his pictures. He was the perfect beach boy with his blond hair and blue eyes, although he wasn't as tall as she'd thought he'd be.

Claudia shoved thoughts of Henry aside, forcing herself to pay attention. She needed to make a good impression on her co-stars. They already thought she was a princess because she was the only one with her own two-roomer and a full-time assistant. It wasn't her fault that her wardrobe comprised of corsets and bustiers that were impossible to get into on her own.

And it wasn't her fault that thoughts of Henry, flashing his confident grin, crowded her mind, making it impossible to concentrate.

8

The Bet

Henry

HENRY SAT under the wide umbrella at the makeup station, allowing Margie to apply burn ointment to his face.

"Hold still, will you?" Margie pinched his jaw with firm fingers and tilted his face toward the light. Her fingers danced along his face. When she grazed the bridge of his nose, a riot of pain exploded behind Henry's eyes. He must have banged it in the crash. He'd broken it twice within as many years, and it smarted with pain even on good days.

"Sorry." Margie patted the ointment into Henry's cheeks, making little sounds of disapproval. "You should have gotten out sooner, Champ."

"I'll remember that next time." Henry closed his eyes as relief from the ointment soothed his skin.

When he opened his eyes again, the pain had subsided enough for him to focus. He glimpsed a woman in a minidress strolling toward the new two-roomer, and he turned his head, but Margie pinched his chin and turned his face back toward hers before he could get a proper look.

"Who's that?" he asked. Only big names got their own trailers with two rooms. "She famous?"

Margie scoffed. "Have you been living under a rock for the last year, man?"

"More like *on* a rock," he said.

The locals sometimes referred to Oah'u as The Rock because that was basically what the island was—a big floating rock formed by two ancient shield volcanos. Henry loved Hawaii, but sometimes he missed the conveniences of living on the mainland. It took forever to get mail, and a phone call home cost a fortune. And there was only one movie theater on the island.

"That's Sissy Saxon," Margie said. "Haven't you seen *Jezebel?*"

"I don't watch those chick movies." Henry wanted to see action at the movies, not romance.

Margie laughed. "More men saw *Jezebel* than women, all because of Claudia Montgomery."

The name didn't ring a bell, but Henry rarely went to the movies. The only theater in Honolulu didn't show Henry's favorite Kung Fu movies. "I thought you said her name was Sissy."

Margie gave him a stern look. "Sissy is the character she played in the movie. Don't you know anything?"

He shrugged. "Guess not."

Margie's expression softened. She turned away and rooted around in one of her drawers. "For the pain," she said, pressing two white pills into his palm.

"What are they?" Henry smoked a little grass and drank a little too much sometimes, but he didn't mess with the hard stuff. He'd seen too many friends get messed up with pills and more.

Margie raised an eyebrow. "It's just aspirin tablets," she said. "You're going to have a headache later. I almost peed my pants watching that stunt."

Henry grinned, grabbing Margie in a hug as he stood from the chair. "It was out of this world, wasn't it?"

Margie squealed when he turned her in a circle and then set her down. She jabbed him in the chest with her index finger. "Don't scare me like that again. My heart can't take it." She swatted him with her brush. "Thanks for helping out Debi." She reached for a cigarette, and Henry offered her a light. "She sure appreciates it. I wish she'd find a good guy like you instead of that bum she hangs around."

"She'll learn," Henry said. "She's young. You gotta get your heart broken early and get it out of the way. Then the fun can start."

"That what happened to you, Champ? You get your heart broken?"

"Yep," Henry said. He grabbed Margie's hand and kissed it. "You break it every damn day."

"Hush." She swatted his shoulder, but she smiled and even blushed a bit. "Don't forget to come see me in the morning. I'll doctor you up again."

"Thanks."

He made his way across the lot to the craft table, where the caterers were busy setting out a second lunch. The food was always different and always plentiful. Today was Portuguese. Bowls of spicy sausage and sweet rice, stuffed peppers, and malasadas lined the table. He grabbed a malasada and sank his teeth into the soft dough. Sugar and cinnamon exploded on his tongue.

"God bless the Portuguese," he mumbled in appreciation.

The set crew was on a break and filled their plates with the new offerings.

"Did you get a load of those gams?" one of the grips asked, grabbing a malasada.

"I was too busy looking at her rack," said the art director.

Henry glanced at the two-roomer across the lot. He didn't have to be a genius to know who they were talking about.

"Did you see *Jezebel?*" asked Stan Beatty, their leading man.

"Who didn't?"

"That pool scene?"

"What about the shower scene? Holy shit!"

They argued over which scene they liked best, and Henry regretted that the only movies he'd seen in the past few years featured Chinese men and violent swordplay.

"Eh? What are you boys talking about?"

Everyone fell silent as Albert Skidmore, the stunt director of *A Long Road Home*, joined the conversation. Albert was a haole recently transplanted from California, but he'd adopted the Hawaiian slang of adding *eh* at the beginning of a sentence and *yeah* at the end, hoping to sound more like a local.

"Let me guess, you're trying to figure out which one of you is going to make it with Claudia Montgomery first, yeah?"

The crew laughed uneasily. They hadn't quite gotten there yet, but Henry guessed it was coming.

"She ain't hard on the eyes," one of the camera operators said.

"I got some places that are hard," said another.

Henry rolled his eyes as the crew howled in laughter.

"I heard she was into free love and all that hippie shit," the key grip said. "And did you hear about her and the district attorney from LA? Big scandal."

"She can give me some free love anytime she wants," said Stan. "Anyone want to make a wager on who gets in her pants first?"

"She ain't wearing pants."

Everyone laughed again.

"I'll bet on myself." Stan puffed up his chest.

"That ain't fair," said Jake. "No betting on yourself."

"All right," said Stan around a bite of pork. "How's this gonna work?"

They all eyed each other to see who would speak first.

"We should pick a candidate for each other. The best man wins."

"Wins what?"

"Besides a great lay?"

Henry stuffed another donut in his mouth and eased away from the table.

"Stan, you've got Jake," the cameraman said.

"No way."

"What? He's a decent-looking kid."

"He doesn't know how to talk to women," Stan said. "I'd rather have Koa. I bet she'll go for a big burly Hawaiian."

Henry took another step away from the table, hoping to escape before anyone noticed him, but his luck ran out before he could get away.

Stan grabbed him by the arm. "How about you take Champ, Albert?"

"No way," Henry said. "I'm not getting roped into this bullshit."

"You're telling me you don't want any of that?" Stan cocked his head at Claudia's trailer.

Henry shook his head. He might flirt with his coworkers, but he looked elsewhere for dates. Other than taking in a show at a club with some of the crew, he didn't mingle with his coworkers.

"Come on, Champ. Have a little fun."

"Champ's not getting laid with that ugly mug," said Jake.

Everyone howled with laughter.

Henry bristled. "I get plenty of chicks."

Stan snorted. "Yeah, the fat, ugly, or blind ones."

Henry forced a laugh. "I like 'em in all shapes. All sizes."

"He's in, yeah?" Albert declared, grabbing Henry's arm and tugging him back to the table. "And the wager is a thousand bucks. Eh? Anyone else in, or what?"

The key grip winced. "Too rich for my blood."

A few others placed their bets or bowed out.

Henry glanced at Claudia's trailer with a sinking feeling.

The poor woman had no idea what had just transpired at the craft table. He had half a mind to knock on her door right now and tell her.

"Eh? Why so down?" Albert asked. "It's just a little fun and games."

"Tell that to her." His appetite gone, Henry headed for his trailer.

Albert followed closely behind him. "So you're not gonna even try? I just bet a thousand big ones on you."

Henry glared at him. "I told you not to."

"Well, I can't back out now, so I would appreciate a little help, yeah?" Albert followed him into the trailer. "Tell me what you want."

Henry grabbed his duffel bag and hitched it over his shoulder. "I don't mess around with coworkers. And there's nothing I want enough to make me change my mind."

He reached for the door, but Albert got there before him. "You're dying to direct a fight scene."

Henry felt like he'd been punched in the gut. Albert had zeroed in on the one thing Henry had been wanting for almost a year.

"You almost met your maker today in that crash." Albert leaned against the door, blocking Henry's exit. He pointed at Henry's singed eyebrows for emphasis. "It's a long climb up to the director's chair. Maybe I can help you with that."

Henry clenched his jaw. He hated it, but Albert was right. Nothing came easy in this industry. Even though he deserved a shot at directing stunts, he wasn't likely to get it without Albert's help. He eyed Albert warily, trying to figure out his angle. "What's in this for you?" he asked.

Albert shrugged. "I like to win."

Henry ground his teeth together. He didn't want anything to do with Albert winning. "Too bad."

Albert snorted. "I get it. You don't think you can score a girl like her."

Henry's eyes went cold. "Nah, I don't. And you're crazy if you think I have a chance. A famous hotshot won't want anything to do with me."

Albert elbowed him in the ribs. "Have a little faith in yourself, man. I'll help you out." Albert pursed his lips, and Henry could see the wheels turning in his brain. "I've got the perfect setup." He narrowed his eyes at Henry. "But you gotta help me too."

Indecision warred in Henry's mind. He knew it was wrong to try to seduce a woman for the sake of a bet, but he couldn't pass up this chance. The whole thing was a long shot, very unlikely to happen. But… what if he did manage to win? His heart raced at the thought of directing. He loved performing stunts, but he needed a backup plan. He was thirty years old. How many more years could his body take? He'd broken so many bones, he no longer kept count.

"I'll think about it," he agreed.

Albert stepped back to allow Henry to leave the trailer. "Eh? Don't think too long."

9

This Ain't Hollywood

Two days later
Claudia

THE MAIN FILMING location for *A Long Road Home* was a warehouse on the southeastern side of the island, far away from the bustling tourist district of Waikiki.

The location was the size of a small city complete with bathrooms, offices, food catering trucks, motor homes and equipment trailers. Giant generators fueled the lamps, cameras and sewing machines, and a special effects truck with enough explosives to blow up an entire neighborhood was parked at a safe distance from the soundstage.

It wasn't the biggest set Claudia had ever seen, but it was definitely the most unique. Even surrounded by equipment and crew, the location felt like the middle of nowhere. A grove of banyan trees with aerial roots sprouting from broad branches looked like something out of a fairy tale. Tropical flowers the size of dinner plates bloomed from lush shrubbery, saturating the air with their musky perfume.

An entire can of hairspray couldn't protect Claudia's hair

from the heavy humidity. Margie had created a stiff bouffant on top of Claudia's head, but it didn't stand a chance against the Hawaiian weather.

After hours of filming in the heat of the day, Claudia doubted the wisdom of accepting the role as Melanie the Witch.

The costume was ridiculous. The hours were brutal. And so far, the only fun she'd had in Hawaii was skinny-dipping with Henry—the stuntman who'd been strangely absent from set the last two days.

Keoni Makai was nowhere to be found.

Everyone knew him, but no one knew where to find him.

Claudia was beginning to think the only chance she had of finding him was to hang around Waikiki hoping for a surf lesson. It had worked six years ago.

Flyaway pieces of hair clung to her neck, and beads of sweat dripped between the mounds of cleavage created by the corseted bodice of her costume.

When Benji called cut, Claudia sighed with relief. She didn't have another take in her to save her life, and if she didn't get out of her costume as soon as possible, her breasts might suffer permanent damage.

Crew members swarmed the set, rolling back the moveable wall to transform the library into the living room.

Claudia was halfway to her trailer before she heard Benji calling after her. She was tempted to keep walking. So far, she wasn't impressed with the famous director. She suspected he might be in Hawaii for similar reasons as her.

Not to find the love of her life, but because he'd been black-listed in Hollywood. The man was a tyrant. He was the most demanding director Claudia had ever worked with.

"Claudia, wait."

She had no excuse not to stop. Pasting a smile on her face, she stopped and waited for the director.

"I need to discuss a few things with you," he said.

Claudia's shoulders inched up, and a frown creased her forehead. "Is everything okay?"

Besides Stan Beatty being an incompetent ass, and the bodice of her costume being more than one size too small?

"Albert!" Benji yelled, waving at the stunt director. "Get over here." When Albert joined them, Benji clapped him on the shoulder. "Tell Claudia your ideas," he said, checking his watch. "Fill her in, I gotta go make sure Koa has the truck ready."

Albert steered Claudia away from her trailer toward the equipment storage building. "Let's take a walk, eh?"

Claudia suppressed a sigh and let Albert lead the way toward a garage that housed the cars used on the show.

"This ain't Hollywood," Albert said.

"No," she agreed.

"We are a little more limited in resources. That's why I have to ask you something that I don't normally ask of the actresses. It may be uncomfortable for you."

Claudia didn't like the way Albert was eyeing her cleavage. She hoped he hadn't believed the rumors circulating in the industry that she was loose. Rick had dragged her name through the mud, but anyone who'd ever worked with her knew she didn't sleep with crew members, especially not directors. She'd turned down some great parts because she didn't want to have a roll on the casting couch.

"Eh? We don't have any stunt men with your—" He cleared his throat and cupped his hands at his chest. "Proportions, yeah?"

She narrowed her eyes at him. "Yeah?"

"A man in a wig with a couple of grapefruits will not cut it, yeah?"

It dawned on Claudia what Albert was asking. "You want me to do stunts?"

"Yeah." Albert steered her around a flood lamp closer to the garage.

"What kind of stunts?" The image of Henry climbing out

of the burning car filled Claudia's mind. This would definitely qualify as something dangerous to check off her list.

"Don't you worry, now. I'm gonna get you some training." They stopped near a group of men bent over the open hood of a car. "Eh? Is Champ around?"

"Under here," said a voice from under the car. "Whatchu want?"

The sound of Henry's deep voice made Claudia's heart skip a beat. The moment she'd been anticipating for days had finally arrived. She was going to see Henry again.

"I need to talk to you, yeah?"

"Hand me a wrench, will you?" A muscled forearm shot out from under the car. One of the men gave him a wrench, and his hand disappeared under the car again.

Albert squatted and peered under the car. "Come out here, yeah?"

There was a clang of metal, a grunt, and a curse of frustration.

Claudia held her breath as Henry inched out from under the car. His dusty boots gave way to a pair of legs clad in faded denim and then a white T-shirt stained with grease. His broad shoulders and neck appeared, and finally his face.

He was just as she'd remembered him. Too rugged to be called handsome, he had a bump in his nose and a stubborn chin. A backward baseball cap covered his bright hair, and a frown creased his brow.

"I'm in the middle of something." He glared up at Albert, wiping his hands on a rag. His gaze flicked over to Claudia, and a slow grin curved his generous mouth. "Janice?"

"Claudia," she corrected.

His eyebrows shot up, and a blush stained his cheeks. "Claudia Montgomery?"

The way he gaped at her made Claudia think he hadn't known who she was the other night. Had he really believed she was just a girl named Janice?

"That's right, yeah?" Albert said. "This is Claudia."

Henry tore his eyes away from Claudia and got to his feet. "What do you want, man?"

Albert clamped a hand on Henry's shoulder and grinned at Claudia. "Champ is our best stuntman. He's jumped out of helicopters, ridden wild horses, crashed into parked cars... You name it, Champ has done it."

"Nice to meet you... Champ." Claudia extended her hand.

One eyebrow arched as he reached for her hand. "Nice to meet you... Claudia." He shook her hand and then turned his back on her to lean over the open hood of the car.

"I want you to take Claudia under your wing," Albert said. "Show her all your tricks, yeah?"

"I'm in the middle of something," Henry said without looking away from the car.

"Eh? Let the mechanics do that," Albert snapped.

"They can't."

Henry leaned over the car to tinker with something, and Claudia tried hard not to stare at his ass, displayed nicely in the tight denim. Megan had been right about his jeans, they ought to be illegal.

"Eh? This is your chance," Albert said.

Henry stood and shot Albert an icy glare. "I don't think so."

Tension zinged between the two men. Claudia began to think that she had misread Henry when they'd first met. She'd taken him for an easy-going type of guy. Maybe she'd been wrong.

"It's not negotiable." Albert dropped his affected speech. "I need Claudia ready for a fight scene. And I need you to teach her. Got it?"

Henry's shoulders inched up to his ears, and a muscle ticked in his jaw. "Got it, Boss." His voice left no doubts about how much he liked the idea. He shifted his gaze to Claudia, and a hint of a smile crept back into his eyes. "You wanna learn how to crash a car?"

Her heart leapt at the suggestion. It sounded like just the danger she craved. Their eyes locked, and Henry's smile grew.

"Nah, nah, nah," Albert replied. "Just a few fight moves, yeah?" He demonstrated by boxing in place. "Maybe a headlock? This is your chance, man. Don't waste it, yeah?"

Henry ignored Albert. "How about jumping onto a galloping horse?" he teased.

Claudia's eyes went round. She'd never considered performing stunts before, but it might be the perfect way to resurrect her flailing career. No one would be thinking about her scandal with Richard Dunlap while watching her take down a villain in a headlock.

She smiled up at Henry. "When do we start?"

10

Chilly Water

Henry

"HOW ABOUT NOW?" Albert suggested.

Henry liked to live dangerously, but Claudia's stare was cutting him to pieces. He didn't want to work with her. He couldn't trust himself to be in the close quarters he knew were required to teach her a fight sequence. He struggled to keep his eyes on hers. They were firing lasers at him. And her chest? It was only a short dip over smooth, creamy skin to the rounded swell of her glorious tits.

"I'm in the middle of something important." He ripped his eyes away from Claudia's hot stare and gestured at the low-slung car. It was the tow-behind Stan Beatty pretended to drive. Cameras mounted to the back of a tow truck captured Stan cruising along the coastal highways, but it was Henry in a blond wig who did the real driving in the real version of the car. "She's leaking oil."

"Eh?" Albert snorted. "We have mechanics for that."

Henry's back stiffened. He was sorely tempted to announce

Albert's true reasons for inventing a fight scene and end the ridiculous bet.

"What does this fight scene entail?" Claudia asked.

Her expression barely concealed her curiosity. The excitement on her face made Henry's smile curve wider. This was *Janice*, the girl who was up for new experiences. She didn't shy away from what she wanted, conventions be damned.

"I never taught a girl to fight before," Henry said. He couldn't help throwing out the challenge. He knew it would piss her off, and he wanted to see the spark ignite in her chocolate-brown eyes. When she arched one eyebrow and fired her furious gaze at him, Henry's lips curved in a smile. "You might mess up your hair," he teased.

The flame in her eyes sparkled. Her chin came up, and she gave him a smile so sexy, it shot straight to his dick. God help him. His gaze strayed down to the mouthwatering display of her breasts.

"Just pretend I'm your sister," she said sweetly.

Henry couldn't suppress the laugh that bubbled up in his chest. There was no way he'd be thinking of his sisters if he got Claudia in his arms. Her little joke reminded him of when they'd undressed on the beach. Did she remember every moment as vividly as he did?

Her voice was like honey and whiskey. Sweet with spice. And coming from the perfect feminine pout of her mouth, it was like a siren's song, drawing him in. Her mouth was full and luscious like the rest of her body. Classy and sexy, Claudia Montgomery was pretty much every man's dream girl.

Henry would do better to stay away from her. As far as he could get. "Aries still needs to be exercised."

Albert waved his hand in the air. "The grooms can do that."

"He likes me." Henry's tone dropped to a dangerous level.

Albert squared his body to Henry, eyes boring holes into him. Henry stared right back.

"I need Claudia ready for this fight scene in a week." Albert was no longer playing around. Authority dripped from his voice. "Get it done."

"We will," Claudia chirped.

Henry glared at her. She had no idea what she was getting into, and Henry was sorely tempted to spill everything. Albert had seized his victory and left them alone. It was the perfect opportunity to tell Claudia everything.

"Don't look so glum," Claudia said. "This is going to be a blast. You're not afraid to teach me to fight, are you?" Claudia assumed a fighting stance, raising her fists and setting her feet. A gleam of challenge flashed in her pretty brown eyes. "Scared I might hurt you?"

Her feet were all wrong, and her thumbs were tucked into her fists, but she looked adorable. The determination on her face made up for the imperfections of her stance. And the spark in her eyes? Henry was loath to kill it with news of a sleazy bet.

He took off his hat and mopped his forehead with the rag again. "Why don't you go change? I'll meet you in ten outside your trailer."

Claudia smoothed a hand along her skirt. "Perfect."

Henry watched her walk away with a deep sigh. He took his time changing into sweats and a clean T-shirt, then stocked up on sandwiches at the craft table before heading to Claudia's trailer. Training was hungry work, and he'd missed lunch. He unwrapped the wax paper on a ham sandwich and took a healthy bite before rapping his knuckles on Claudia's door.

No one answered. He knocked again, and called, "Claudia? You in there?"

The doorknob rattled and then the door cracked open. Claudia's face filled the small gap. Her cheeks were flushed, and her hair was half-undone, floating around her neck and shoulders. She blew out a frustrated breath, stirring the bangs stuck to her forehead. "I'm having some trouble," she said.

His brow creased, and he took another bite of his sandwich. "What's the problem?"

She pulled the door open a few more inches and turned around, presenting him with her back. "I can't get out of this by myself."

Henry nearly choked. Her corset top was mostly undone, except for a few hooks in the middle that she couldn't reach. Her back was nearly naked, covered only by a swatch of her dress hooked together at middle of her back. She'd managed to undo the hooks at the top and the ones at her waist, leaving all that creamy skin bared.

A bolt of desire shot straight to his cock. It stiffened, and he cursed the fact that he was wearing sweatpants. There was no way to hide what the sight of Claudia's nearly naked back was doing to him.

He went up the stairs into her trailer. The place was neat and orderly, but everything was pink. Ruffly pink curtains fluttered over the window above the sink. Pink cushions adorned the long bench running down the length of the trailer. A pink vase held a dozen pink roses.

Henry closed the door behind him and set the sandwiches on the small table next to an ashtray and a copy of *The Feminine Mystique.*

"Lots of hooks," he mumbled, crossing the room toward Claudia.

"I know." She held her hands over the front of her dress as Henry reached for the hooks on her back. "This costume is impossible. And the shoes?" She stuck her foot out from under the hem of her skirt to show him her pointed-toe heels. "They're a size too small."

Henry focused on her feet and not the smooth skin revealed with each hook he unclasped. His fingers were clumsy, and the hooks were tiny. It took longer than he'd expected to work each one free. Focusing on her feet did nothing to discourage the bulge in his sweatpants. He'd bet a week's paycheck that Claudia had adorable feet to go with the rest of her.

He struggled with a stubborn hook and cleared his throat. "I can put in a word with the costume department for you."

Claudia glanced at him over her shoulder. "Would you?"

Henry finished with the last hook, and Claudia stepped away from him with a swish of her long skirt. "Thanks."

"No problem." Henry took a seat on the long bench that ran the length of the trailer as she went into the bedroom to change.

"Are those sandwiches?"

She'd left the door open a crack, and Henry could hear her moving around. He imagined her slipping out of the costume, which only made his dick harder.

"Um… yeah." He grabbed a pink pillow and placed it on his lap.

A splash of water sounded from the bathroom, and a moment later, Claudia came out of the bedroom wiping a wet washcloth across her face. She was gorgeous with no makeup, wearing a simple pair of denim shorts and a plain white T-shirt.

Henry's mouth dropped open. He'd never seen shorts and a T-shirt look so good before.

"What kind?" she asked, wiping the lipstick from her mouth.

"Um… what?"

"The sandwiches?" Claudia tossed the washcloth into the sink and picked up Henry's half-eaten sandwich. "They aren't octopus or anything, are they?"

Henry had forgotten all about his sandwich when his dick had started misbehaving. "They're ham," he said.

"Half that stuff on the craft table is unrecognizable." Claudia unwrapped the other half of Henry's sandwich and took a healthy bite, chewed, and swallowed. "You didn't want this, did you?"

"No," he said. He pointed at the counter. "There's another one right there."

Claudia put the sandwich down and picked up the other one. She unwrapped it and sniffed, wrinkling her nose. "Tuna salad. Yuck."

Henry leaned forward and plucked the sandwich from her hand. "I'll take it."

"I didn't eat lunch." Claudia picked a piece of crust from the edge of the bread and popped it in her mouth. "We had to do retakes all day. That Stan Beatty is an imbecile."

The mention of Stan did the trick on Henry's stiffening dick. He was no longer aroused. Now, he just felt guilty.

"Sit down," he told Claudia, patting the bench beside him. There was nowhere else to sit in the small trailer.

"I know it's rude to eat standing up." Claudia grinned around her mouthful of food. "My mother was a stickler for manners. She would have twisted my ear for this." Claudia shuddered as if reliving a bad memory. "Ladies don't eat like horses," she said in a haughty tone.

Henry smiled, imagining Claudia as a little girl. No doubt she'd been adorable. He lifted a hand and rubbed his chest where a persistent ache throbbed.

"So, I think I know what you're going to say," Claudia said, coming to sit next to him on the bench.

Henry's heart rate kicked into high gear. He doubted she knew what he was going to say. Unless… maybe Claudia already knew about the bet. Wouldn't that be nice? Relief softened the tightness in his chest. Maybe he wouldn't have to be the one to hurt her…

"You're embarrassed," Claudia said.

Henry's thoughts froze. "What?"

"That water was very chilly." Claudia flicked an innocent gaze at Henry.

He bit back a laugh and agreed. "It was."

"I get it. You never thought you would see me again. I never thought I would see you again either."

Thank God they'd seen each other again. Henry had been thinking about Janice non stop. "Why did you say your name was Janice?" he asked.

She smirked. "I don't believe I did. Why did you pretend not to know who I was?" she countered.

Henry shook his head. "Believe it or not, I didn't know you who you were." He figured he was the only guy on the planet who hadn't seen *Jezebel,* which was a real shame. "You didn't act famous."

Claudia laughed and took the last bite of the ham sandwich. "I guess that's a compliment."

"It was." Henry hated going out with some of the actors on the show who flaunted their celebrity status in order to get free drinks and women.

"You told me your name was Henry, and you worked on a farm."

"My name *is* Henry." He took a big bite of the tuna sandwich. "And I never said I worked on a farm."

Claudia tossed her trash onto the counter next to her book. "You alluded to it," she said. "And everyone here calls you Champ. Megan doesn't even know your real name."

Henry chuckled. "Champ is short for my last name, Longchamp."

"Oh. That makes sense. I thought it was because you were the best at something."

His chuckle turned into a full-blown laugh at the doubtful tone in her voice. "The nickname goes back to my football days. Everyone on the team had nicknames."

"You played football?" she asked. "My brother played too."

He knew he should be telling her about the bet, not his glory days on the team, but he couldn't bring himself to break the news. She would hate him for it, and he just wanted a few more minutes of her liking him.

"My feet are killing me," Claudia said, lifting her foot into her lap to rub her toes.

Henry glanced at her foot and was glad the pillow was still in his lap. His dick even liked her feet. They were slim and dainty, and with polished pink toenails. She really did love pink.

"Let me do that." He abandoned his sandwich and reached for her foot. "I'm pretty good at it."

"Ahh." Claudia lay back on the bench as he pressed his fingers into her instep. "You *are* good at this."

"Five sisters, remember? They used to pay me a nickel to rub their feet." He smiled, remembering how they used to line their coins up on the kitchen counter and take their turns. "And I rub the horses down almost every day."

"Are you comparing me to a horse?" she asked, snorting playfully.

He pressed his knuckles into her instep, and she moaned. The noise sent a zigzag of lust through his body. Nope. She was nothing like the horses.

"Did you get to watch any of the surfing contest?" he asked.

She sighed. "No. I had to work all day, and by the time I got, off it was over."

"Your buddy Declan won."

"I heard. It was all over the news." Claudia moaned, tilting her head back as Henry worked his fingers into her arch. "You missed a spot," she teased.

Henry tickled her instep, making her giggle. "Did you meet up with your friend who was going to show you the island yet?" he asked.

Her pretty lips pouted. "I'm having trouble finding him."

"Did you try the phone book?"

"Of course I tried the phone book." She closed her eyes, moaning again. "He isn't in it."

"What's his name? I might know him." Henry tried not to look at her face. She was far too sexy. He tried not to think about the stupid bet or the fact that they worked together. "What?" he asked when she pressed her foot into his leg. "I know a lot of people."

"You want to help me find a man I'm looking for? Why?"

"I happen to be a nice guy," he said. Plus, if he hooked her up with someone else, she would be off-limits. He could forget all about the bet.

"It's Keoni," she said. "Keoni Makai." Claudia sat up and propped herself on her elbows. "You know him?"

Henry swallowed roughly. "I know him all right." Keoni had been one of the first friends he'd made in Hawaii. Everyone knew Keoni. Everyone loved Keoni, especially the ladies. Of course Keoni was the man Claudia was looking for.

"Can you help me find him?"

The hope on Claudia's face was like a knife to Henry's chest. "You sure you want to get involved with him? He doesn't seem like your type."

"How would you know my type? You don't even know me."

Henry stopped rubbing her foot and met her gaze. "You may be right, but I know Keoni."

She shifted her feet off his lap. "What's wrong with Keoni?"

Henry could tick off quite a few things. Just last week, Keoni had been hooking up with Henry's friend who'd been visiting from the mainland. And then he'd stood Henry up for a deep-sea dive that had nearly ended in disaster because they were a man short.

"Keoni's cool, I guess." *If you're into charming surfers.* Henry rose from the bench and reached for Claudia's hand. "Break's over. We should get started."

Claudia let him haul her to her feet. "Can you help me find Keoni?" she asked.

Henry wanted to say no, but when he looked down at Claudia's face, so sweet and so full of hope, he couldn't. "If that's what you really want," he said, already knowing he was going to regret it.

11

Fight Lesson

Claudia

HENRY WAS A METHODICAL TEACHER. He started from ground zero, showing Claudia exactly how to stand. Left foot in front, pointed at twelve o'clock. Right foot planted slightly behind and pointing at two. He showed her how to balance her weight on her back foot, how to twist and rotate, and how to power through with her punch.

He demonstrated each move with an endless supply of patience, gentle guidance, and fair critiques. After working together for a half hour, Claudia already had the basics of blocking and punching.

Once she had the basics down, they moved on to the fight scene. She was following along okay, feeling pretty confident until it was time to learn how to escape a headlock.

When Henry grabbed her and turned her in his arms so that her back was snug tight to his chest, Claudia lost focus.

His body was so hard, she felt bruised just from brushing against it. The man didn't have an ounce of fat clinging to his physique. His arm was like a vice around her waist, and his chest muscles rippled against her back. The bulge of his bicep flexed against her ribcage just under her breasts, and she felt her knees go weak.

"You okay?" His voice was near her ear, and the rough scrape of his beard nuzzled her cheek.

"Fine." She gritted her teeth and tried to remember to breathe.

Henry shifted his arm up her chest and locked his elbow around her neck. "And now?"

She was trapped in the crook of his elbow, her back flush against his chest. His masculine scent enveloped her. He wasn't wearing cologne, and his natural scent was enough to invade her senses. He smelled like clean cotton with a trace of engine oil, and something sweet like hay.

"You still okay?" He prompted when Claudia didn't answer.

Claudia tried not to think about how close his crotch was to her ass. "I'm okay."

"Good." He tightened his hold. "Tuck your chin and grab my arm with both hands."

Claudia pulled in a breath and followed his instructions.

"Don't lean forward," he said, pulling her hips tighter with his free hand. "Press back against me."

Her heart thudded. Pressing into him would destroy what was left of her focus. She did it anyway, ignoring the way he smelled, like fresh cotton and engine oil, so masculine it made her knees weak. A bolt of pleasure zapped down her spine.

"Now step your foot behind mine. Feel my calf against yours?"

She felt it. His calf was an iron bar against hers. "Yes."

"That's the perfect position."

Claudia resisted snuggling closer into him. She had to agree; it felt pretty good being held so tightly in Henry's strong arms.

"If you were really fighting for your life, you would want to bend your knee and give me a swift back kick to the groin." He chuckled uncomfortably. "We aren't going to practice that. But just remember to always go for the groin."

Her heartbeat sped up. "I'll remember."

"Push off your front leg and turn one hundred eighty degrees. Push your hips back into me and flip me over your leg."

Claudia's mouth went dry. "What?"

Henry released her and turned, stepping around to face her. "I know it sounds like a lot, but I'll do most of the work. Stunts are eighty percent illusion. But it's a stuntman's job to convince the audience they are one hundred percent real." He raised his hand at one of the crew members walking by. "Hey, Koa, come here a minute."

A big, square-shouldered Hawaiian man walked over to them. "Hey, Champ," he said.

"I'm teaching Claudia a stunt, and I want to show her what it looks like. Put me in a rear headlock."

Koa shrugged and stepped behind Henry. He was much bigger and broader than Henry, and when he grabbed Henry in a chokehold, it nearly lifted him off his feet. Claudia's stomach dropped when Koa tightened his elbow around Henry's neck and used his other hand to secure the hold.

"Tuck your chin," Henry said, demonstrating. "Grab his arm. Slide your leg behind his. Calf to calf. Got it?"

"I think so."

Claudia watched in fascination as Henry performed each step with fluid grace. He stomped his foot to the side, pushed his hips back, and flipped Koa over his thigh. The burly man rolled over Henry's leg and fell flat onto his back, expelling a huff of surprised breath when he landed.

Henry glanced up at Claudia with a hopeful expression. "Got it?"

Claudia swallowed roughly. "You made it look so easy."

"Want to see it again?" Henry asked.

Koa groaned from his prone position.

"No," Claudia said. "I think I've got it."

Henry reached down and offered Koa a hand. "Thanks, man."

Koa pushed to his feet and placed a hand on his back, stretching. "Sure," he muttered. "Anytime, man."

Claudia watched Koa shuffle off, then turned toward Henry. "Eighty percent illusion?" It had looked a lot more real than that.

"That's right. Do you want to try?"

Claudia set her jaw and fisted her hands. "I can do this."

Henry smiled. The skin around his eyes crinkled, and his gaze softened. He took a step forward and reached for both her hands. "I know."

His assurance bolstered her confidence. She squeezed his hands.

"Ready?"

"Ready."

He moved faster this time. After snaking an arm around her, he spun her body so that her back collided with the hard wall of his chest. His arm encircled her neck, and his legs bracketed hers.

Claudia was so disoriented by his sudden movement and the smell of his fresh cotton scent enveloping her that she forgot everything he'd taught her.

"Step. Bend. Flip," Henry said in her ear.

Those words shouldn't sound erotic. They shouldn't get her heart pumping and liquid pooling between her thighs. Her nipples hardened to stiff peaks under the vice of his arm, and goose bumps rose along her neck where his rough chin scraped her skin.

He tightened his hold, pulling her closer, snug against his hard body. "You can do this," he said.

Claudia cleared her mind and shifted her leg behind Henry's. When her calf rubbed his, she pushed off her front foot and pivoted. She yanked his arm, and in one swift move, Henry flipped over her leg.

He rolled smoothly to his feet, beaming. "Perfect!"

Claudia looked up at him. "You did all the work."

He ran a hand through his messy hair, giving her a confused look. "I'm supposed to. That's the point."

A spark of anger flared to life in her chest. "I want to do it on my own."

Henry laughed. "Why? You did what you needed to do."

Claudia ducked out from under his arm and crossed her arms over her chest. "Don't patronize me, Henry. I want to be treated like every other stuntman. I didn't get this far in my career by accepting favors." She threw back her shoulders and puffed up her chest. "Let's do it again. The right way."

Henry's gaze dropped over her, a smile twitching on his lips. "I think we need a break," he said, strolling over to the craft table. He grabbed a big chocolate chip cookie and sank his teeth into it.

Claudia grabbed a cigarette from the tray on the table. Before she could light a match, Henry took the pack from her trembling fingers and struck one for her. She leaned in and touched the tip of her cigarette to the flame, her eyes clashing angrily with his.

"I'm sorry," he said, flicking his wrist to put out the match. "If you want me to show you something harder next time, I will. Maybe you need more of a challenge."

Claudia exhaled a thin stream of smoke. Her nerves calmed as Henry's soothing voice washed over her. "You really think I did okay?"

His smile bloomed. "You were great." He stuffed the rest of the cookie in his mouth and dusted his hands together. "We can have another lesson in a few days."

Her heart sank. She wasn't ready for the lesson to be over. "I thought we were just on a break. Are you in a hurry to get out of here?" she asked. She was the one who needed to go. She needed to find Keoni. "Do you have a hot date?" She was teasing, but when Henry shrugged, she felt a stab of disappointment.

Henry shrugged. "Just meeting someone for drinks."

Jealousy coiled in her chest, but she crushed it down and slapped a smile on her face. "I'm hoping to get out to the beach before dark anyway," she said.

"Gonna catch some rays?"

"I'm hoping to find Keoni. Maybe he's giving surf lessons at Waikiki."

Henry choked on a laugh. "Keoni giving surf lessons? At Waikiki?"

"What's so funny?"

"I can't imagine him giving surf lessons. He would never let anyone touch his surfboard. It's his most prized possession."

"I've touched his surfboard," Claudia bragged.

Henry's smile faded. "Let me guess, he played guitar for you?"

"Maybe," she admitted.

He shook his head. "Works for him every time."

Claudia crushed her cigarette into an ashtray. "I don't like what you're insinuating."

Henry took a step closer. "Let me guess, he offered to show you the *real Ha-vhy-ee.*" He mimicked the local accent. "Starting with a surfing lesson and ending with his bedroom."

Henry's nearly accurate guess infuriated Claudia. Before she realized what she meant to do, she raised her hand and struck him across the face. The sound of her palm striking his cheek cracked like lightning.

A red mark in the shape of her palm blazed to life on Henry's cheek. Claudia's eyes widened as she realized what she'd done.

The tips of his ears turned a shade of pink that matched his cheek. "I apologize," he said, his eyes downcast. "That was out of line."

Claudia crossed her arms in sulking silence.

Henry shuffled to an ice chest and grabbed two bottles of soda. He offered one to Claudia. "Truce?"

Claudia took the bottle, her eyes shooting to the red mark on Henry's cheek. Her anger disappeared as quickly as it had risen. She tapped her bottle to Henry's. "Truce," she said.

Henry grinned. "Guess we can skip the slapping lesson. I think you've got that down."

Claudia unscrewed the cap and took a swallow of the cold soda. She suppressed a smile as Henry rolled the cold bottle onto his cheek. She probably should apologize, but honestly, he'd had it coming.

"Have fun on your date tonight," Claudia said, deciding to be the first to walk away.

"Thanks." Henry lifted his bottle to her as she headed toward her trailer. "Good luck finding your man," he said.

Claudia glanced back at Henry over her shoulder. Even though the sentiment was sincere enough, she thought she detected a note of jealousy brimming in his words.

Serves him right.

————————————————

12

79

The SurfRider

————————————————

Henry

IT DIDN'T TAKE LONG for him to realize he was being stood up. Henry sat on a stool at the bar at The SurfRider, Waikiki's oldest, most prestigious hotel, nursing his second martini.

The live band on the small stage played a popular swing song from his parents' era. Like everything in Hawaii, the music was a blend of native and mainland influences. The result was a uniquely Hawaiian blend that made Henry wish he had a beautiful woman to lead onto the dance floor.

He checked his watch again and sighed. His date was forty-five minutes late. Not a good sign.

Henry took another small sip of his drink. The vodka was top-shelf smooth, but it was going to his head. A pleasant buzz infiltrated his thoughts, which was fine with him. He couldn't seem to get out of his head tonight. He was feeling a bit sorry for himself. Another fifteen minutes and he could officially say he'd been stood up. Leilani was a local girl he'd met a few days ago at the supermarket in the produce section. She'd helped him pick out the best mangoes, and he'd offered to buy her a drink.

He lifted his glass and drank. Dave really did make the best vodka martinis on the island. He was on his second, and they were going down way too easily.

He checked his watch again and saw that only a few minutes had passed. Maybe Leilani had gotten stuck in traffic. He sighed heavily, thinking of the empty house that waited for him. His house seemed bigger since Penny and her friend had gone back to the mainland. He didn't miss their wet swimsuits hanging from his shower curtain, and he was glad to finally have his bed back after sleeping on the sofa for two weeks, but he missed them. He missed the way their laughter filled his kitchen in the morning, and he missed having someone to talk to after a long day at work.

Maybe he should get a dog.

He wondered how Penny was doing. Did they miss Hawaii yet? Penny was Henry's favorite cousin. She was a redhead like him—the only two redheads in the Longchamp clan. Everyone liked to tease that maybe they had the same milkman for a father. While Henry was easy as a breeze, Penny had a redhead's passionate temperament. Penny was Katharine Hepburn: head-strong, independent, and passionate.

Penny had managed to fall in love with Bones while she was in Hawaii, which was nothing new. The island inspired love connections, the sultry nights turning friends into lovers and enticing strangers to swim naked.

Henry's lips twitched into a smile as he thought of Claudia. The smile disappeared when he pictured her and Keoni together.

Henry frowned into his drink. Keoni had his role as Casanova down pat. A seductive song on his guitar, a charming story about ancient Hawaii folklore, and off came the panties. Women practically threw themselves at the handsome surfer. Meanwhile, Henry was being dropped like an over-ripe mango.

He tossed back his drink in a long swallow and set his glass on the bar with a clatter.

"Another one, Champ?"

Henry looked up at Dave. "Not tonight."

He slid his credit card out of his wallet and placed it on the bar. The little piece of plastic was a happy reminder of how far he'd come. Henry Longchamp, youngest child and only boy of Dale and Vi Longchamp, had a credit line of five thousand dollars with Bank of Hawaii. Even though he'd just been stood up, at least he had made it. Henry Longchamp was a success. And even if he never got the chance to direct a series, or even a single stunt, he was the best in the business.

"Holy B-52s! Check out the bombers on that one," Dave said, gesturing with his chin at the entrance to the bar.

Henry swiveled on his barstool and saw Claudia standing at the hostess desk. Suddenly, the room went quiet. The buzz of conversation faded into the background, replaced by the hum of his blood in his veins. His cock went rock hard, painfully swelling against the seam of his jeans.

She sauntered into the bar, mesmerizing every male in the vicinity with the sway of her luscious hips. The short hemline of her dress swished across her legs, revealing a tantalizing glimpse of tanned thighs with every step. Her long hair was pulled back into a high ponytail, and a fringe of wispy bangs fell over her forehead.

Claudia looked beautiful wearing a pair of shorts and a T-shirt without a stitch of makeup on her face, but dressed up and wearing dramatic makeup, she was the sexiest woman Henry had ever seen.

Henry froze when the beam of her gaze swept across the room and landed on him. Her mouth curved into a smile, and his heart jumped into his throat. Adrenaline shot through his veins. He'd only had two drinks, but one smile from Claudia and Henry was as high as a kite.

"Hi, Henry." Claudia's candy-pink lips looked good enough to lick. "What happened to your date?"

Henry winced. "I think I've officially been stood up. Do you care to join me?"

When Claudia shrugged and slid onto the stool next to him, Henry picked up his credit card and slid it back into his wallet.

"Another vodka martini, please," he told Dave. "And Don Julio on the rocks with a twist of lemon for the lady."

Claudia smiled, sharing their secret. "You remembered."

"Put hers on my tab."

"You don't have to do that. The studio is picking up my bill."

Henry shook his head. "When you're sitting next to me, I pay."

"Why, Henry," Claudia said in a Southern belle voice. "I never knew you were such a gentleman."

Dave placed their drinks on the bar.

"Cheers to that." Henry lifted his glass and drank. The vodka burned his throat going down. He grimaced and swallowed. He decided not to beat around the bush and asked what he was dying to know. "What happened with Keoni?"

Claudia plucked a cigarette from a silver case and pinched it between her lips. "I haven't had any luck finding him."

Relief filled Henry's chest. He felt like he'd dodged a bullet. He grabbed a pack of matches and struck one for Claudia.

"I thought he'd be easier to find," she confessed, her eyes bright against the flare of the match.

Henry bristled at the thought of Claudia and Keoni together. "He doesn't deserve a woman like you."

Claudia's eyebrows rose. "How can you say that?"

"You deserve a man who shows up for his friends. When Keoni ditched us for that dive this weekend, it wasn't cool." That was the understatement of the year. Bones had almost died. Henry scowled into his drink, thinking about how Keoni had seduced Lou while they'd been visiting. Lou had fallen for Keoni. Penny had fallen for Bones. Love was in the balmy air all right. Both women had fallen for their Hawaiian hosts. "You deserve a man who doesn't take advantage of a sweet girl who doesn't know any better."

Claudia took a long drag off her cigarette and lifted her chin in the air to exhale a stream of smoke. She eyed Henry thoughtfully, her hand fluttering to his arm. "I don't think anyone's ever said anything so nice to me. Thank you."

Guilt stabbed Henry's chest. He'd been talking about his cousin and her friend, not Claudia, but he could hardly admit that now. "You're welcome."

She tapped ashes into the ashtray and leaned her elbow on the bar. Every man in the place was looking at her right now, but she hardly seemed to notice. "When Keoni and I met six years ago, it changed my life. He encouraged me to go after my dreams. If not for him, I may have never made it in Hollywood."

"So you just want to find Keoni to thank him?"

Claudia took a drag off her cigarette. "Not exactly."

"Oh." Henry nodded, wishing he didn't understand. "Okay."

She swiveled on her stool to face him. "Keoni was the first man who made me feel alive. I'd had other boyfriends by then, but I felt nothing for them. And truth be told, I haven't felt much for anyone since." She frowned, her pink lips forming the sweetest pout. "My dating life is mostly controlled by my agent. Especially since…" Her voice trailed off, and her shoulders stiffened. "Never mind."

Henry's eyebrows drew together. "Sounds like you never really gave anyone a chance."

Claudia bit her lip, staring at something in the distance. "I just have this feeling that Keoni is the right man for me. We are meant to be together."

Henry pressed a hand to the ache in his chest as if he could rub the pain away. He didn't want Claudia to be with Keoni, but he did want her to be happy. He took a long swallow of his drink and then signaled the bartender. "Can you bring me the phone?" he asked.

Dave grabbed the phone from beside the register and stretched the cord down the length of the bar until it reached them. "Not long distance, is it?"

"No."

"Who are you calling?" Claudia covered his hand with hers. "Keoni?"

Henry pressed buttons. "Not Keoni, but the next closest thing."

The phone rang four times before Bones picked it up. "Hello?"

"Hey, man. It's Henry."

There was a long pause. They hadn't spoken since the dive in Maui. Finally, Bones cleared his throat and asked, "Howzit, Henry? I been meaning to call you."

"Good." Henry wasn't going to get into a deep discussion about the unfortunate events of the coral dive, not when Claudia was leaning into him, hanging on his every word. "You seen Keoni around?"

"Nah," Bones said. "Not for a few days. I can barely hear you over the music, cuz. Where you at?"

"I'm at the bar at The SurfRider."

"Whatchu want with Keoni?"

Henry darted a glance at Claudia. "I know somebody who's looking for him."

"Somebody like who?" Bones growled.

"Somebody beautiful." And smart and sexy. Somebody who made Henry laugh.

Bones laughed. "Oh, yeah?"

"What's his phone number?" Henry gestured at Claudia to get a pen. She reached in her bag and scrambled around, then came up with a tube of lipstick. He grabbed a napkin and wrote the number down in pink lipstick. "Thanks, man. Laters."

"Laters. If you talk to Keoni, tell him I'm looking for him, kay?"

Henry agreed and pressed the button on the phone to hang up. "You want to call him now?" He offered the receiver to Claudia.

She took the phone and held it to her ear, then gave Henry the go-ahead. He punched each button calmly, as if his heart weren't ripping out of his chest.

13

Swing Dancing

Claudia

CLAUDIA FIDGETED with the hem of her skirt, crossing and recrossing her legs as the phone rang. Each shrill ring in her ear made her heart beat faster. The noises from the bar disappeared, and all she heard was the sound of her heavy breathing and the incessant ringing of the phone.

Biting her lip, she replaced the receiver with a nonchalant lift of her shoulders. "He's not home," she said.

"You have his number now," Henry said practically. "You can call him later."

Claudia took another sip of her drink. Her heart was still stuck in her throat, and she swallowed roughly. She glanced at Henry, who was signaling the bartender to take away the phone. Curiosity filled her mind as she stared at him.

"What?" He raised a brow when he caught her staring.

Claudia narrowed her eyes at him. "What exactly happened on that dive?"

Henry drew in a sharp breath and shook his head.

"Was it dangerous?" she asked, prodding as she turned to face him. "Tell me, Henry."

He took a big swallow of his drink and set it on the bar. "We were diving for black coral," he said in a soft voice that she had to lean in to hear. "It's not exactly legal."

Claudia sucked in a surprised breath and glanced around. "Go on," she said, leaning closer.

"Bones knows a spot where it grows on the bottom of the ocean near Maui. The trees are worth a fortune, but they are down deep."

"How deep?"

Henry cracked his knuckles and clasped his hands on the counter. "Deeper than I know how to dive. That's what Keoni was for. He's been diving since he was a teenager. He and Bones were going to dive as a team, and I was there to man the boat. I've never dived over fifty feet, and this was…" He glanced around furtively. "Five times that deep."

Claudia's eyes went wide as she quickly calculated the distance. "Two hundred and fifty feet?"

Henry cleared his throat. "Yeah."

"Geez. That sounds like suicide."

Henry shuddered visibly. "That's why I couldn't go with Bones. I would have been useless. If I was trained—" He broke off, jamming a hand through his hair.

Claudia touched his arm. "It's not your fault." It sounded like it was Keoni's fault. "Then what happened?"

"The boat drifted while he was under, and I lost sight of him." Henry blinked rapidly as if reliving the nightmare. "I waited for him as long as I could, but the longer I waited, the more daylight was ticking by. I didn't want to call the coast guard, but in the end, I had to."

"You had to," Claudia said in agreement, knowing that the story had a happy ending, seeing as Henry had just talked to Bones on the phone.

"And then I had to sail home alone and tell everyone in Bones's family what happened."

Claudia put her hand on his arm and squeezed. "That must have been horrible."

He raised his eyes toward hers. Dark blue and fringed with long lashes, Henry's eyes weren't smiling for once. "It was one of the worst moments of my life."

Claudia had judged Henry for a good-time Charlie, but the look in his eyes told her she'd been wrong. There was a serious side to Henry that he kept hidden. His eyes were full of secrets that she had the insatiable urge to unravel.

The band broke into a Hawaiian version of "Pennsylvania 6-5000," and in a blink, Henry's eyes flashed with his trademark smile. He slid off the stool and grabbed her hand. "This conversation is getting too heavy," he said. "I don't do heavy." He tugged her off her stool. "Do you want to dance?"

Claudia felt like she had whiplash from the sudden change in Henry's mood, but she was beginning to understand something about him. He didn't dwell in dark places longer than necessary.

"It just so happens I won a dance-off to this song," she said, allowing Henry to steer her away from the bar.

"You know how to swing?" he asked in a reverent tone.

"I do," she confirmed. "Do you?"

"Five sisters, remember?" He tucked her hand in the crook of his elbow. "They used to take turns with me since I was the only boy. Plus, my mom said dancing is the way to win a girl's heart."

From the way her heart was beating out of her chest as Henry twirled her onto the dance floor, she had to agree that Henry's mother was a wise woman.

Henry spun Claudia in a circle, then passed her behind his back, showing off a bit of fancy footwork.

"You do know how to swing!" she cried.

With a victorious smile, he swung her to the center of the

floor. One of his big hands went to her back, just under her shoulder blade, and the other gripped hers loosely at her waist.

When she placed her hand on his shoulder and triple-stepped with a little flounce, Henry's smile beamed. He extended his elbow, allowing her room to rock back before pulling her forward again.

After steering her in an underarm turn, he switched to a handshake hold so that she could spin in a circle. He did it all smoothly, as if dancing the swing was something he practiced every day.

Less ambitious dancers stepped aside to give them room, and a crowd formed in a circle to watch.

Claudia felt like a beam of light had swallowed her whole as Henry spun her around and then clasped her hand again. Their shared connection sent a buzz of excitement racing down her spine.

There was something exhilarating about dancing with a man who knew how to move. No wonder Henry was such a good stuntman. Anyone who could dance like him could trick the audience into believing a fake fight was the real thing.

Butterflies stirred to life in her belly, and a flush stained her cheeks as Claudia wondered what Henry would be like in bed. She shut the thought down, surprised at herself. She should be thinking about Keoni, not Henry.

But his effortless moves made her thoughts spiral toward the bedroom. His hips rocked against hers. His touch was light but commanding. His eyes never lost contact with hers. A man who could move with such fluid strength on the dance floor had to be fantastic at sex.

He raised his arm, directed her underneath, and brought her back in close. Claudia spun like a yo-yo, then ended with her arms crossed in front of her chest and Henry's front snug against her back in a cuddle hold.

She tilted her head back in a throaty laugh as he pulled her close against his shoulder.

"Sliding doors?" he whispered in her ear.

His chin brushed her cheek, and his scent enveloped her. Cedarwood and cotton. Henry smelled like a naughty picnic under the sun.

"Sliding doors," she replied.

Henry dropped her hands and slid behind her, allowing her to pass in front. She took his offered hand, and they switched positions. They grinned at each other, sliding back and forth in front of each other to a round of applause.

Claudia was breathless as the song wound to a close. Ending on a grand gesture, Henry spun Claudia into his arms and dipped her over his knee. She felt weightless in his strong hold, arching her back over the steel of his thigh. His hands held her firmly, one wrapped around her waist, the other cradling her back.

The lightness in her chest bubbled up in a laugh. She wound her arms around his neck and threaded her fingers through his hair.

He stared at her mouth, and she licked her lips, suddenly craving his kiss. He felt so good against her. The hard length of his thigh supported the arch of her back. His arms were tight around her, holding her as if nothing could tear her from his grip. And his mouth… His mouth was close. So close.

Then it was on hers.

The kiss was cool at first. A casual brush of his lips. Then, his firm mouth moved against hers, sliding softly, hungrily. He nibbled at her bottom lip, teasing her mouth with his teeth.

A blaze of heat scorched through Claudia. Her heart skipped. Her thoughts scrambled. Kissing Henry felt like touching a live wire. She felt electrified from head to toe.

He pulled back and spun her upright in a dizzying turn. Their audience clapped enthusiastically, and Henry winked at her, indicating they should bow.

Claudia suddenly felt clumsy as she slid one foot behind the other and tucked her chin in a bow. She stole a glance at Henry and felt peevish at his easy grin.

He'd been playing it up for the crowd, and the kiss was just a bonus for more applause. Her temper flared. She'd been fueling fantasies of Henry in bed, and he'd been acting all along. Claudia felt foolish for getting lost in the music and the hum of energy on the dance floor.

The band broke into a Hawaiian-style rendition of "Brown Eyed Girl," and Henry reached for her hand.

"They're playing our song," he said, tugging her closer.

Claudia stepped back before he could reel her in. "We don't have a song."

Henry brushed his hair back from his forehead where it had fallen into his eyes and looked down at her. "What's eating you?"

"Not a thing." She fired a bright smile at him. "I have an early shoot tomorrow." She turned to go and left him solo on the dance floor. "Thanks for the drinks and the dance."

His eyes burned into her as she walked away. She grabbed her handbag from the bar and went up to her room. As she wiped off her makeup, she realized she'd accomplished what she had in mind when she left her room earlier. She'd wanted a distraction and a bit of a good time. Henry had provided both, plus a little more than she'd bargained for.

It wasn't until she was dressed in her pajamas and settling under the covers with a book that she remembered she'd left the napkin with Keoni's number at the bar.

14

Since We Kissed

Henry

IT WAS JUST A KISS. Nothing to sweat over. So why couldn't Henry get it off his mind? Because he never should have done it. He never should have given in to his desires. He should have left Claudia alone and steered far away from her, both for his own safety and because of the stupid bet.

Four days had gone by since he'd seen Claudia. Four long days since he'd set foot on the seventy acres of property A Long Road Home shared with two other television shows.

He'd been so busy working at the stables, training the new stunt horse, that he'd barely thought about her. That was a lie, but it was what Henry told himself. Repeatedly.

Usually Henry loved being at the stables—the rolling paddocks reminded him of home—but not now. Not when Claudia was on set and he wasn't.

It was almost four o'clock, officially quitting time. Thank God it was Friday. He finally had an excuse to drop by the set for his paycheck.

He fed Aries a carrot and let himself out of the horse's stall.

Aries protested with a whinny, and Henry turned around with a smile.

"You know I've still got one left, don't you?" He held the last carrot under the horse's muzzle and laughed as the ex-racehorse daintily snuffled his hand for the treat.

He'd had enough of the horses for a few days. Every muscle in his body ached. Every bone was dead tired. Even his teeth hurt.

Aries had proved to be as stubborn as he was photogenic. Since his arrival a month ago, the horse had bitten two grooms and bucked everyone who tried to ride him—except Henry.

"Good night, Aries." Henry signaled the stable hand to take over. There wasn't time to brush Aries down. It wasn't part of Henry's job to groom the horses, but he usually did it to relax. Today, all Henry wanted was to get to the set and see Claudia.

He sped the few miles along the coastal highway back to set and pulled into the lot in record time. The first thing he noticed was that Claudia's trailer wasn't in its usual spot. His heart seized in panic. His mind jumped to the worst conclusion—that she was gone and he'd never see her again.

And then he saw her, walking across the lawn in her costume, chatting it up with Stan.

Henry's heart skipped to life, racing at an alarming rate.

The two of them looked deep in conversation. Henry hoped they were simply discussing a scene, but just the sight of them head-to-head made him uncomfortable.

He watched them walk across the lawn, and he spotted Claudia's trailer under a little grove of trees. It was shady there, and private.

Henry lost sight of them when they walked around the other side of the trailer to the door.

His heart pounded as he imagined the conversation between the co-stars. Was Stan telling Claudia about the bet? Henry knew he should have told her when he had the chance, before anyone else was able to. But there had never seemed to be a right time, and Henry had been a coward.

No more. He hopped out of his car and slammed the door. It was time to tell Claudia the truth, admit his role in the sordid affair, and suffer the consequences. Unless Stan had already told her. Then the plan would be to grovel at her pretty feet.

Stan was nowhere in sight when Henry stepped up to Claudia's trailer and knocked on the door.

"Megan?" Claudia called from inside. "Is that you?"

Henry cleared his throat. "It's me," he said, whisking off his hat. "It's Henry."

A moment later, the door swung open. Henry's shoulders relaxed when he saw Claudia was alone. Then he remembered his purpose and tensed again.

"You're always showing up just in time to help me out of my clothes," she quipped, turning around to present Henry with the back of her dress. "Can you help me out of this?"

His mouth was too dry to speak, so he stepped forward and tossed his hat on the counter, then reached for her.

This time, he sped through the hooks with nimble fingers. He didn't want to linger. Touching Claudia only added fuel to the fire of his fantasies.

"What did Stan want?" he asked, undoing the final hook that held her dress together.

Claudia fired a curious gaze at him. "Why?"

Henry crossed his arms over his chest. "Just wondering."

Both her eyebrows rose, but she went into the bedroom without answering.

Henry blew out a breath of frustration, his mind churning out the worst-case scenarios. If Stan had told her, he was going to beat the man to a pulp. He didn't stop to examine his volatile reaction. He only knew he wanted to punch anyone who'd hurt Claudia, including himself. He braced his hands on the kitchen counter and stared at the pink curtains covering the window over the sink. The ache in his chest smarted, reminding him of the mistakes he'd made. He should have told Claudia about the bet from the beginning. He shouldn't have let himself get involved. He shouldn't have kissed her…

Claudia came out of the bedroom wearing shorts and a T-shirt. No bra. His heart pounded, and his cock stirred.

"I'd ask what's got your shorts in a wad," she said. "But I don't think you're wearing any."

Henry managed a strangled laugh and casually leaned his hip against the counter. "I just wanted to know what you and Stan were talking about. That's all."

Claudia's eyebrows shot upward. She reached for a cigarette and leaned forward, allowing Henry to strike a match for her. "If you must know, Stan wanted me to rehearse with him." She blew a puff of smoke into the air. "One-on-one."

Henry didn't know whether to be relieved or outraged. He settled for relieved. At least Stan hadn't spilled the beans about the bet. "What did you say?"

"I told him I didn't need rehearsing," she said, stepping around him to open a cabinet above the counter. "I was born perfect."

Henry flushed, watching the way the T-shirt molded to her breasts when she reached up into the cabinet. Claudia was right about one thing. She was perfect. Every man's dream girl. She had a body for sin, a sweet mouth, and a biting wit.

She pinched her cigarette between her lips and pulled down a bottle of tequila and a glass. "I can handle men like Stan Beatty."

Henry's jaw tightened. "You shouldn't have to. Men like him make me sick." He'd been out to clubs with Stan before. He'd seen the way Stan treated women, as if they were there to serve him.

"Men like Stan are usually compensating for something." Claudia lifted her pinky finger and wiggled it in the air.

A bark of laughter escaped Henry's mouth, then died away when he remembered his purpose for coming to Claudia's trailer. He picked up his hat and slid a finger around the felt brim as he searched for the right words. When he started to speak, his throat closed up.

"You want a drink?" Claudia blew smoke into the air between them. "I've got whiskey too."

"Sure." A drink would help loosen his tongue and maybe make the news easier for Claudia to swallow. He snagged a lemon out of a bowl on the counter and gestured for Claudia to sit. "I'll fix them."

"You missed your calling as a bartender." Claudia sat on the bench and took a drag off her cigarette. Squinting up at him, she slowly exhaled. "Where have you been the last few days?"

Since we kissed? The unspoken words hung heavy between them.

Henry turned and rummaged in the drawer for a knife. He wouldn't think about that kiss anymore. He couldn't. But a grin tugged at the corners of his lips anyway when he remembered the soft curve of her mouth yielding under his.

Maybe Claudia had missed him too. Maybe she was thinking about that kiss right now, just like he was. He snuck a peek at her as he sliced the lemon. She was studying him.

"I've been working with the horses."

"Oh? So that's the smell."

Henry laughed and sniffed his shirt. "Is it bad? I'm so used to it, I don't notice anymore."

"It's not bad." Claudia let her eyes drop over him slowly. "I'm really digging this whole cowboy getup. Especially the hat."

Henry swept the hat on his head and dipped his chin. "Thank you, little lady," he said in his best Western drawl.

Her lips curved in a smile as she accepted her drink. "Much obliged, Champ," she said in a smokey voice.

A jolt hit him in his heart and then zigzagged down to his cock. His pulse throbbed. There wasn't a woman on Earth sexier than the one sitting two feet away from him. Her long legs were bare and crossed at the knee. Her feet were bare, her toenails painted candy pink.

It was torture being this close to her, knowing she was off-limits because of that stupid bet, which he'd yet to figure out how to tell her about. And they worked together. There were too many reasons to stay far away.

Henry splashed whiskey into a glass for himself and turned around to face Claudia. It was a bad idea. He couldn't look at her. He was all for women's liberation, but right now, he needed Claudia to be wearing a bra. The tiny pebbles of her nipples pressing against the fabric of her T-shirt was too distracting.

Instead of looking at her tits, he tore his gaze up to her face. Another mistake. The rosy pout of her bottom lip practically begged to be kissed. Again. Next time, he'd take his time with that plump bottom lip, sucking it into his mouth and running his tongue along the seam.

"Why are you really here, Henry?" she asked.

He was there to kiss her, of course. Wasn't he? No. He was definitely not.

A sharp knock sounded on the door to the trailer, and a moment later, the door burst open.

"Sorry it took me so long—" Megan stepped into the trailer and froze. Her gaze darted from Claudia sitting on the bench to Henry leaning against the counter, and her entire demeanor changed. A flush rose up her neck to her cheeks. "Hi, Champ."

Henry tipped his chin at Megan. "Howzit, Megan?"

The blush on her cheeks flamed brighter. "I'm… It's… uh…" She giggled and blushed brighter. "It's good," she said, glancing at Claudia. "Sorry it took me so long, but I guess you didn't need my help?"

"I managed to get out of that straitjacket without your help."

"Sorry," Megan muttered. "I was talking to Koa. He knows that guy you asked about." Megan handed Claudia a piece of paper. "That's his address."

A bright spot flashed in front of Henry's eyes. Heat speared his chest. He watched the way Claudia's eyes lit up as she leaned forward to take the paper, and his chest tightened painfully. He rubbed a hand over his heart to soothe the ache and drained his glass of whiskey in a single gulp.

"I gotta go," he said, setting the empty glass on the counter. "Thanks for the drink."

He managed to smile at both women and get out the door before he did something stupid, like rip the paper with Keoni's address on it out of Claudia's hand and tear it to pieces.

15

Dangerous Diving

Henry

BY THE TIME Henry turned into his neighborhood, he had almost convinced himself he'd done the right thing by not telling Claudia about the bet.

What did it matter if the cast and crew were betting on who'd be the first to sleep with her when she was dead set on finding Keoni?

She wasn't going to sleep with Stan or Koa or Jake, not when she could have Keoni, the hero of O'ahu who'd saved more people from drowning than all the lifeguards at Waikiki added together.

He drove up the winding road to his hilltop street, barely noticing the expansive views of Eastern O'ahu bathed in twilight. Henry's house was a modest one-bedroom bungalow built on top of the ridge, with a spectacular view of Diamond Head Crater.

The view was the only reason he'd paid the outrageous price to buy the place. That and the shower wasn't bad either.

Henry was looking forward to a hot shower, a beer, and a

night of reruns on television. His list of Friday-night activities wasn't the most exciting in the world, but being in show business wasn't all glamour and glitz. Sometimes it was ten- and twelve-hour days in the scorching sun, training a horse to drop and roll without injuring the man riding on his back. Sometimes, it was grueling and thankless. And exhausting.

Henry's plans for a low-key evening came to a screeching halt when he saw the woodie station wagon with the surfboard strapped to the top parked in his driveway.

Bones's car.

Henry hauled himself up the driveway. Bones was the last person Henry wanted to see right now. Scratch that, he wanted to see Bones's cousin Keoni even less. He opened the door to his house, thinking it could have been worse. It could have been Keoni sitting on his sofa leafing through a magazine and drinking a Primo.

Screw Keoni. If he saw him right now, he'd put his fist through his pretty face. It had been Keoni's fault the coral dive had gone to shit. His fault if Bones would have died.

Bones looked up from the magazine when Henry slammed the door. "Eh? This the kind a trash you like to read?" He tossed the magazine to the coffee table. "You're worse than my sisters, brah."

Henry grabbed the magazine and stuffed it in a drawer in the kitchen. It was a rag mag he'd picked up at the supermarket. Claudia was on the cover. He moved to the fridge and opened the door.

"You bring any more of those beers, man?" he called to Bones.

"You know it." Bones came into the breakfast room and sat on a stool across the counter from Henry.

Henry's living room was one big room divided by a kitchen counter. The furniture was sparse and cobbled together, but it was tidy. He'd gotten the chrome-rimmed table and chairs at a yard sale, and the previous owner had left the sofa. The only personal touches were the books on a bookshelf and a few framed photographs.

"It's good to see you in one piece," Henry said, popping open a beer.

"It's good to be in one piece." Bones lifted his can in salute.

They drank to Bones's life.

"You seen Keoni yet?" Henry asked, hating to even say his name.

"Yeah. It's all cool, brah. We're cool."

Heat crept up under Henry's collar. He usually let things slide right off, but this time, he couldn't. His anger with Keoni burned in his gut.

"You almost died," Henry said. "Fuck Keoni."

Bones's glare hardened to black diamonds. "Don't talk shit about my cousin. We shoulda stayed back. It was my fault for diving, not Keoni's." He took a long swallow of beer. "I'm hard to kill though, brah. I'm still here."

When Keoni hadn't showed up the morning of the dive, they'd been stupid to think they could go without him. In Henry's defense, he hadn't known Bones was planning on diving two hundred and fifty feet deep. The current had pushed him farther from the boat, and he'd ended up swimming all the way to the nearest island of Moloka'i. Six miles away. It had taken him all day. Meanwhile, Henry had thought he was dead.

Part of him wanted to punch Bones for putting him through that. A bigger part of him wanted to punch Keoni.

In the end, he was too tired to fight. He leaned against the counter and drank his beer. "What are you doing here?" he asked Bones. "You come for the view?" He nodded at the panoramic view of the sunset from the sliding glass doors.

Bones tossed a fat envelope onto the counter beside Henry. "I brought a peace offering, awright?"

"What's that?"

"Just open it, cuz."

He opened it and whistled as he thumbed through the stack of bills. "What's this for?"

"I heard the way you handled my family, brah. I owe you one."

Henry scrubbed his hands along his face, too tired to argue. He wanted a shower, another beer, and his bed. He wouldn't mind if a woman were in it either. A specific woman with blonde hair and more curves than the Pali Highway popped to mind, and he pushed it farther away. What he didn't want was Bones's money.

He slid the envelope back across the counter. "I can't take that."

"Why the hell not?"

Henry shrugged. "I didn't do anything."

"That's a thousand bucks, man." Bones laughed. "You're not turning it down. You're taking it. End of story."

Bones gave him a stern look that said he wasn't taking no for an answer.

One thousand dollars. It was the same amount Albert had bet on him. If he gave Albert the money, then he could get out of the bet.

He reached across the counter for the envelope of money. "I'll take it on one condition," he told Bones.

"What's that?"

"I want in on the next dive."

"Yeah, yeah, yeah." Bones waved his hand in the air, no big deal. "You can drive anytime."

"No," Henry said, hefting the envelope. "I don't want to drive the boat. I want to dive with you."

Bones's dark eyes appraised him. "You ever done any divin'?"

"Nope."

Bones sat on the stool and leaned forward, resting his elbows on the counter to level Henry with a glare. "It's not an ordinary dive, man. I been divin' since the day I was born, and it about killed me."

"What almost killed you was not having a dive partner."

Bones's eyes sparked fire, but he held his tongue. There was no point arguing over Keoni anymore. Bones would never say a bad word about his cousin. The blood they shared was too thick and spanned too many centuries.

"Diving deep is some dangerous shit," Bones warned.

Henry laughed. "No shit, man. I like danger. Look at what I do for a living."

"Kay den," Bones said. "I guess I can teach you to dive. How's Friday next week?"

Henry looked at his work schedule, which was pinned to the fridge. He tapped his finger on the following Friday. He happened to be off. "Works," he said.

"I'll pick you up at seven."

"I'll be ready."

Bones stood to go and then hesitated at the door. "You heard from Penny?" he asked.

Henry hadn't thought Bones was going to ask about Penny. Things had ended badly when she'd left. And then Bones had disappeared and scared everyone half to death.

"I called her to tell her you were alive."

Bones grimaced. "How did she take the news?"

Henry shrugged. "She might have liked you better dead." He grinned when Bones shot him a dirty look. "She's good, man. Don't worry about Penny."

"I'm not."

"Next time I talk to her, I'll tell her you said hi."

"No. Don't tell her that. Eh? Tell her to forget me."

Henry nodded solemnly. He understood perfectly. There were some things better off never mentioned again. They also never had to talk about Keoni again as far as he was concerned.

When Bones left, Henry grabbed his address book and the

phone. He dialed the stunt director's number and thumbed through the bills while the phone rang.

"Hello?" Albert said.

"It's Henry." He took a swallow of beer and launched right into his plan. "Listen, man, I came into some money. How about I buy my way out of that bet?"

Albert was silent for a moment and then burst out laughing. "Fat chance!" he said and then hung up.

16

Hale'iwa

Claudia

CLAUDIA ZIPPED along the country roads in her baby-blue Thunderbird convertible. The top was down. The music was loud, and the tank was full.

She sang along to every song, even the ones she didn't know. The wind whipped through her hair. The sun shined on her face. Warm humidity clung to her skin.

She was finally going to see Keoni.

She hit a pothole so hard, it made her teeth clack together. *Ugh.* Didn't they maintain the roads out here? She was in the middle of nowhere, driving along a country road that cut a swatch through the center of the island.

Her heart stuttered, and she faltered over the words of "Ruby Tuesday," even though she knew the lyrics by heart.

Keoni was only a few more miles down the road. Soon, she would see the man she'd dreamed about for six years. With each mile, those years melted away, and Claudia felt like her eighteen-year-old self again, experiencing love for the first time. She and Keoni had been nothing but kids. She was fresh out of high school with ambitions to make it big, and he was determined to be the most famous surfer in the world.

A lot had changed since then. Claudia was a woman now, not some naïve country girl with grandiose dreams of making it big in Hollywood. She'd actually made it, and Keoni was still home. He hadn't been selected to compete in the contest that Declan had won.

Claudia had achieved her dreams, and clearly Keoni was on a different point in his journey. Would he resent her for that? Most men would. Most men didn't like a woman to make more money than them. It was one reason Claudia never dated. She'd yet to find a man who could swallow her success without choking, and the few times she'd dated men as successful as her, they were assholes.

Her agent arranged fake dates for her so the press could report on her social life. Claudia hadn't had a proper date in years. The closest she'd come to a date was at The SurfRider with Henry.

There had been drinks and dancing and even a kiss. A slow smile spread across Claudia's lips. As far as dates went, it had been more than satisfactory. But Henry hadn't meant that as an actual kiss. He'd been playing it up for their audience. Which was fine with Claudia. She wasn't interested in Henry. He wasn't even that good looking. Too rough around the edges. Not serious enough. Not even her type.

His mouth was too wide, his nose was crooked, and his hands were big and clumsy.

Claudia flushed when an image of Henry undoing the hooks on her dress flashed into her mind. The calloused pads of his fingers had been hot and rough against her skin. She imagined those hands everywhere, hungrily touching her skin, leaving a trail of fire in their wake.

Claudia slammed on the brakes, almost missing the turn to Hale'iwa. Keoni's town. His neighborhood. His street.

She gripped the steering wheel tightly in both hands, driving at a snail's pace down the street of tiny cottages. Each house had a postage-size front yard strewn with water toys. Surfboards and canoes leaned against palm trees, and boats were as prevalent as cars. She smelled the ocean, heard the distant cry of gulls, and tasted the salt in the air.

She almost missed the tiny house painted a cheerful shade of green. It was about the same size as Claudia's pool house in the hills of Hollywood. What it lacked in size, it made up for with charm. Flowers spilled from baskets on the porch, the grass was freshly cropped, and a wide porch with rocking chairs welcomed guests.

Claudia's heart raced as she pulled into the driveway and parked behind a faded VW Beetle. Keoni's car.

She wiped her sweaty hands on her dress and rehearsed her speech one last time. In Claudia's mind, her soliloquy started with an apology and ended with a kiss. Uncertainty coiled in her stomach. Claudia reached for a cigarette and lit the tip with trembling fingers. A few deep inhales and exhales later and she felt almost ready to get out of the car.

She stared at the house, imagining Keoni lounging in the hammock, strumming his guitar on the porch, or mowing the lawn.

Doubt crept in, treading lightly on nimble feet through her mind.

She shouldn't have come. After all, Keoni hadn't come for her. Six years, and she hadn't heard a word from him. He probably hated her still. Or worse, he'd forgotten all about her.

Only one way to find out. Claudia crushed her cigarette in the ashtray and got out of the car. She marched up the stairs and raised her hand to knock on the door.

"You lookin' for Keoni?"

Claudia turned and saw a woman standing on the neighboring porch. She wore a flowered muumuu and held a watering can in one hand.

"He ain't home," the woman said, tilting her head to squint

at Claudia. "Anybody ever tell you you're a dead ringer for Sissy Saxon in *Jezebel*?"

Claudia smiled tightly. "A few times." She walked to the edge of the porch. "Do you know when Keoni will be back?"

"Nah. He don't check in with me. I don't know everything in his life."

Claudia glanced at the Beetle in the driveway. "Is that his car?"

"Yeah, but I wouldn't bother waiting. If the surf is up at Waimea, he be gone for days, you know?" The woman watered more of her plants. "I heard surf was up at Waimea."

Claudia dug in her purse for a piece of paper, then had a better idea. "Can you give him a message for me?"

The woman lowered her watering can to glare at Claudia. "Humph. I look like a secretary to you?"

Claudia took out her wallet. "What if I make it worth your time?" She plucked a twenty out of her wallet and walked across the lawn between the houses. "If you see him today, tell him to meet me at Sans Souci tomorrow at sunrise."

The woman leaned down and snatched the bill. "Who should I say is waiting for him?"

Claudia turned to walk away. "You don't have to say. He'll know."

17

Legends

Henry

LEGENDS WAS MORE crowded than usual because Ryla Aikau was playing.

Ryla always attracted an enormous crowd. Locals and tourists came out to see her. It was only a matter of time before she was discovered and catapulted to international fame. For now, Ryla Aikau was Hawaii's hidden gem.

Except, tonight, it seemed the entire island had come to the seedy bar just a block past the tourist district of Waikiki Beach. Henry had always thought of Kahala Street as the dark side of Waikiki. The street was full of pawnshops, liquor stores, and bars. The lights were often burned out, and drunks stumbled along the trash-littered sidewalks.

Legends smelled of stale smoke, and the floors were sticky with yesterday's beer, but the bartenders poured generously, and the music was the best the island had to offer.

Most of the crew from *A Long Road Home* was here tonight. Jake and Koa were at the bar. Megan and a few others were lighting up the dance floor. Ryla Aikau was lighting up the stage.

It was the perfect recipe for a fun night, but Henry sulked in the corner, unable to shake his dark mood.

"Howzit, Champ?" Koa asked.

"Been worse," Henry said.

Koa nodded his head to the music. "You made any headway on that bet?"

Henry's blood ran cold. "I don't know what you're talking about, man."

Koa's laugh boomed over the loud music. "Don't make A," he said. "Everyone knows about the bet."

Henry considered denying it again but decided not to bother. "Everyone except Claudia," he said.

"I don't think either one of us has a chance with her."

"Nope." Henry had already come to that conclusion. Not with Keoni in the picture.

All day, he'd been thinking about Claudia going to Keoni's house. She had the day off, while he had to do the first takes with Aries. He hadn't been able to concentrate during the shoot and mistimed a jump. He'd narrowly missed landing on the back of the wagon pulled by the horses and could have broken his neck. After they'd wrapped, Albert had praised him for taking the risk, and Henry had walked off the shoot to a round of applause.

Henry and Koa fought their way to the bar, where they ordered more beers and commiserated with the grumpy bartender over the presence of so many tourists.

"You don't like tourists?" asked a pretty brunette with the telltale pink sunburn of a visitor.

"Yeah, what's wrong with tourists?" asked her friend, a cute blonde who looked a little like Claudia if Henry squinted.

"We love tourists." Koa raised his bottle to them, touching the rim of their glasses in turn.

"I'm a tourist too," Henry said. "I came to visit a few years ago, and I never left."

The women giggled. Introductions were made and then the

foursome hit the dance floor. The band was playing an up-tempo tune popular on the radio, and the crowd surged to their feet. For a little while, Henry forgot about Claudia. He danced with the tourists, forcing himself to pretend everything was the same as it had been a few weeks ago, before he'd met Claudia.

When Ryla belted out the last note of her final encore, Henry went to the bar to pay the tab. Tina, the blonde from Chicago, followed him. "Is it true you know Stan Beatty?"

"Yep." Henry slapped his credit card on the bar counter.

"What's he like in person?" Tina pressed closer. "Is he dreamy?"

"He's shorter than you'd think," he said. It wasn't true. Stan was well over six feet, taller than Henry by a few inches. But Tina wasn't likely to ever know the truth.

Her jaw dropped. "But he looks so tall."

"Don't believe everything you see on television." Henry paid for everyone's drinks and pocketed his card.

Tina pressed closer. "You didn't have to do that, Champ."

"No worries," he said. "Enjoy Hawaii."

"I hate to ask," she said, pressing even closer. "But do you think you can give us a lift? Libby is too drunk to walk all the way back to the hotel."

Henry's eyes narrowed. "You shouldn't be walking in this neighborhood stone-cold sober."

"So you'll do it?"

"I'll give you a lift. Where to?"

"The SurfRider."

Henry groaned. Claudia was at the SurfRider. He'd just stopped thinking of her. It had been for a record time of about thirty minutes. Now, she was back, firmly lodged in his mind.

"I'm happy to take you," he told Tina. "But promise me you won't walk down this way again. This area isn't for tourists."

"I'm glad I came." She looped her hands around his neck and brushed a kiss on his jaw. "Or else I wouldn't have met you."

Henry placed his hands on her hips, intent on pushing her away. Someone brushed up behind him, forcing him to step closer. And the result wasn't terrible. Tina's hips were feminine and full under his hands. She felt nice. It had been forever since Henry had held a woman in his arms.

It was high time he ended his dry spell, and from the way Tina was pressing her soft curves against him, she was game.

Henry drove Tina and her two friends back to the hotel and walked them to their door. The other women went into the room, while Henry and Tina lingered in the hall.

"I would invite you in," Tina said. "But I'd rather be alone with you."

Henry almost laughed. She certainly wasn't subtle about what she wanted, but he liked that. The problem was he didn't bring women home to his place. He liked to keep his space private.

Tina reached up and brushed back a lock of hair that had fallen onto his forehead. "I've never met a television star before."

Henry laughed. "I'm not a star. Not even close."

"But you're on TV. If I watch the show, I'll see you."

Henry shrugged. "You won't know it's me."

Henry did all the dirty work for none of the recognition. He was the stand-in. He'd always been fine with that until recently. Now he hungered for more. He wanted to be the man calling the shots for once. The man someone drove across an island to find.

Tina leaned up on her tiptoes to lace her hands around his neck. "I'd know you anywhere."

As he bent his head to kiss Tina, they were interrupted by a bellman coming down the hall with a bouquet of flowers.

The bellman worked as an extra on the show sometimes. Henry recognized him but couldn't remember his name.

"Hey, Champ," the bellman said, giving him a broad wink as he walked past them.

Henry watched him curiously, wondering who was getting a delivery of flowers this late at night. The bellman stopped down the hall and knocked. The door swung open, and Henry forgot all about the woman in his arms.

Claudia stepped into the hall to accept the flowers. She smiled at the bellman and then her eyes found Henry and widened slightly. Their eyes locked for a long moment, and Claudia turned and went back into her room.

The look she gave him before she slammed the door was one he knew well. Pure jealousy.

18

Counting Slowly

Claudia

A HOT SPEAR of light burned behind Claudia's eyes, blurring her vision. She stumbled across the room and set the vase of flowers on the table. Her hands groped in the pocket of her robe and found a pack of cigarettes. She pulled one out of the pack and pinched it between her lips, staring blindly at the colorful flowers.

The image of that little hussy with her arms wound around Henry's neck was burned in Claudia's brain. Even if she squeezed her eyes shut, she couldn't erase the picture.

Her fingers shook as she reached into her pocket for a book of matches but came up empty.

Dammit, there was never a light when she needed one.

She stomped to the nightstand and rummaged around in the top drawer for a pack of matches.

What was Henry doing right now? Had he gone into that woman's room? Were they kissing?

And where the hell were her matches?

She smothered a scream of frustration and fell back onto her bed with a dramatic flounce.

Her head throbbed, and the banging of her heart echoed in the silent room. She rubbed her chest where a deep yearning pulsed.

What she hated the most was how good Henry had looked.

He'd been wearing those tight jeans, and she could see the outlines of his rugged body. His muscled thighs. His lean hips. His perfectly sculpted ass.

Claudia squeezed her eyes closed tighter, but she couldn't stop seeing that woman draped all over Henry, running her fingers through the thick strands of his hair, climbing him with her leg.

A knock sounded at her door, and Claudia's eyes flew open. She sat up and tossed the cigarette aside. If it was the bellman again, she was really going to scream. Her heart thudded hard at another possibility… Maybe it wasn't the bellman. Maybe it was Henry.

She swung her legs off the bed and adjusted the sash of her robe before going to the door. Halfway across the room, she stopped and fluffed her hair. It would never do to look too eager.

She tucked the unlit cigarette back in her pocket and counted slowly. Five. Four. Three…

Her heart stuttered as the knock sounded again. This time, a low voice accompanied it.

"Claudia?"

Lust rose, licking a path up to her core. That was no bellman. Only Henry's voice did that to her, cut quick like a sharp knife through her inhibitions. That voice was pure sex.

Claudia swallowed thickly and stepped up to the door.

"Who is it?" She peeked through the peephole and saw Henry's bright shock of red hair. His hot blue gaze flashed up to the peephole, and Claudia ducked as if she'd been burned through the door.

"It's Henry," he said. "Can you open the door?" There was a soft thump. "Please?"

Desire danced down her spine. She tried not to rush opening the door, but suddenly, she had to see him. She pulled the door open.

Yearning throbbed in her chest, shooting fire to her core.

God, he looked sexy. Adorable. Henry leaned against the doorframe, his head close to the door. The soft thump she'd heard must have been his head resting against the wood.

"What are you doing here?" Years of training as an actress came in handy. Claudia's voice was smooth and steady, despite her racing heart.

Henry lifted his head and flashed her a sheepish smile. "I was in the neighborhood."

Both Claudia's eyebrows shot upward. "Was your tongue taking a detour down that woman's throat?"

Henry laughed softly, his eyes sparkling. He looked like the epitome of sin in tight jeans and a button-down aloha-style shirt.

Was he even wearing underwear? It didn't look like it. A thousand butterflies took flight in Claudia's stomach as she imagined Henry naked under the faded denim.

The elevator dinged, announcing they would have company in a moment. Claudia snapped out of her lust-induced trance and glanced toward the alcove of the elevator just as voices drifted down the hall.

"Get in here before someone writes a story about us in the rag mags." She grabbed Henry's arm and tugged him into her room.

His gaze swept around the suite as he shut the door behind him. "No company tonight?" he asked.

Claudia bristled at his tone of voice. Was he judging her? After the spectacle she'd just witnessed in the hall?

"That's none of your business." Her voice betrayed her this time, going just past shrill.

Henry's lips curled into a wicked smile. He glanced down at where Claudia's fingers wrapped around his forearm in a tight grip. "You can let go of me now."

Instead of letting him go, Claudia gripped him tighter. She wasn't ready to let him go. Not yet. His muscular forearm rippled under her touch. She leaned closer. "You smell like the floor of a nightclub."

Henry's eyes crinkled in the corners. "Is that better or worse than the horses?"

"Are you drunk?"

He shifted his hand to link their fingers. "I had a few beers."

The hammering of her heart drowned out her thoughts as she stared at their entwined fingers. "I'd offer you a drink, but it's late. I was just going to bed."

Henry's gaze drifted along her silk robe with a sinful gleam. Tension coiled low in her belly. The way Henry was looking at her made her skin tingle.

A line formed between his brows, and his eyes darkened. "Who sent you the flowers?"

Claudia lifted her chin and met his bright-blue eyes. "Jealous?"

His smile quirked. "Hell yes." A bitter laugh escaped his mouth. "Pathetic, aren't I?"

A flush stole up Claudia's neck. He wasn't the only one who was jealous. It made little sense. Nothing made sense when it came to Henry. She shouldn't even be attracted to him, but all she could think about was kissing him again.

"Very pathetic," she said in a barely-there whisper.

His eyes swept downward to linger on her mouth. "I should go," he said. "I don't know what I'm doing here. I just got you off my mind."

Claudia couldn't say the same about him. Henry had been lodged in her mind for days.

"You've been ignoring me long enough," she said.

His gaze flashed hungrily over her face. "I haven't been

ignoring you, Claudia." He swallowed thickly. "I couldn't if I tried."

Claudia slid her other hand to his collar, to toy with the top button of his shirt. "I heard you'd rather be with the horses."

Henry chuckled. The low sound vibrated between them. "Who told you that?"

"Everyone says you like them better than your co-stars."

"That isn't true." His hand came to her hip. "I'd much rather be with you."

Standing so close, she could smell the clean masculine scent of him under the stench of stale beer. She slid her fingers beneath the fabric of his shirt and stroked the smooth skin along the hollow of his throat.

Claudia's heart jerked in response to his wild pulse. She slid her fingers to the top button of his shirt and worked it free.

"Jealousy is a nasty thing," she said, stepping closer.

Henry's breath hitched, and the little noise encouraged her. She took another step. Undid another button. His masculine scent invaded her senses, made her throb with longing. She slid her hand beneath his shirt and ran her fingers along the crisp curling hairs of his upper chest.

Desire pulsed between them.

Henry's fingers curled tighter at her hip and dragged her closer. "We still have some practicing to do for the fight scene," he said.

Claudia reached up and combed her fingers through the thick waves of Henry's hair, smoothing it away from his forehead where it always seemed to fall with lazy abandon. He was too rugged to be called handsome. Too rough around the edges to be the leading man.

"I thought you showed me everything."

Henry's laugh erupted. The sound was quickly becoming one of her favorite things. "Not everything."

He curled his hand around her neck and pulled her flush against him. From her chest to her thigh, she felt the hard crush of his body. The outline of his erection branded her low belly.

He brushed his lips across her jaw to the sensitive spot below her ear. Hunger flared to life. She'd been aching for his kiss for days.

He was so hard. Every inch of him was like a brick wall. Only his mouth was soft as it glided along her skin, bringing up shivers.

His big hand captured her wrist, and he lifted her hand to his mouth. He kissed her palm. She felt the soft scrape of his beard. Firm lips. The nip of his teeth.

"I can't stand the thought of hurting you," he said.

"So don't."

"I think we should talk," he said.

Claudia tugged her hand from his and found the buttons of his shirt again. His body stiffened as she trailed her fingers down his chest, down to his taut stomach.

The lower her hand dipped, the more labored his breathing became. She glanced up and saw his eyes had drifted shut and his lips had parted.

"I don't want to talk." She dragged her hand down, palmed the bulge in his jeans through the fabric.

A low moan tore from his throat.

"Good thing you don't smell like horses, or I definitely wouldn't be doing this." She pressed her lips to his collarbone. "Or this." She ran her tongue lower, along the top of his chest.

She kissed lower, spreading his shirt open and finally all the way off. Her heart raced frantically as she looked at his naked torso. Henry had been carved by a skilled hand, his muscles etched from a slab of stone.

She looked up at his face and saw the flames burning in his blue gaze. He curved his hand around her neck and pulled her close so that their mouths met. His lips crashed onto hers.

Finally. Hot. Hungry. Demanding. He devoured her with his kiss.

Shockwaves of pleasure burst through her.

Claudia had never known a kiss could feel so good. The electric current passing between them threatened to burn her up. She needed more of him. Now.

She rose onto her toes and wound her arms around his neck, shamelessly grinding against him.

Henry's hands came between them to the knot of her robe. He tugged it open. The robe fell off her shoulder, revealing what she wore underneath—nothing.

Henry went very still and then a growl tore from his throat, and he took her mouth in another hungry kiss.

19

Never Stop

Henry

HENRY KNEW he was moving too fast, taking too much. He couldn't stop himself. When it came to Claudia, he didn't seem to have control.

He pushed the robe from her shoulders and let his fingers roam over her delicious skin. She was satin and silk and heat. The robe fell to her waist, and he couldn't breathe.

She was more perfect than he could have ever imagined. Her breasts were full and heavy, with rosy nipples. She had a tiny waist he could wrap his hands around. He reached for her, but she shook her head, wagging her finger in his face.

"Now you." Her fingers fumbled with the buttons on his shirt, but she wasn't quick enough for Henry.

He tore it right off. A few buttons bounced onto the carpet as he tossed the shirt to the floor.

It had been too long since their last kiss. Now that he'd had a taste of her, he couldn't get enough.

The way she kissed him back—hot and wet and demanding

like she couldn't ever get her fill of him either—was like nothing he'd ever known.

He skimmed his hands up the sides of her body, brushing the outside swell of her breasts. She shivered, responding to him as if they were born for each other.

He moved his mouth against hers, teasing her lips open, sliding his tongue into her mouth with little licks. He wanted to devour her whole, eat her like his favorite dessert.

Her mouth was hot and wet, so demanding he didn't think he could keep up. Didn't think he could stop.

She was his. All his.

She was sweetness and spice, and so much heat.

"These too." She slid her finger under the waistband of his jeans, then flicked open the button. "I'm dying to see what you have on under…" Her words died away as her fingers found out.

Henry wasn't wearing anything under his jeans. He never did. His cock stiffened painfully as her fingers dipped lower, exploring.

She wrapped her hand around him, and his heart stopped beating. For one long second, he died. Ecstasy engulfed him, leaving him to swim through waves of pleasure back to the surface of reality.

"I was right." Claudia pushed his jeans over his hips. "I knew you weren't wearing any underwear."

"You thought about that?" He sucked in a sharp breath as she squeezed his cock, making him even harder.

"Every girl on set has," she assured him.

Henry groaned as she tightened her grip. "I only care about one girl on set."

Her hand was doing wicked things to him, making him lose his mind. He cupped her ass, filling his hands with her sweet cheeks. He couldn't believe this was happening, that this woman was in his arms, touching him with sure and steady strokes that made a moan escape his lips.

"Get these off." Claudia pushed impatiently at his jeans.

Henry barely contained his laughter as her greedy hands slid along his skin. He shucked his shoes.

Claudia watched him with a flushed face, the robe still tied at her waist.

"You really haven't been wearing underwear all this time on set?"

He chuckled. "No." His eyes dropped toward her bare breasts. "You never wear a bra either."

"Not when I don't have to," she said in agreement.

He undid the knot of her sash, and the robe fell to the ground. "Thank God for women's liberation."

"Especially when it suits you."

Henry laughed and gathered her in his arms. "It always suits me, baby. I love empowering women."

Claudia linked her arms around his neck and pressed into him. The tight buds of her nipples brushed against his chest. "Never stop laughing. The world would be a sad place without your laugh."

"You like my laugh?" His heart pounded so hard, he couldn't hear his thoughts over the whoosh of his blood. No woman had ever said she liked his laugh. He'd been told it was too loud, obnoxious, annoying... Even his sisters teased him about it.

Claudia threaded her fingers through the hair at the nape of Henry's neck and pulled his face back to hers. "I love your laugh. It lights me up."

A frisson of heat sparked to life in Henry's chest. He'd never wanted a woman as badly as he wanted Claudia right now. He couldn't stop looking at her, touching her, wanting her. It was like she'd gotten under his skin, inside his veins. He gazed down at her beautiful face, wondering how the hell he'd gotten so lucky.

Claudia looked back at him with her velvet brown eyes. Her

lashes were impossibly long. Without makeup, she looked so innocent. So young.

How could a woman who basically oozed sex appeal come across as an angel at the same time? It was her mouth, Henry decided. The neat little package of her mouth, which he desperately wanted to unwrap, looked as sweet as cotton candy.

He bent his head to capture her sweet lips. For now, it was all his. Henry was no longer the stand-in. He was the hero, the leading man.

He kissed Claudia long and deep, sweeping his tongue along the seam of her perfect mouth to tease and taste until she moaned against him.

The kiss started gently, but it quickly turned rough as Claudia's hands blazed across his body, exploring every inch.

Henry scooped Claudia into his arms and carried her to the bed. He deposited her on the mattress and knelt on the floor in front of her.

He pressed gently on her thighs, and her legs fell open. He stared at her with hungry eyes. Henry wasn't an overly religious person, but looking at Claudia's beautiful pussy spread before him was almost a spiritual experience. She'd obviously been created by a higher power, one who knew how to create supreme beauty. Blonde curls shimmered over the mound of her sex. Her pink lips were plump and blushing, shiny with slick juices.

Knowing he was the cause for that glistening wetness made his cock as hard as an iron spike.

He ran his hands up her thighs, touching her reverently. Her skin was molten hot and silky smooth. She sighed as he bent his head to kiss her leg, then higher and higher, until he settled at the apex of her thighs. He licked his lips in anticipation of lapping up all that sweet cream. Her smell intoxicated him. She was vanilla and honey. Sweet and spice.

He slid a finger up her seam, and she shuddered. God, she

was hot. Her skin was on fire. Dipping a finger inside, he flicked his tongue against the swollen bud of her clit.

"Henry," she said on a moan.

Henry fought the wave of lust that made him want to plunge inside her.

First this. First, he wanted her to come on his tongue. He stroked her, sliding another finger inside her wet heat. He gave her one long, slow lick and then sucked on the tight little bundle of nerves before delivering another teasing lick.

Claudia thrust her hips off the mattress, crying out. Pleading. *His name.*

"*Henry.*" Her voice pleaded. "I can't take that."

"Do you want me to stop?" he asked, teasing her clit again.

"God, no!"

Henry rubbed his jaw across the soft mound of her curls, inhaling the sweet, musky scent of her desire. He was so hard. He'd never been so hard in his life. He could feel every beat of his heart in his cock. The ache was painful.

He flattened his hand to her belly and pinned her to the bed while he took his time adoring her sweet, pretty pussy.

She said his name again, and Henry preened.

It made him a selfish bastard, but he wanted to erase the memory of every other man who'd worshiped at her altar. He wanted to bury himself inside her. But first he wanted to lap up her sweet cream.

Her sheath was tight and scalding hot, slick with wanting. She writhed against him, clutching his head between her thighs. Henry stroked her harder, his tongue soaking up her honeyed juice. Her fingers pulled painfully at his hair as she begged incoherently.

He didn't have to ask what she needed. He knew: more. She needed more. He curled his fingers inside her and hit the spot that made her lock her legs around him and cry out.

Her body pulsed and throbbed as he fastened his mouth on her clit and sucked.

The climax overcame her, but Henry didn't stop. He kept up his pace, prolonging the orgasm as long as possible.

Finally she went still, and Henry withdrew his fingers. He eased his mouth off her clit with a final kiss.

Claudia pinned him with a wide stare, her eyes glossy with shock. "Where did you learn to do that?"

Henry laughed and lifted her higher onto the mattress. He crawled up her body, his cock so hard, it was a weapon. She was flushed pink and glistening with a sheen of sweat. Henry let his eyes linger over her full breasts with their rosy tips before dragging his gaze up to her face.

He liked very much that it was him who'd put the little smile on her lips.

Claudia reached up, tangled her hands in his hair, and pulled his face to hers. "What else can you do?" she asked.

20

Resurrection

Claudia

HE HAD A WICKED TONGUE, and he knew how to use it. Claudia felt like she'd been kissed by a fire.

His heavy erection dragged up her thigh. *Finally.* She reached for him, but he tugged her hand away.

Clasping her wrists over her head, he bent to kiss her breasts. Her thoughts were no longer her own as he feathered gentle, teasing kisses along the undersides of her breasts. Her nipples ached as his wet mouth circled closer. Licking and teasing seemed to be his specialty. And making her feel like a queen. He did that well, too. His tongue worshiped her. His lips praised. His teeth punished.

She squirmed. Never had she been so aware of her stiff nipples. She needed his mouth on them immediately.

She arched and wiggled, on the verge of swearing if he didn't give her what she wanted. And then the rough scrape of his jaw rasped against her piqued flesh. The wet slip of his tongue bathing her tortured nipple only stoked the fire from her breasts to her belly to her sex. Electrifying every frayed nerve between.

There was no breath at all in her lungs as he sucked hard on one nipple, then pinched the other at the same time.

Lightning scored through her. A noise she didn't know she could make ripped from her throat as a powerful orgasm crashed over her. Lifted her on a giant swell.

She floated down only to ride high again as he pulled hard on her nipple, toyed with the tight petal.

Behind her closed eyelids there were sunbeams. Her heart banged in her chest. Her toes curled. *This* was being alive.

And they hadn't even had sex yet. She'd just had one of the most powerful orgasms of her life, and Henry had only touched her breasts.

The roar in her ears faded, replaced by the deep rumble of his laugh. Her eyes snapped open, and she saw him braced above her. His hair fell over his forehead, and his eyes gleamed with male satisfaction. His wet mouth curved in a grin more roguish than usual.

"Holy shit, Claudia. I knew you'd be a pistol."

He was hard and heavy, nudging her entrance. She smiled wickedly and pushed him over onto his back. "You ain't seen nothing yet."

His eyes darkened as she slid her hand down the flat plains of his abdominals and wrapped her hand around his iron-hard cock.

He was hot enough to brand her palm. She needed that heat inside her more than she needed to breathe. Her sex throbbed just looking down at his delicious body. All those rippling muscles and smooth flesh. She wanted to trace her tongue down the thin trail of hair and suck him into her mouth.

Later.

She would devour him as he'd done her later. Now she needed him in her pussy, branding her from the inside.

She straddled him.

Henry gripped her hips and stopped her before she could take what she needed.

"Wait," he said. His eyes were hooded. "I need to cover up." He swore under his breath. "My wallet's in my car."

Claudia leaned down to take his mouth in a feverish kiss. "I have a prescription. Long live women's lib, remember?"

His mouth chased hers as she pulled away. "You sure?"

She slid her hands down his chest, his ribs, his tight belly, delighting in the way his muscles rippled, responding to her touch. Her hand circled the girth of his cock. "I'm sure. It costs me six dollars a month."

He groaned as she pumped him, then bit back a terse laugh. "You know what I mean, Claudia."

She guided his stiff erection to the notch between her legs. When the head of his cock brushed the swollen bud of her clit, she nearly cried out.

"What do you mean?" Her eyes flashed to his. "Tell me."

He reached up to frame her face, his big hands rough and calloused, caressing her. "We can stop right now if this is too much. It's not too late."

Her eyes filled with tears. "Don't be sweet. Not now." Not when she was flayed open.

Henry's thumbs brushed her jaw. His eyes darkened. The smile that permanently lived there was gone. "You can say no, babe." His thumbs were hot little pads against her cheeks, smearing wetness over her skin.

Claudia hadn't realized she was crying. She blinked down at Henry, who was gazing up at her as if she was a fragile orchid blossom. She was hardly a flower blossom, more like the stalk. She was tough and unflappable. Always.

But not now.

Because Henry was giving her something no man had ever offered Claudia. Besides a couple of orgasms, he was also giving her a choice. Some people thought Claudia had slept her way to the top, but it wasn't true. She was so selective that she could hardly remember the last man she went to bed with.

But this was different. *Henry was different.*

She leaned closer, pressed a kiss to his lips. "If I told you to stop right now, would you?"

He nodded, looking pained. "Of course." His hands slid down to her hips and lifted, putting space between them. "Is that what you want?"

"You wouldn't be mad?"

His eyelids lowered, and his jaw clenched. "No. Maybe it's better if we don't." He shifted under her. When he opened his eyes, they were burning with regret. "We shouldn't."

She smiled down at him, her eyes still glistening with tears. "Henry?"

He blinked up at her. "Yes?"

"I don't want to stop." She bent to kiss him, using her tongue to trace the shape of his mouth until he opened for her. She stabbed her tongue into his mouth, and he groaned, hands tightening at her hips. She rocked against his hips and felt his erection throb. Reaching down, she wrapped her hand around the silky length of him. His cock jerked in her palm, growing even stiffer as she stroked him with her hand, her tongue in his mouth mimicking her hand's movements.

When a low moan tore from his mouth and his fingers tightened painfully on her hips, Claudia guided him closer to her entrance.

"This is mine," she said, tearing her mouth from his. She positioned herself over him, thighs braced against his hips, slick seam poised over his rigid cock. "This is my cock, Henry." She lowered herself an inch, and he growled her name. "Don't tell me I can't have it ever again."

His eyes flashed up to hers, molten blue lava. Sensual lines carved his mouth into a wicked smile. His hands bruised her hips, and he thrust up just as she slammed down.

They cried out together. So loud, she hoped the entire floor of the hotel heard it. Especially that little twit a few doors down. Claudia hoped she heard it and knew exactly who it was and that she was never getting any of it for herself.

Buried deep inside, Henry felt so hot and big. So right.

He began to move, and her world tilted off center. Each thrust made her come apart a little more.

His hands cinched her waist, lifting her and moving her exactly how he wanted.

He knew instinctively what she needed. A slow grind of his pelvis, a sensual roll of her hips. He moved her up and down as he thrust up from the mattress.

Claudia thought she'd be in control while she was on top of Henry, but it was the opposite. She was blinded with need. He was beautifully restrained.

She would have thought him unaffected except the flush on his chest and the tightness of his mouth gave him away.

He moved faster, grinding harder, driving deeper. She clamped tight around him, losing what little bit of control she had as he reached up to knead her breasts and pinch her nipples.

One thrust more and all control was lost. Fragmented beyond repair. Her muscles tightened on him, pushing uncontrollably as wave after wave of pleasure crashed over her. For the third time that night, Henry made her come. She looked down at his face as she fell apart on top of him. His expression was somewhere between ecstasy and agony.

He gritted his teeth and pushed her off of him, his hands gentle and firm at the same time. Corded veins stood out on his neck as he pumped, shooting hot jets of cum onto his muscular chest.

His face—mouth open, eyes squeezed shut—was the most erotic thing she'd ever seen. His groan—deep and animalistic—was the hottest sound she'd ever heard.

Claudia collapsed beside Henry on the bed.

"You didn't have to do that," she said. "I told you I was on the pill."

He grunted, opening his eyes to look at her. "I don't like to take chances."

Claudia raised an eyebrow. "The first time I saw you, you crashed into a car."

Henry sat up and tossed a grin over his shoulder at her. "The first time we met, you took off all your clothes."

She laughed. "That was Janice."

He went into the bathroom. "I liked Janice. She was a gas."

Henry came out of the bathroom. A loose towel clung just above his hips, revealing everything that he packed into those tight jeans.

She sat up and reached for him, pulling him by the hips closer to the bed. Trailing her fingers down the line of hair below his navel, she pushed the towel lower.

"What about Claudia? What do you think of her?"

Henry grinned. "She'll do."

Claudia scooted over and made room for him, then lit a cigarette. He stretched out beside her and stared up at the ceiling, at the tendrils of smoke. There should have been an awkwardness between them, they were practically strangers, but it didn't feel awkward to Claudia. It felt right. Henry felt right.

He looked right—lying next to her on the rumpled sheets, his hair mussed and his cheeks flushed—he looked exactly right.

"I know you think I probably do this all the time, because I'm taking the pill and because of… well, because of Richard Dunlap and all, but I don't." Her cheeks flushed, and she was glad Henry was staring up at the ceiling into the cloud of smoke so he didn't see. "Have sex with men I barely know on a regular basis. I just don't want to get pregnant. Not now…" She realized she was babbling and shut her mouth.

Henry turned on his side to look at her. "Who's Richard Dunlap?"

"What? You don't know who he is?"

Henry chucked her under the chin, raised her face so their eyes met. "Why are you talking about another man while I'm in your bed?" He smiled, letting on that he was teasing.

"Be serious, Henry."

"Never." He tickled her neck with the scruff of his beard. Gathering her close, he bit her earlobe gently. "Who is this Richard Dunlap guy and do I need to kill him?"

Claudia stiffened. "I think it might be a federal offense to kill a United States Senator."

"He's a Senator?" Henry pulled back to look at her.

"Not yet, but it's happening."

"What did this guy do to you, babe?"

Fingers of ice chilled Claudia's veins as she thought of Rick and the story he'd told the press. "He told lies about me. He used me to get ahead in politics. No one would hire me. That's why I'm here in Hawaii, trying to resurrect my career."

Henry went very still. After a long moment, he plucked the cigarette from her fingers and crushed it in the ashtray. Without a word he gathered her close and just held her. His arms were a solid comfort around her. His broad shoulders took the weight of her disappointment.

"You're more than an actress, Claudia. You're talented, and gorgeous and funny. You sparkle. When you walk in a room, everyone wants to get near you, hoping some of whatever you've got will rub off on them. You're the most incredible woman I've ever met."

Claudia looked up at Henry and saw the smile in his eyes. His heart was in every word. Something in her chest shifted as her heart swelled. Joy filled her soul. Henry had just checked off another item on her list.

21

Old Fashioned

Henry

THEY'D LEFT the balcony doors open, and a sliver of moonlight was all that lit the room. Claudia's hair shined silver in the darkness.

"You want a drink?" she asked.

"You got any whiskey?"

She sat up, sliding her feet to the floor. "I've got a full bar, but no ice."

"That's fine."

She stood and walked to the bar. Henry liked that she didn't cover up, and he liked what he saw. Watching Claudia fix drinks while naked might be one of his favorite things, right up there with the Fourth of July and overtime pay.

She had an amazing ass. Firm and round and shaped like an upside-down heart, with two dimples riding high at the small of her back.

She caught him staring and smiled. "Keep looking at me like that and I won't let you get any sleep tonight."

"Come here."

She carried the glasses back to the bed and kissed him, then reached for a cigarette.

"You smoke too much."

"I like to smoke after sex."

"And after breakfast, lunch, dinner…" He propped himself up on his elbow and smoothed her hair away from her face. "Those things will kill you."

"Don't believe everything you see in *Reader's Digest*." She touched a finger to the bump in his crooked nose. "I'm not the one crashing cars for a living."

Point taken.

She settled down beside him with her drink. "Are you old-fashioned, Henry?"

His eyes popped open. "Why?"

She brushed his hair off his forehead. "You don't believe the pill works."

Pain stabbed his belly, and his body tensed. "I'm not old-fashioned." He pulled the sheet up to his chest and laced his fingers on top. "I'm just careful."

She tapped her fingers on his chest playfully. "Says the man who crashes cars for a living."

He caught her hand and laced their fingers together. Electricity hummed between them. Even after hours of making love, neither one of them had gotten enough.

Henry lifted her fingers to his mouth and kissed each knuckle. "When I was in college, I got a girl in trouble." His voice was soft and gravelly, full of regret.

"Geez, Henry. What happened?"

He laughed bitterly. The hurt was still there, as sharp as if it had happened yesterday. "It's a long story."

"I'm not going anywhere."

He took a moment to gather his thoughts and get his courage to tell the story. One look at Claudia's pretty brown eyes and he was spilling his guts.

"I was a football star in high school," he said, twirling a lock of her hair around his finger. "I got a free ride to UCLA."

"What position did you play?"

"Tight end."

She slid her hand under the sheets to grab his butt. "Groovy."

"Do you know what a tight end does?"

"Catch the ball?" She squeezed his cheeks.

"I mostly blocked, but I caught a few." He sipped his whiskey. "Anyway, I blew my knee out, and my career was over. Then to top it off, my girlfriend broke up with me."

"That's a bummer." Claudia snuggled under his arm against his side. "She sounds like a bitch."

"You have no idea. When she broke up with me, I figured it was because I wasn't on the team anymore." He shook his head. "She disappeared, but I just went on with my life. I dropped out of school, started working with horses on *Turner and Ditz*. Remember that show?"

"My dad used to watch it."

"Damn, how old are you?"

"Twenty-four."

"Geez, you are just a kid."

She yawned and stretched. "How old are you?"

"I'm thirty."

She kissed the scruff of his beard. "Ancient." She kissed a path to his ear. "What happened with the girl?"

"I ran into her a few years later, and she told me everything. Turns out she didn't disappear because I was off the team." Pain inflated his chest, making it hard to breathe. He downed his whiskey in one gulp and put his empty glass on the nightstand. He forced himself to finish the story. "She had a baby," he said.

Claudia gasped. "Your baby?"

Henry rested his head against the headboard and closed his eyes. "Yeah."

"You have a kid?"

"Yeah."

"Boy or girl?"

"Little girl. But that's all she would tell me. She gave her up." Henry squeezed his eyes shut, as if it could help hold back his emotions.

"Oh, sweetie."

The mattress shifted when she moved. He heard the clink of her glass on the nightstand and then her arms were around him. She held him tightly, soothing what was broken inside him.

"I'm so sorry."

His arms went around her and he held on. Claudia felt so small in his arms. He wanted to protect her almost as much as he wanted to bury himself inside her. With Claudia, he was all urges and no restraint. All emotion. No thought.

She stroked his hair and murmured soothing words.

It's not your fault. You were so young. You didn't know.

Henry had told himself all those things a million times, but he still could never forgive himself. He could never make things right.

Hearing Claudia whisper those words and more didn't erase his mistake, but it did ease the brunt of his pain.

He breathed in her scent. Expensive perfume, cigarettes, and sex.

He didn't know why he was telling Claudia about his bastard child when it was something he hated thinking about. He'd pushed it so far back in his mind, he hardly thought about it at all. He'd never told anyone, and here he was spilling his guts to a woman who was very likely the most enjoyable one-night stand he'd ever had.

Except it didn't feel like a one-night stand. It felt like more. It felt right.

She fit nicely against him, her leg thrown over his hip, her head cradled on his chest. He ran his hand along her hip and she sighed. He trailed his fingers up her arm, keeping his touch light. She snuggled closer, hooking her leg over his.

"Do you want to have more children someday?"

Henry pulled her close and dropped a kiss on her hair. "Yes," he said. "I want children. Someday."

She wrapped her arms around his waist and burrowed against his chest. "How many?"

"A whole brood of them," he said with a soft laugh. "A football team of them."

She squeezed him. "You think you'll have all boys, then?"

"Maybe." He pulled back and grinned down at her. "What about you? Do you want kids?"

"Sure."

"Not worried about ruining your career?"

She shook her head. "The man I choose to have kids with won't expect a wife who stays at home to bake cookies. He won't care if his wife works outside the home, if she makes more money than him, if she's successful."

His low laugh rumbled. "I never took you for a baker. But for future reference, chocolate chip cookies are my favorite."

"Shut up!" She swatted him on the shoulder.

Henry smiled and brushed his lips against her temple. He pulled her closer and nuzzled her neck with his chin, whispering sexy suggestions that involved naked baking, melted chocolate, and the kitchen counter.

Claudia laughed, and the sound rippled through him like a sneaky wave that pulled him under when he wasn't looking. He couldn't hold back anymore. He was falling for her.

22

Flowers

Henry

HENRY WOKE to Claudia kissing him. Her mouth was soft and warm on his chin, his cheeks, his jaw… He opened his eyes and pulled her into his arms, then rolled so she was pinned beneath him.

To his surprise, she was fully dressed.

"Going somewhere?" He nuzzled her neck.

"Yes. I didn't want to leave without telling you."

He peeked over her shoulder out the window. The sun wasn't even up yet. "Where are you going so early?"

Claudia dislodged herself from his arms and rolled off the bed. She went to the mirror over the dresser and tidied her hair.

"I'm meeting Keoni at Sans Souci."

All the air left his lungs. "What?"

Claudia turned away from the mirror and faced him. "It's not what you think."

He scooted up against the headboard, his heart pounding so hard in his chest, he thought he might need an ambulance. "Oh, yeah? What am I thinking?"

"That I want him." She crossed her arms over her chest and shot him a defiant glare. "It's not like that."

Henry's heart didn't like her answer. It continued to knock and bang against his chest in a bruising rage. "What's it like?"

"I need closure. I came out here to find him. I need to see him."

He squinted at the clock on the nightstand. It was 5:30 a.m. "Now?"

She nodded. "I left him a note, Henry. I told him to meet me at sunrise." She shrugged. "It was our thing, watching the sunrise over the beach at Sans Souci."

Henry would never think of the little beach at the foot of Diamond Head in the same way again. He suddenly hated Sans Souci, fine sand, calm waters, and all. He hated sunrises too.

Claudia sat on the mattress beside him and smoothed a lock of hair off his forehead. "Don't pout."

Henry couldn't decide if he wanted to push her away or pin her to the sheets.

His arms went around her, his fingers tightening around her waist. She was wearing a minidress that showcased miles of legs. He'd kissed every inch of those legs. He hadn't missed a spot.

His heart calmed as he remembered the spot behind her knee, so warm and smooth against his lips.

She pressed a kiss to his forehead. "I need to do this, Henry. You understand, right?"

He didn't. His jaw ached as he ground his teeth together and nodded. "Sure." The single word burned more than anything he'd ever said.

"I didn't have to wake you up, you know?" She pulled back to spear him with a sharp look. "I could have just slipped out, and you would have never even known."

Part of him wished she would have done just that. He didn't want to know. He liked ignorance. It didn't steal his breath and make his chest burn. He pressed his hand against the ache. Somehow he thought he would have known, even if she hadn't told him. Claudia couldn't hide a thing like meeting another man, not after the intimate night they'd shared.

Claudia tucked him back into bed and kissed his cheek. "I'll be back."

He sat up and let the sheet fall to his waist. "I won't be here."

Her face fell. "Don't be that way."

Henry's ego liked the disappointment on her face, even though his heart still hurt. He reached for her hand and toyed with her fingers. "I have an early shoot on location at the Pali Highway." His arm snaked around her waist, and he tugged her down onto his lap. "Otherwise, there's nowhere else I'd rather be."

Claudia put her arms around his neck. "Another car chase?"

Henry nodded. His ego was a monster. It liked the concern stamped on her features and the lack of color in her cheeks. The way her brows furrowed made hope bloom in Henry's chest. He wished he could keep Claudia right where she was, in his lap, all day.

"Be careful," she said. "It's nerve-wracking, thinking of you speeding down that winding highway."

He chuckled softly. "You don't have to worry about me, baby. I know what I'm doing behind the wheel." Although, the thought had occurred to Henry that he would have to navigate the curves of the Pali Highway while knowing Claudia was with Keoni. "I'll be done at noon," he said, pulling her closer. "Meet me after?"

For a long beat, they looked at each other. Her eyes were liquid drops of chocolate, dark kisses against the cream of her skin. Henry hadn't known he could get lost in a woman's eyes. Truthfully, he'd never paused long enough to look for longer than a hot second.

Henry liked fast music, faster cars, and a good time. Staring soulfully into a chick's eyes had never been his thing.

Until now. Until her.

His pulse leaped in his throat. Each breath felt like five evers of waiting. *Say something. Anything.*

"Where do you want to meet?"

His shoulders relaxed. He could breathe again. "Have you been to Diamond Head?"

"No."

"We have to fix that. You can't come to Oah'u and not hike to the top of Diamond Head. It's like skipping out on the Empire State Building in New York."

Claudia bit her bottom lip.

Henry pressed a kiss to her mouth. "You didn't go to the Empire State Building in New York, did you?"

She shook her head. "I didn't have a chance. I was working the whole time."

"You're not working today," he said. "You're going to explore this beautiful island with a local."

Claudia laughed, wriggling out of his arms to stand. "You're from California."

"I've been here four years. That's local enough."

"I'm not much of a hiker." She bent to retrieve her platform shoes and held them in the air by the straps. "I don't have the right shoes."

Henry watched her step into them. The wooden and leather clogs were all the rage in fashion magazines, but they wouldn't do for hiking. "You might need to visit the gift shop."

Claudia smiled. "You don't have to twist my arm to go shopping." She bent to buckle her shoes. "I better go."

He gritted his teeth. "You wouldn't want to be late."

"Be careful leaving," she said, opening the door. "I don't want anyone to see you."

Henry fisted the sheet in his hands. "I will."

When she was gone, Henry sighed heavily and rolled out of bed. He went into the bathroom, where Claudia's perfume still hung in the air, used the toilet, and splashed water onto his face. His jaw was thick with scruff, and his eyes were bloodshot. He needed a shower, a shave, and a few more hours of sleep. He also needed Claudia to forget about Keoni, who probably still looked like a bronze god on two hours of sleep.

Henry felt ancient, alone, and truly pathetic.

How the hell was he going to speed down the Pali Highway knowing Claudia was with Keoni?

Henry slammed his palms onto the counter and hung his head. He'd do it because he had no choice. Claudia may have been his for the night, but she wasn't *his*.

Claudia was a modern woman. She could meet Keoni or whomever else she wanted.

Henry went into the bedroom and found his clothes stacked in a neat pile on a chair by the window. He stood for a moment, looking out at the half-mile stretch of sand between him and Sans Souci.

In the water was a lone canoe, paddling toward the pinkish horizon. The sun was already on the rise. Claudia was going to be late. And Sans Souci was a fine beach for a picnic or snorkeling, but it was a stupid place to watch the sunrise.

Didn't Keoni know anything? Diamond Head Crater completely blocked the view of the sun breaking the horizon.

Henry knew of much better places to watch the sunrise, including the deck of his own house.

Images of Claudia and Keoni's long-awaited reunion flashed through Henry's mind. He pictured them holding hands, watching the sunrise. He pictured them sharing an intimate look, a gesture, a roll on the sand…

He snapped his eyes shut and pulled on his jeans. The worst of the images were still stuck in his mind as he shrugged into his shirt. He wanted to punch something. He wanted to do something stupid like burst out of the room and run down to Sans Souci.

His gaze landed on the bouquet on the table. Claudia had never said who they were from. The white card peeked out from the exotic blooms, tempting him.

Henry plucked the card from the bouquet. Before he could talk himself out of it, he slid his thumb under the seal and pulled out the card.

CLAUDIA,

I hope you are enjoying our little paradise. I would love to show you more.

Stan

HENRY'S STOMACH CLENCHED. He crumbled the card and stuffed it in his pocket.

The bet.

He'd completely forgotten about the bet.

23

Sans Souci

Claudia

CLAUDIA DIDN'T KNOW what she was doing. It was a new feeling for her, and she didn't care for it.

Claudia always knew what she was doing. She always had a plan.

She'd come to Hawaii knowing exactly what she wanted. She had a whole list, and finding Keoni was the most important thing on it. She wasn't leaving without seeing him.

"Always so stubborn," her mother had said.

Claudia had been the kind of child who would sit all night at the dinner table, refusing to eat her peas. She'd slept in the dining room more than once over asparagus. She'd refused to quit ballet even though she hated it because she wasn't a quitter.

She'd come to Hawaii to find Keoni, and she was going to find him.

Henry was great, but Keoni was the man she'd obsessed over for years.

It wasn't fair to compare the two men. Keoni had a natural

advantage. He was taller and better looking. He played guitar and sang. He surfed like a Hawaiian god.

But Henry made her laugh. And God, he was sexy. He had a mouth made for sinning. His hands were rough but gentle. Claudia's steps faltered.

Was she crazy for leaving Henry—who made her laugh and doled out orgasms in the multiples—in her bed? Naked?

She was definitely crazy. But she was more stubborn.

Henry made her feel alive. He did amazing things with his tongue. His hands. And don't get her started on his cock. He was somewhat of an expert in all things sex. Just as she'd suspected when they'd danced together, Henry had all the moves.

But it didn't mean she didn't want to see Keoni Makai. One night of hot sex with a skilled lover couldn't erase six years of pinning for Keoni.

Her footsteps halted.

She was crazy. Certifiable.

She was also at Sans Souci. She almost didn't recognize the tiny beach. Where there had once been only a patch of pristine sand, there was now a towering condominium building. Like the rest of Waikiki, Sans Souci had changed.

The only thing that looked the same was the looming crust of Diamond Head Crater, sloping into the sea at the furthest edge of the sand.

The sky was pink, and the beach was deserted. Claudia turned in a circle, scanning every inch of the area.

No Keoni.

Orange stripes of light zigzagged over the horizon as the sun pushed out of the sea. It was officially sunrise.

Knots of tension coiled in her belly.

Claudia remembered her last day in Hawaii all those years ago. She was supposed to meet Keoni at Sans Souci to say good-bye, but the night before, she'd stayed up fretting over it.

Blinded by love, she was bound to do something stupid when she saw him. So she hadn't gone to Sans Souci.

She'd stood Keoni up, and now he was returning the gesture.

He wasn't coming.

Claudia stared at the sunrise, shading her eyes with her hand.

A man walked along the beach in the distance. Butterflies took flight in her belly.

He was tall and broad-shouldered. Tan enough to be Hawaiian. Claudia's heart pounded harder with each step he took closer to her.

Anticipation curled inside her, ready to lash out like a whip. Time ticked slowly as the man came nearer. He was close enough that she could see the shape of him. Big shoulders, broad chest, strong legs…

Her heart raced as the man broke into a jog in her direction. She could see his face clearly now. Chiseled jaw. Full mouth. Deep-set, dark eyes.

Not Keoni.

He jogged past her and climbed onto the lifeguard tower behind her back. "Howzit?" he asked with a friendly nod.

Claudia released the breath she'd been holding. Surprise mingled with relief. Maybe she didn't want closure with Keoni after all. Maybe she wanted a certain stuntman instead.

HENRY WAS GONE when Claudia got back to her room. She hadn't expected anything else, but still, she was disappointed.

She stood on the balcony, watching the beach fill with early-morning tourists. Surfers paddled out to the deep channel and bobbed on their boards while they waited for the perfect wave.

Keoni had taught her to surf on those very waves. Or he'd tried. She'd been more interested in seducing her instructor than learning how to stand on a surfboard.

She'd been a child.

Now she was all grown up and ready to admit her failure. It was time to quit. Her quest for Keoni ended now.

She crushed her cigarette in the ashtray and hauled her suitcase to the bed. It was full of dresses, swimsuits, and sandals. None of it would do for hiking.

Shopping would give her something to do instead of counting the hours until she saw Henry again.

She couldn't stop thinking about him. The look on his face when he'd told her about his daughter had crushed her.

Claudia's life hadn't been easy, but a tragedy of that magnitude had never happened to her. She'd never gotten close enough to a man to have her heart broken. Her social life had taken a back seat to her career.

She'd never realized how sad that was until now. All these years, she'd been clinging onto the fantasy of Keoni so she didn't have to connect with anyone.

Henry had snuck up on her, wormed his way into her heart with his easy smile, his dancing skills, and his eagerness to please in bed.

She smiled as she rode the elevator down to the lobby to shop for something appropriate to wear on a hike.

The hotel hadn't changed much since Claudia's previous visit. Dark wood floors gleamed under antique carpets, and a wide curving staircase led to a second-story hall supported by tall white columns. Walking through the lobby felt like taking a trip back in time to the opulent 1920s, when the hotel had been built.

Servers in crisp linen offered cocktails with umbrellas to well-dressed guests. Claudia plucked a cocktail from the tray and meandered down the long hall to the boutique.

Shopping for herself was a pleasure Claudia hadn't indulged in for a long time. Her agent picked out her clothes, and her assistant delivered them. Claudia wore designer gowns, one-of-a-kind swimsuits made in New York, and hundred-dollar shoes.

Even her personal items had been hand-selected by her agent.

Excitement bubbled up as she entered the shop and took a long look around. Her agent would definitely not approve of the loud colors or the wild patterns, but Claudia was delighted.

She bought an aloha-print wrap dress, thong sandals, and a bright orange terrycloth shorts set. The saleslady talked her into white sneakers that she wouldn't be caught dead in at home in Hollywood.

On her way out of the shop, a Hawaiian print shirt caught her eye. It was deep, dark blue—the same blue of Henry's eyes.

"I'll take that too," she said impulsively. She'd give it to Henry when she saw him at Diamond Head.

24

Diamond Head

Claudia

CLAUDIA WAS EARLY. Or maybe Henry was just operating on Hawaii time. Either way, she arrived first to the dusty parking lot in the center of Diamond Head Crater.

It had been a harrowing drive up the side of the crater that sloped into the sea at the southern-most tip of the island. Then, the road had flattened out and veered left into a tunnel. Claudia realized in the darkened space of the tunnel that she was inside Diamond Head Crater, surrounded by the crusty ridge of an ancient landmark.

When the bright light of day hit her on the other side, she blinked and noticed everything was brown. This wasn't the lush side of the mountains where they filmed *A Long Road Home*. Here, there was nothing but the burnt crust of a volcano ridge, a blister of earth.

She parked her car and got out, feeling awed that the divot of ground where she stood was the scar left by a natural disaster.

Claudia had nothing but respect for Mother Nature. She lavished her attention on a whim, and she never failed to leave her mark. Diamond Head Crater was a perfect reminder of what happened when things got too hot: they exploded.

Under the shade of a Banyan tree, there was a man selling shaved ice out of a cart. Claudia bought herself a cup of thinly chipped ice doused in sugar and fruit juices and strolled back to her car to wait for Henry.

Fifteen minutes past noon, he finally pulled into the parking lot. Claudia paused in the act of lifting the spoon to her mouth to check him out.

He was dressed for hiking in a pair of short shorts, a tank top, and a baseball cap turned backward. His hair stuck out from under the cap in waves, and his dark sunglasses gave him a bit of a mysterious look.

He looked good enough to eat.

Her gaze lingered on his brief shorts. She didn't have to guess if he was wearing underwear. She could see he wasn't.

Henry slid next to her onto the hood of the car and draped an arm around her shoulders. Helping himself to her spoon, he took a bite of her shave ice.

"Mango," he said with a grin. "My favorite."

He gave her back the spoon, and electricity darted up her arm to spread through her chest. She hardly had time to recover from the vibrations and set her cup on the hood before his mouth settled onto hers in a firm mango-flavored kiss.

At first his lips were cold, but the heat between them rose rapidly. Claudia clutched his shoulder, and his tongue licked the seam of her lips. She nearly jolted with desire.

It seemed the chemistry that had flared between them the night before wasn't just a fluke. Henry was the real thing. And those shorts? They were killing her. They were worse than the jeans. They showed everything.

"Don't look at me like that, Claudia, or I swear I will take you right here in the parking lot." He brought her close and kissed her again, softer this time, more appropriate to them being in the middle of a parking lot full of tourists. His smile curled at the corner. "That would definitely get your picture in the magazines."

Claudia slid his sunglasses off his face, letting her eyes wander over him. "I'm glad to see you're all in one piece," she said, curling her fingers in his hair.

"Don't worry about me, baby. It was a piece of cake."

"Says someone who jumps out of two-story windows onto a wagon being pulled by a horse."

He grabbed his sunglasses and tucked them into the neck of his shirt. "Heard about that, did you?"

Claudia put her hand on his arm and was reassured by the solid bulge of his muscle. "I know you think you're invincible, but you could have died."

"It's all part of the job. Remember what I told you? Eighty percent illusion."

She nodded. But Henry had a knack for making everything look 100 percent real.

He took a spoonful of ice into his mouth and glanced around at the parking lot filling with tourists. Claudia could feel the tension in Henry's posture. He held his jaw in an uncharacteristic clinch that didn't suit him.

Claudia figured he wasn't a fan of tourists.

Then his gaze flicked back toward her, and she gasped. She'd never seen Henry's eyes so intense before, and she'd been wrong about the color. They weren't navy as she'd thought. They were the exact color of a midnight sky, so dark they were nearly black, with a burst of lighter cobalt circling his pupils.

The look in those vibrant eyes was nothing short of anguish.

Claudia felt an electric charge dance along her skin. Henry blinked, and his expression softened. The insanity in his eyes oxidized. It was as if he'd flipped a switch and nonchalant Henry was back.

She felt bereft in the sea of his mood change.

"How was the sunrise?" he asked, spooning up another bite of mango-flavored ice.

Heat scored her chest as she watched Henry lick the spoon. "It was lovely."

"Hmm." He offered her a bite. "You know, there are much better places to watch the sunrise."

Claudia plucked the spoon and the cup and deposited them on the hood of the car. She turned back toward Henry and laced her arms around his neck, then threaded her fingers through the thick waves that sprung from beneath the bill of the backward ball cap.

"Would you care to show me a better place to watch the sunrise?"

His eyes darkened. "I couldn't let you leave Hawaii without seeing all the best it has to offer."

A flush stole over her cheeks. "I want to see everything."

His hand slid down her back, tracing her spine to the waist-band of her shorts. "We really need to talk." His thumb made a slow circle on the patch of skin exposed between her top and her shorts.

She knew what he was going to say. He wanted to talk about Keoni. *She* did not.

Claudia ran her fingers through the soft tufts of hair sticking out from the cap and tugged his mouth a few inches closer.

Henry was having none of it. "This is important, Claudia. We need to get a few things straight."

She sighed heavily. "I know what you want to talk about, but we don't have to discuss it, okay? We don't ever have to talk about Keoni again."

Henry's eyes widened. "We don't?"

"No." She pressed a kiss to his cheek. "Because you're the one I want to watch the sunrise with, okay?"

Then his mouth was on hers, pressing hard, cool. And then soft and melting.

It was wonderful what Henry could do with his mouth, the way he could turn one little kiss into a panty-melting fantasy.

He really had the most talented mouth.

His hand shifted to her hips, and a bolt of pleasure scorched through her veins. She may have pushed him down. She may have climbed on top of him and pinned him to the hood of her car. She had absolutely no control over herself when Henry kissed her.

He made her lose her mind.

He kissed like he did everything—exuberantly. Henry was full throttle without any brakes.

A few minutes later, it was Henry who insisted they stop.

"You're going to get me arrested," he said in a raspy growl, dislodging himself from her clutches.

The sound of voices penetrated Claudia's fog of lust. Behind them, someone cleared their throat and giggled.

Henry replaced his sunglasses—it was a miracle they hadn't been crushed—and flipped his hat around so that the bill shaded his eyes. "You're damn distracting."

She slid off the hood. Her sneakers hit the ground, and she looked up at Henry with innocence. "Me?"

His soft chuckle sounded. "Let's get going before all these tourists beat us to the top."

Claudia spotted her cup of shave ice on the pavement, melting in the midday sun. She put her hands on her hips and frowned down at it.

"I'll buy you another one on the way out," Henry promised.

Claudia batted her eyelashes at him. "Big spender."

He smacked her playfully on the butt and grabbed her hand to tug her to the trailhead.

Claudia eyed the ridge of the crater towering over them and sighed. "You might have to carry me."

Henry tipped his imaginary hat. "It would be my pleasure, ma'am."

25

Get to the Top

Henry

HALFWAY UP THE TRAIL, Henry stopped to wait for Claudia. He shaded his eyes against the sun and called down to her. "You okay?"

Claudia raised her head and gave him a thumbs-up. "Go ahead," she said, panting slightly.

Henry found out she hadn't been kidding when she said she wasn't much of a hiker. But he couldn't help but admire her determination. A determined frown marred her smooth forehead, and a strand of hair clung to her cheek. Sweat stained her top between her breasts. No bra.

Jesus. She was killing him.

A man jogged up behind Claudia, passed by her, and dashed by Henry with a cheerful "Howzit?"

Henry lifted a hand in response. "Howzit?"

He walked back down the trail to a vista point and rested his hands on the iron railing. "This is a nice spot for a rest," he told Claudia when she joined him.

It was a day like every other in Hawaii. Pure paradise. Seventy-five degrees and not a cloud in the sky.

"See all the way out there?" He put his hand on the small of her back and turned her a little more east.

She squinted.

"That's our nearest neighbor, Moloka'i."

"Have you been there?"

Henry shook his head. "No one goes to Moloka'i. It has a bad history."

Claudia stared at the distant island. "Is that where John Cook died?"

Henry shook his head, surprised she knew some Hawaiian history. Then he remembered Keoni. Keoni was full of stories about Hawaii. He'd probably told her about the English explorer.

"That was The Big Island. Moloka'i was used as a leprosy colony. About a hundred years ago, they sent people to there to die." Anger clenched his jaw. "They were never allowed to leave. If they had children, they took them away from their parents."

Claudia slid her arm around his waist and rested her head on his chest, giving comfort. She knew how to comfort him without saying a word. Ever since he'd told Claudia about his daughter, he'd been thinking of it all day. He pushed the nightmare to the back of his mind, hoping it would stay put this time.

Henry spotted a group of tourists gaining on them from below, and it was just the distraction he needed.

"I owe you a ride," he said, turning around to crouch down.

"You can't carry me up this mountain."

"It's not a mountain," he said. "It's a crater. Now get on. I want to be alone with you at the top for a minute, and those tourists will catch us if we don't get a move on."

Claudia climbed on. He felt the heat of her body through her clothes, and he wished they were back in her hotel room, in her bed where he could spread her legs and taste her heat. He settled for turning his head to capture her mouth in a kiss. More could wait for later.

Her arms linked around his neck, and he stood with an exaggerated groan.

Claudia swatted his arm. "I'm too heavy. Put me down."

Henry secured his hands beneath her knees. He wouldn't have cared if Claudia weighed more than a ton of bricks; he wasn't putting her down. She was all curves and feminine perfection pressed against his back. Having her close was worth the pain of carrying her to the top.

He grunted. "Good thing I'm strong."

Claudia cinched her legs around his waist. "Just for saying that, I'm making you carry me the whole way."

Gladly.

They hiked up a series of switchbacks, making enough time on the tourists to allow for a quick pause at the lookout over Diamond Head Lighthouse.

"I hear they have some great parties," Henry said, indicating the dwelling where the lightkeeper lived. The sprawling home with a wraparound deck was separated from the lighthouse tower by a well-manicured stretch of lawn. It was the perfect spot for a large party.

"You think we could get an invitation?" Claudia asked.

"You, maybe. Me, hell no." Only the elite ever saw that manicured lawn up close. "You want a lift again?" he asked.

"Nope." Claudia strode ahead of him, continuing toward the top, her ponytail swishing against her shoulders.

Henry let her get ahead a few feet as he admired the view.

"You coming?" she asked, tossing a teasing glance over her shoulder.

"Right behind you," Henry muttered, wondering how he was going to keep his eyes on the trail with Claudia as a distraction. Those soft shorts hugged her curvy ass and showed off her long legs.

The jogger who'd passed them earlier appeared at the end

of a switchback, and Henry saw his face as he recognized Claudia. He'd come up behind them before, and had surely noticed her, but had probably thought she was just another pretty girl. Pretty girls were abundant in Hawaii. But now that he got a glimpse of her face, there was no mistaking the Hollywood star.

The jogger's step faltered, and his mouth dropped open. As he ran by Claudia, he turned to get another look at her and nearly plowed into Henry.

"Sorry," the jogger said.

"No sweat." Henry stepped aside to let the man pass. He could commiserate. The man wasn't the only one to suffer from whiplash trying to get a look at Claudia.

The jogger asked, "Is that—"

"Yeah," Henry said, interrupting.

"She's with you?"

The man's gaze dropped over Henry. Assessing. Judging. Henry's chin inched up, and his jaw tensed. "Yeah, she's with me. You got beef with that?"

He'd been in Hawaii long enough to pick up some of the slang, and apparently the jogger had too. The man's face cleared, and Henry saw the grudging respect in his eyes. "Nah. No beef, man."

Henry's shoulders didn't relax until the jogger had passed out of sight. When he turned back to the trail to catch up with Claudia, Henry's chest was tight and his throat burned. He knew he wasn't the type of man Claudia was usually seen with. The rag magazines had linked her with handsome actors, successful athletes, and wealthy businessmen, not stuntmen with a face for radio. He didn't blame the jogger for doubting that Claudia was with him, but it still stung.

He came up behind Claudia, who'd stopped at the base of a narrow flight of concrete stairs. There was no one around, so he slipped his arm around her waist and pulled her back against his front. His heavy erection pressed against the base of her spine.

A gasp tore from her throat, and she pressed back against

him. He stiffened even more at the feel of her soft curves. His hand came to her hip, his mouth to her neck. He traced the shell of her ear with his tongue.

"You can't possibly be thinking about sex right now." Her voice was soft and throaty. She always sounded like she'd been yelling too much and her throat was sore. It was incredibly sexy.

"Did I tell you I like your shorts?" He pressed against her, showing her how much.

"You can borrow them," she teased.

"I don't want to wear them. I want to rip them off you."

"God, Henry." She breathed hard, arching into him. "Can we get out of here?"

"You're just saying that because you don't want to climb those stairs." He laughed as he released her and adjusted his shorts to relieve the ache. "I promise it's worth it when you get to the top."

"It better be." She began the trudge up the stairs.

Henry poked her in the back. "Hurry. Those tourists are catching up. And I think one of them was on crutches."

Claudia turned to glare at him. "Shut up, or I'll make you carry me up the rest of these stairs. God." She huffed. "How many are there?"

Henry knew it was a rhetorical question, but he told her the answer. "Ninety-nine."

Claudia stopped abruptly and turned to look at him. "How do you know that?"

"I've counted them." He stroked his chin. "It always bothered me that there weren't a hundred. Couldn't they have put one more in to make it even?"

She started climbing again. "How many times have you been up here?"

"I used to come a lot when I first moved here. I didn't know anyone, and I was working all the time. I needed something to do."

"So you climbed a mountain for fun?"

"It's not a mountain," Henry said, reminding her. "It's a volcano tuft." Henry frowned, remembering who had told him the story of Diamond Head a long time ago—Keoni. "It's like an explosion." Henry used his hands as he struggled to describe the phenomenon. Keoni had told a story about a war of the gods, making it sound like something out of a fairy tale, but Henry didn't have his way with words. "Like when a blister pops."

Claudia's nose wrinkled.

Henry shrugged. He wasn't Keoni in more ways than one.

"Just through this tunnel and we'll be there," Henry said, changing the subject. He didn't want to think about Keoni right now. Henry and Keoni had been friends, but he didn't think they could be anymore. After Claudia went back to the mainland, Henry wouldn't forget her. And Keoni would be a painful reminder.

They came out of the tunnel at the base of a spiral staircase. Almost at the top. Henry couldn't wait to see Claudia's reaction. He grabbed her hand and pulled her up to the concrete platform that had been built during the war.

From there, they could see the entire southern coastline, including all of Waikiki. Clear skies, sandy beaches, and turquoise water unfolded in every direction. The tourists hadn't caught up to them yet, so for the moment, it was just him and Claudia on top of the world.

"There's The SurfRider." Henry pointed at the small white hotel surrounded by high-rises.

"It looks so tiny. So beautiful."

It had been the finest hotel on the beach, and now it was dwarfed by towering buildings. Construction cranes littered the shoreline.

It was beautiful and poignant, and tragic in a way. He imagined what the view had looked like centuries earlier, when those warriors had clashed swords right where they stood. His heart ached for them. They could have never guessed what would become of their island.

Claudia reached up on her toes to kiss him. Soft and sweet, her lips still tasted like mango. Her kiss took his mind off the plight of the island.

She kissed one corner of his mouth, then the other. She kissed his cheek, his chin, and his jaw. Slow, soft kisses that were meant to soothe. They quickly turned heated. No matter how gentle a kiss started with them, it always ended the same way—hot and out of control.

A clamor of noise on the metal stairs announced the family had arrived.

Henry eased back and set Claudia away from him. He hopped over the railing onto the dirt just as the tourists clattered onto the platform.

"That's dangerous," the mother warned her children.

"Don't worry," Claudia said. "He's a stuntman."

Henry reached up and snagged Claudia by the waist. She giggled as he lifted her down from the platform into his arms.

"Are you a stuntman too?" asked the little girl.

Claudia raised her eyebrows at Henry.

"Yes," he said definitively. "Of course she is."

26

Gentleman

Claudia

"THE TRIP DOWN IS QUICKER," Henry said in promise as they started down the stairs.

"It better be."

He tugged on his hat. "You should give up those smokes. Then you'd be able to beat me to the top."

"Stop nagging."

"I'm just looking out for you is all. Plus…" He reached for her hand and tugged her back into his arms. "I like tasting mango on your tongue better than menthols."

"Hmm. At least I don't smell like a barnyard half the time."

He sniffed her neck. "You're a little sweaty right now."

She laughed and hooked her arms around his neck. "You still want to kiss me."

"You're right."

"Kiss me."

He dropped a kiss on her nose. "Here?" When he pulled away, she chased his mouth with hers. He grinned. "Here?

What about here?" He peppered soft kisses on her face, much as she'd done to him on top of the crater.

"You missed a spot." She shifted so their lips lined up.

He gripped her chin and planted a kiss on her lips. Hard. Possessive. "What are you doing for the rest of the day?"

"Why?"

"Because I want to keep kissing you." He lifted his head and glared behind them. "Dammit, those tourists move fast. Let's go."

"Hey!" She tugged his hand. "Thanks for dragging me up here."

"You're welcome."

"You owe me ice chips."

"It's called shave ice."

"That's what I said."

He smirked at her and started down the trail again. "Coconut okay with you?"

"Sure."

Henry was right. The trip down was a lot quicker than the trip up. They bought another shave ice once they made it to the bottom.

Claudia liked mango better than the coconut flavor, but she didn't want to hurt Henry's feelings.

"I got something for you," she said when they got back to their cars.

"I like the sound of that."

He grabbed for her, but she swatted his hands away. "Not that. I got you a present."

His hands fell away, and his blue eyes widened. "What kind of present?"

"You'll see." Claudia reached in the car and grabbed the bag from the boutique. Heat crawled up her chest to her cheeks as she handed it to him. "It's nothing really," she said, seeing the look of amazement on Henry's face.

A grin spread across his mouth as he unfolded the shirt.

"Do you like it?"

"I love it. I'm going to wear it right now."

"You don't have to. I can take it back. I'm not sure what I was thinking."

His hand curled around her neck, and he pulled her close for a kiss, shutting her up. "Thank you."

He stepped back and whipped off his shirt, giving her a show of solid muscle and smooth skin before he shrugged into the shirt. He didn't bother buttoning it but instead left it hanging open. The tantalizing view of his chest was almost too much to resist.

"What are you doing for the rest of the day?" he asked again.

"I need to train a little more. The fight scene is in a few days."

His smile slowly beamed. "It would be my pleasure to train with you. I know the perfect spot." He opened his car door for her. "We need to make one stop first."

The stop turned out to be a corner grocery store, where Henry bought a bag of carrots and some sugar cubes.

"Hungry?" Claudia teased.

"They aren't for me."

They drove along the coastal highway that overlooked the pristine white beaches of eastern Oah'u and turned into Niu Valley.

"This is my favorite place on the island. It's where I come when I'm feeling low."

The road narrowed and cut a path between the foothills. Claudia had expected Henry to take her to the beach, but this was the middle of nowhere.

Tension knotted her belly. "Are you feeling low?"

He reached for her hand and brought it to his mouth for an absent kiss. "Never when I'm with you."

They passed a lone house with a red tin roof, where a man sat on the porch. He waved at Henry as they drove by.

Wooden fences lined each side of the road, separating vibrant green pastures. A craggy mountain range stood tall in the distance.

Henry stopped the car in a grove of flowering trees next to a red barn.

Claudia spotted a familiar quarter horse grazing near the barn. "That's Rusty!"

"He's my favorite. He's been on the show for two years and really enjoys his job. He knows just what to do."

They got out of the car and went to stand at the fence. Rusty lifted his head, snorted, and trotted over.

Henry stroked the horse's chestnut coat and fed him a carrot. It warmed Claudia's heart to see Henry interacting with the horse.

"You guys have a special bond."

Henry laughed, his eyes dancing as he patted the big horse's neck. "My pockets are full of treats."

It looked like more than that to Claudia.

When it was clear to Rusty that he wasn't getting any more carrots, he wandered off to graze under the trees. Henry and Claudia walked along the fence to a flat spot in the shade.

"You ready?"

Claudia set her feet and raised her fists. "Ready."

The next thing she knew, she was in a headlock under Henry's arm. She hadn't expected him to move so fast, and she temporarily froze.

"Stomp my foot," he said to encourage her.

She remembered what she'd learned, and they went through each motion of the fight scene until everything was perfect.

Henry dodged her punches. Claudia broke his hold. They moved in perfect harmony, their pretend fight nearly as seamless as their swing dance.

Even though Henry was bossy and demanding when he was training, Claudia liked it.

The sexual charge between them sharpened their moves, heightened the tension.

When Henry pulled her into a headlock, she felt the tight coil of his muscles at her back. She wanted to spread her palm against those muscles, feel them tighten and watch his face as she stroked his skin.

But she also wanted to get the scene right, so she focused on the work. She was a professional. She could handle a little lust, especially if she knew she was getting what she wanted later.

Over the smell of horses, hay, and grass, Claudia could still smell Henry. He smelled like sunshine and spice. She wished she could bottle that smell and take it with her when she went back to the mainland.

She stopped fighting and nuzzled his chest, filling her lungs with his clean, masculine scent.

His hand roamed along her back, tracing the curve of her spine. Claudia was acutely aware of his body pressing into hers. The hard planes of his chest against her soft curves felt so right.

Somehow, Henry had worked his way into her heart. His smile lit the dark places inside her. His laugh shattered her defenses. His touch sparked a fire that only his kiss could quench.

Pressed tightly against him, she was acutely aware of his need for her. His erection pressed against her belly. His arms wrapped around her tightly like strong, thick bands.

She lifted her face, needing to see the desire stamped on his. His eyes were tight, his mouth set in a determined line.

"Do you have plans tonight?" he asked, fingers tightening at her waist.

Doubt trembled in his voice. Henry hadn't even asked about Keoni. If she'd seen him at Sans Souci. If they'd arranged to meet again. She guessed he didn't want to know.

"Are you asking me on a date, Henry?"

"Are you saying yes?"

Claudia reached up on her tiptoes and pressed her mouth to

his. "I'd love to go on a date with you." She rubbed her lips across his mouth. "But only if you take me back to your place after and screw me all night long."

His eyes widened and then his laugh sounded, rumbling against her chest. "Are you gonna let me sleep at all?"

"Not likely."

His cock liked that and stood at attention. "Then pack a bag."

Hoof beats sounded nearby. The ground thundered. Claudia turned to see a magnificent horse racing beside the fence. Head high, tail flicking, he was terrifyingly beautiful.

"That's Aries," Henry said, following her eye. "He's an ex-racehorse who doesn't realize he's retired." He placed his thumb and third finger in the corners of his mouth and whistled. "Come over and say hello, Aries."

Aries lifted his head, his nostrils flaring as he assessed them. Henry rattled his shirt pocket, and the horse's ears perked. A moment later, he trotted over.

"Good boy." Henry fed Aries a sugar cube.

"No carrots for him?"

"He likes these better." Henry pressed a sugar cube into her palm. "Try it."

"He won't bite me?"

Henry winked. "He's a gentleman."

Claudia held her hand the way Henry had done, palm up. Aries bent his neck and brushed his soft muzzle against her hand. His whiskers tickled her palm as he ate the sugar cube.

When he was done, he snorted and tried to stick his nose in Henry's pocket. Henry laughed and gave Aries the last sugar cube.

"That's it for you."

Aries lifted his head and trotted off to the other side of the pasture. Henry leaned against the fence, watching the horses graze. He seemed lost in thought, as though he had forgotten she was there.

"You okay?"

He turned to look at her, a ghost of a smile playing on his lips. "We should go so you can get ready."

"Ready for what?"

"We're going to a luau."

27

Velvet Eyes

Henry

HENRY DIDN'T SEE Claudia in the lobby, but he knew she was there. He could feel her presence. There was an electric charge in the air when Claudia was near, and he felt it now, even though he didn't see her.

Henry's gaze skipped over a group of tourists dressed in their vacation finery and settled on a young woman seated on a velvet settee.

Claudia. He almost didn't recognize her under the enormous hat and sunglasses hiding half her face. Then he saw her legs, and he knew.

Desire flared. Passion burned.

She looked up and spotted him. He couldn't see her eyes, but he knew by the slow smile that took over her mouth that she'd seen him.

God, she was pretty. His cock noticed the pretty dress she wore, the abundance of tanned legs, and the sin in her smirk and tried to embarrass him by going instantly hard. Henry forced himself to ignore his body's barbaric reaction to Claudia and put one foot in front of the other as if each step didn't chafe miserably.

Damn these jeans. They were so tight, he couldn't hide a thing.

Henry did his best impression of a man who didn't have a growing erection in his pants and strode across the lobby.

"Have you seen a gorgeous girl named Janice? She's supposed to be my date tonight, but I think she may have chickened out."

Claudia reached down to adjust her sandal. Her eyebrow rose, an accusing arch, and she said, "Maybe she figured out you were lying to her."

Panic surged in Henry's gut. His mouth couldn't quite form words.

He wasn't exactly lying. He was just leaving something out. He'd been a breath away from telling her about the bet a half dozen times, but he just hadn't been able to do it. He knew he was a coward. A dirty, low-life bastard…

Henry cleared his throat. "Lying about what?"

Claudia lowered her sunglasses and looked at him. Her eyes burned so brightly, he thought his skin might melt.

"Admit it," she said.

His heart lurched. "Admit what?"

"You knew who I was that first night."

Henry's shoulders inched back down. He picked up her hand and kissed her knuckles. "I know you're the most famous woman in the world," he teased, "but I had no idea who you were. I've never seen *Jezebel.*"

Claudia gasped in mock horror. "You don't say."

"I'm sorry. I'm more of an action flick fan."

Claudia lifted her chin and looked down her nose at him "You promise?"

"I promise. I love Kung Fu."

She laughed. "I meant you promise you didn't know who I was."

"I swear on my life, I didn't know who you were. Why? What does it matter?"

"I don't like the idea of you fooling me."

Tension balled in his chest. "We should go. The party has already started." He stood and held a hand down to her. "Did you bring a bag?"

Color rose into her cheeks. "Yes."

He wanted to kiss her, but not in the hotel lobby where everyone was watching. It was only a matter of time before someone came up and asked for her autograph, and he didn't want to give anyone a reason to take their picture.

They went outside, where the sky was as colorful as a crayon box and plumeria flowers perfumed the air. An ocean breeze stirred the trees, keeping the humidity at bay.

It was another perfect night in Hawaii, and Henry cherished it even more because Claudia was on his arm. She would be gone soon. Back to Hollywood.

Henry knew one thing for sure. He was never leaving Hawaii. That meant their affair had an expiration date. There really was no need to tell her about the bet.

Henry led Claudia to his car, which was parked under the striped awning that stretched over the half-circle driveway of The SurfRider.

Henry shooed away the bellman and opened Claudia's door for her.

Before he could close the door, she grabbed him by the collar. "You can kiss me now," she said in her breathy voice. "No one is looking."

Her bold smile sent a fresh wave of desire through his body. Henry lowered his head to hers and kissed her softly.

"I don't know how I'm going to keep my hands off you in that dress."

"We could just go straight to your place."

Electricity sizzled between them. He had half a mind to

drag her out of the car and right back up to her room. Screw the luau.

"I promised you a luau."

Claudia took his face between her hands and kissed his lips. "What a bummer."

Henry laughed and tucked her into the car before closing the door.

"You're gonna love this," he said, starting the car. "You can't visit Hawaii without going to a luau. It would be like…" Henry couldn't think of anything to compare with a luau. The food, the dancing, the irrepressible spirit of aloha… "There's just nothing like it."

He pulled out of the driveway onto Kalakaua Avenue and headed toward Diamond Head. After three years in Hawaii, the pace of the island had influenced him. He no longer rushed from place to place. Instead, he took his time, pointing out his favorite spots to Claudia along the way.

"There's the zoo," he said.

"You go there often?"

"I like the peacocks," he admitted.

Claudia smiled. "I wouldn't mind seeing them."

He covered her hand with his free one. "Should we add it to the list?"

"Why not?" she asked. "I have two more weeks."

Henry eased his hand away from hers and back to the steering wheel. It wasn't too late to stop himself from falling for Claudia. He should pull back on the throttle. The problem was Henry didn't know how to do that. He was a full-steam-ahead kind of guy. His family always said he had one speed—fast.

Claudia only had one speed too, and the two of them together were on a crash course for a collision.

Her hand slid up his thigh. "I like your shirt," she said.

He was wearing the gift she'd given him. Tension pinched his shoulders. He might not take this shirt off after Claudia left. "Thanks."

"What's wrong?" She squeezed his leg. "Lay it on me."

His smile tightened. He was dying to tell her everything. The bet. His growing feelings. Keoni. Everything.

Pain stabbed his chest. "Just thinking about that fight scene. I think you need more practice."

Claudia leaned over the console between them and brushed her lips across his jaw. Her hand stole up his thigh. "I can think of something else I'd like to practice."

He picked up her hand and kissed her knuckles. "You have a one-track mind."

"I can't help it. Those jeans are turning me on."

Her kisses stole his breath. "These are the same jeans I always wear."

Her lips found the pulse in his throat. "That's the problem."

She kissed lower, along the column of his throat, and pushed his shirt aside to lick his collar bone. Her hand worked up his thigh.

Henry covered her hand with his own. His body was on fire. His vision blurred. "Baby, I can't drive with you doing that."

She undid the button on his jeans, and he groaned. She teased his zipper down. His cock sprang free.

"You're a stunt driver. You can swing it."

A thrill raced through him. Danger had always been a drug for him. He loved racing on the edge of anything safe. Pushed himself to the extremes.

Gravel filled his throat. He swallowed thickly. "We'll be there in a few minutes."

She nipped his jaw. Tightened her fist. "Is that a challenge?"

His world turned upside down. This girl had been made for him. Cut from his own cloth.

"You think you can get me off that quick?"

Her soft chuckle vibrated against his skin. She kissed her way down his throat, licking and sucking. "Positive," she whispered. "Think you can get us there alive if I do?"

A depraved thrill ran down Henry's spine. This girl was crazy. He loved it. He'd never been more turned on his life.

He glanced away from the road and looked down at Claudia. Desire stamped her pretty features. Her eyes were soft velvet. Her lips parted, and her tongue darted over his swollen crown. He was already leaking, and she lapped up the pearl, her eyes fixed on his the whole time.

He dragged his gaze back to the road. He knew these roads intimately. Every bend. Every curve.

Claudia shifted in his lap. Her tits flattened against his leg, her fantastic ass draped over the console.

With his eyes fixed on the road, Henry slid his hand to the back of her neck and fisted her hair.

He glanced down and caught her wicked smile. She swirled her tongue along his shaft, getting him wet. She shifted closer and slid her mouth down his dick, sucked him to the back of her throat in one swift move.

A hiss escaped his mouth. He gripped the steering wheel tightly and dragged in a steadying breath.

Her mouth surrounded him. A scorching hot fist. She sucked him deep. Her fist worked what she couldn't fit in her mouth. Her ass swayed in the air. Her breasts crushed his thigh.

When he groaned, she laughed. The vibration sent a ripple of pleasure straight from his shaft to his heart.

He drove on autopilot, hugging the tight corners of the switchbacks, downshifting as they climbed up the hills of Puuikena Drive.

Claudia was good at this. So good. Her mouth slid and sucked. Her fist pumped. Her ass jiggled.

At this rate, he would finish long before they arrived at their destination.

Henry wished he could savor what was surely the best blow job of his life, but they were almost there, and he didn't want to rob her of the satisfaction of accomplishing the challenge.

The little noises she made were driving him crazy. Her ass in the air tempted him to fill his hands.

He slammed the car into second and slowed to take the turn into the neighborhood. They were almost there. He was almost there.

His hand stole back to her hair, and he tugged. Warning her. "I'm going to blow."

She sucked hard, then released him with a pop. "Are we there yet?"

Blood roared between his ears. "Next street over," he said with a grunt.

Claudia sucked him to the back of her throat, then swallowed him deeper.

Henry's vision doubled. He slowed the car to a crawl and jerked the wheel. They skidded to a halt at the curb in front of a brightly lit house.

The moment he shoved the clutch into neutral, his cock jerked hard and he erupted, spilling into her mouth. Claudia sucked him deep, her laugh muffled against his dick.

Ecstasy enveloped him. He clung to the final throbs of pleasure pulsing through his veins, wishing he never had to come down from the incredible high. Eventually, his grip relaxed on the steering wheel. His vision slowly cleared.

Claudia shifted back into her seat and wiped the corner of her mouth. The dainty gesture combined with the naughty look in her eye sealed the deal for Henry.

He was falling for Claudia fast and hard.

He didn't like to think about what would happen when she left. He didn't like to think about a lot of things, particularly the sticky situation he was in with the cruel bet.

But Henry being Henry, he shoved all the less-than-attractive thoughts of his into a neat little box and stored it away to be opened later. Right now, they had a luau to attend.

28

So Ono

Claudia

HENRY LEANED over the console and kissed her. He groaned when he tasted himself. "Did that turn you on as much as it did me? I can take care of you."

She kissed him, nipping his lower lip between her teeth. "You will," she said. Her voice was low and needy. Sucking him off had turned her on more than she'd thought it would. The thrill had nearly driven her crazy. She'd handed over all her control. She'd never trusted someone so much or been so vulnerable.

If he touched her now, she'd explode.

"Did we make it to the destination?" she asked.

They were high in the hills, where the temperature was several degrees cooler and the constant humidity was less than pea soup for once. The sounds of laughter and music drifted down the street. Someone was having a party. A car drove by and parked in front of a house a few doors down. Claudia noticed the street was full of cars on both sides.

Henry shut off the ignition. "Almost." He tugged his jeans back in place and zipped up. "We're about three houses down, but I couldn't last any longer."

"So, technically I won."

He leaned over the console and curled his hand around her neck to tug her close. His fingers were warm and calloused, and his touch made her feel like she'd swallowed a cup of butterflies.

"You won." His voice was low and gravelly in her ear. "Name your reward."

Her eyes drifted shut as his lips moved along her neck. "Can I have whatever I want?"

His tongue traced the shell of her ear. "Anything in my power."

Another car drove by, and she relaxed against Henry's warm hand. She wanted something she'd never wanted before: a man simply for the pleasure of him.

Henry couldn't advance her career. He couldn't bring closure to the mistakes of her past.

He made her laugh and trusted her with his secrets.

She just might be falling in love with him.

She eased out of his arms and stared at him as if seeing him for the first time. He wasn't the most handsome man she'd ever dated. Thank God. In Claudia's experience, the most handsome men made horrible lovers. They were so used to women falling at their feet, they didn't know how to be funny or charming. Henry was both. And he had a magic tongue, talented hands, and close to eight inches stuffed behind the zipper of his skin-tight jeans.

"What do you want, Claudia?" He asked, his eyes brilliant blue in the dark interior of the car.

She swallowed roughly. Licked her lips. Her pulse raced. "I want to ride Aries," she said. "Can you teach me?"

Henry exhaled loudly. "That's a tall order. So far, he's only let me ride him, but I'll try."

Claudia flipped down the visor and fixed her lipstick in the mirror while Henry watched. She'd never met a man who wasn't fascinated by a woman putting on her lipstick.

She rolled her lips together and checked her teeth. "I think I'm ready for my first luau."

"I don't think the luau is ready for you. You'll be the most gorgeous girl there."

Pleasure heated her cheeks. "You don't know who else will be there."

"It doesn't matter. If you're in a room, you'll be the best-looking woman in it." He laughed, the sound a wondrous chuckle. "I don't know what you're doing with me."

She did. "You've got a lot going for you, Champ."

He raised an eyebrow when she called him by his nickname. "Why are you calling me that?"

"It suits you."

"That's very nice of you to say." He leaned across the console and kissed her lips with soft, closed-mouth kisses. A bolt of longing exploded in her chest. He pulled back, and she chased his lips with hers. "Now I've ruined your lipstick." He leaned across her legs and opened the glove box, then handed her a napkin. "I'm sorry."

Normally, Claudia would be annoyed if a man messed up her lipstick right before she entered a party. She needed to be picture ready at any moment. But tonight was different. For one thing, there wasn't an abundance of photographers following her around, and for another, this wasn't just any man. This was Henry. And with the way he used his mouth, he could kiss her lipstick off anytime.

She dabbed her mouth with the napkin and leaned in for another kiss. Henry obliged her, and it was another ten minutes before they finally got out of the car and started down the street toward the party. As they neared the house, the hum of noise grew to a loud buzz. Laughter, music, and voices carried along the top of the ridge of the mountain. They were high up in the lush hills. The night breeze was chilly, and the dark sky seemed close enough to touch.

"I need to warn you about the swipe," Henry said, placing his hand on Claudia's back as they walked up the driveway. "Don't drink too much of it."

"And swipe is…?" She'd never heard of it, but it sounded unpleasant, like something that got stuck on your tongue.

"It's Hawaiian moonshine." They approached the tidy bungalow hidden from the street by a grove of trees, and Henry stepped up to the door first. "The locals can handle it, no sweat, but it's not a tourist drink with an umbrella on top. Too much swipe can lead to some very bad decisions." Henry's deep chuckle sounded, and Claudia knew he was speaking from first-hand experience.

Henry reached for the doorknob, but before he could open the door, Claudia put her hand on his and stopped him. She was suddenly overcome with nerves, which was strange because she was well aquatinted with parties and never got stage fright. But right now, her heart was beating too fast, like a film reel running on the fastest speed, flipping out of control.

It had been a long time since she'd been to a party where the entire evening—from what she was wearing to whose arm she hung on to what pictures she posed for—wasn't entirely scripted. A lump rose in her throat, as if she'd swallowed sand. What if she said the wrong thing? She wasn't sure what to do with herself at a party. This was different from that first night at Sunset Beach when she hadn't known anyone. Now she was with Henry.

He turned his hand and captured her fingers. "You okay?"

She nodded tersely, mustering up a brave smile. "Fine."

"You don't have to be nervous about people trying to get your picture or ask for an autograph. These are my friends. They're cool."

That was just what bothered Claudia. These were Henry's

friends, and she was desperate for them to like her. She swallowed the bitter taste in her mouth and squeezed his fingers. "What are you waiting for then? Let's go."

Henry grinned and opened the door without knocking.

In the living room, Henry introduced Claudia to dozens of people. She couldn't possibly remember all their names, and she finally gave up trying. There were more people to meet in the hall, and even more in the kitchen.

Henry dropped a twenty-dollar bill into a fishbowl filled with bills and grabbed them both beers.

"Such a showoff," chided one of Henry's friends, a tiny little thing who came up to Claudia's shoulder.

"What was that about?" Claudia asked, after the woman, whose name she couldn't remember, drifted back into the hall.

"That's the way they do it here." Henry gestured at the bowl of money. "You bring a dish or you bring cash. Since I don't cook, I always bring cash. But you're in for a treat. The food is out of sight."

From the kitchen, they continued down to the basement where even more people were gathered. Claudia had never seen so many people in one place. They lounged on every piece of furniture, leaned against walls, and sat cross-legged on the floor. A group of men stood at the record player, loudly discussing which album to play next.

A haze of smoke filled the upper half of the room and floated up the stairs to the main floor. Conversation, music, and laughter mingled together to create a sound that filled Claudia with energy. It was like being struck by a bolt of electricity. She felt the pulsing music throb through her veins.

Claudia met even more people, was draped in leis, and treated to an impromptu hula dance.

Finally, they got to the food table. It was spread with so much food that it buckled in the middle. Henry grabbed a cup and filled it from a plastic milk jug.

"Try your first sip of swipe," he said, holding the cup out to her. "Be careful."

Claudia smirked. "I bet I could out-drink most people at this party." She was very good at drinking.

"You've never hung with Hawaiians. They all have PhDs in partying."

She sipped cautiously, and her eyes filled with water. She struggled to swallow the burning liquid that tasted of pineapples, sugar, and pure alcohol. Trying and failing not to cough, Claudia squinted at Henry through her tears. "You weren't kidding," she said.

"Nope." Henry laughed and loaded a plate with more food than they could possibly eat. "Let's go outside and find a place to cop a squat."

They went out onto the lanai, and Claudia gaped as she looked around at the view. She'd known they were high up in the mountains, but because she'd been occupied on the drive, she hadn't realized they were *that* high.

The golden-hued clouds were so close, she felt like she could reach up and touch them. There was nothing but pastel sky above and undulating sea below.

"Nice, huh?" Henry asked, staring straight ahead.

Claudia could think of more spectacular words than nice, but none of them seemed good enough either. She had the sudden urge to throw her arms around Henry and kiss him. She was having an amazing time at her first unscripted party in years.

Looking out over the unobstructed view of sea and sky was like standing on top of the world. And there was no one else she'd rather be with.

If someone had told Claudia a month ago that she would be enjoying time with a man in Hawaii who wasn't Keoni, she wouldn't have believed them. But here she was, having the time of her life with Henry.

They found a place to sit, and Henry loaded a fork. "This is Kalua pork," he said. "It's roasted in an underground pit covered with banana leaves for nearly a day." He handed Claudia the fork mounded high with shredded pork. "Reason number one hundred fifty that I'll never leave Hawaii."

Claudia's stomach rumbled in anticipation as the scent of roasted meat hit her nose. She took a delicate bite of the pork and closed her eyes as in delight as she chewed. The pork was juicy with smoke and salt and was so tender. Claudia took another, bigger bite and looked up to see Henry watching her with a knowing grin.

"Best thing you're ever tasted, right?" He loaded the fork with macaroni salad. "Now taste this."

Claudia wrinkled her nose. The dish reminded her of her mother. It was one that had been on frequent rotation at their home growing up. She was going to tell Henry she didn't like macaroni salad, but his eager expression stopped her.

Henry might be thirty years old, but he didn't look it. His expressive eyes and ever—present smile gave him a boyish charm. She took the fork. Bracing herself for the too-sweet, overly done pasta, Claudia took a hesitant bite. She was surprised to find the noodles creamy and full of the earthy flavors of onion and garlic. The noodles were perfectly done. It was actually very good.

"Have you tried poi?" He picked up a dinner roll and tore off a chunk, then dunked it in a purplish mixture that looked a lot like cement.

When she put it in her mouth, she was disappointed to find it didn't taste much better than it looked. Slightly rooty in flavor, it had the consistency of thick baby food.

Henry laughed at her reaction and handed her the plastic cup of swipe. "Wash it down with this."

Claudia took the cup and raised it to her lips. The sweet smell of pineapple hardly masked the strong odor of alcohol.

She took a small sip. This one wasn't as harsh as the first, and she wondered if she was already under its influence.

"What's in this?"

"Secret recipe," he said. "If I had to guess, it's mostly pineapples. They turn to alcohol if you let them sit long enough."

Claudia took another cautious sip, wrinkling her nose. "It's moldy fruit?"

Henry eased the cup from her hand and took a big swallow. He grimaced as it went down. "Don't be a snob. It isn't so bad."

They took turns with the single fork, sampling everything on the plate. Between bites of creamy macaroni salad, spicy grilled shrimp, and gingered kimchee, they sipped the pineapple swipe. A pleasant buzz permeated Claudia all the way to her bones. She didn't know if it was the food, the swipe, or the company that had her feeling so happy. Probably all three.

They saved dessert for last. Henry went back to the spread of food and came back laden with unrecognizable treasures. There was a piece of cake pinker than the Waikiki sunset, a yellow block that looked suspiciously like fudge, a frosted donut with no hole, and a chocolate cupcake.

"I'm too full," Claudia protested.

"This is going to blow your mind." He brought the cupcake to her lips. "So ono, it broke da mouth," he said in his best impression of a Hawaiian accent.

Claudia laughed and leaned forward to take a tiny bite of the cake. It was still warm and gooey in the center, so good she would have considered eating the whole thing if her stomach could take it.

"You have a little chocolate right there," he said, pointing at the corner of her mouth.

Her tongue darted out, and Henry's eyes flared. He lowered his mouth to hers and kissed her. His mouth was warm and firm, quickly heating. Maybe it was the swipe, maybe it was the gentle stroke of Henry's tongue, but Claudia was definitely intoxicated.

His fingers curled around her neck lightly, possessively.

"Want to get out of here?" he asked, reading her mind.

"Yes."

Claudia was learning that with Henry, the answer was almost always yes.

·

29

Luckiest Man Alive

Henry

IT TOOK a lot longer than Henry wanted to say good-bye to everyone at the party. Why now, when all he wanted to do was get out of there, did everyone have something urgent to tell him? His patience thinned to a brittle thread as he waded through the thick crowd. They had almost escaped when someone put on Van Morrison's album. When the first refrains of "Brown Eyed Girl" rang out of the tinny speaker, Claudia clutched his hand and ground to a halt.

"Our song," she said, bouncing in her shoes. "We have to stay for our song!"

Henry repressed a deep sigh. "Now you're admitting we have a song?" The tone of incredulity in his voice was clear. The door was in sight. They were almost there. "Okay," he said. "But you have to dance with me."

"Or else what?" she said flirtatiously, tossing her hair over her shoulder. "You'll throw me over your shoulder, caveman style, and haul me away?"

"Sounds appealing." He reached for her.

Claudia giggled and slipped away. And then she was in his arms again, spinning. He leaned forward, and she shimmied back in perfect sync. They danced, making spectacles of themselves to a cheering crowd. Henry even lifted Claudia off her feet at one point and spun her around in a stiff-armed circle, their bodies barely touching. The crowd went wild. They were natural-born dance partners, made for each other.

At the end of the song, Claudia tipped her head back and laughed, and something in Henry's heart shifted. He spun her back into his arms and held her close for a long moment, knowing something important had changed between them.

They had a song.

"You okay to drive?" Claudia asked when they finally exited the house and were approaching his car. "You did have a lot of that swoop."

He laughed. "It's swipe. And I think I danced most of it off." He opened the passenger door for Claudia and saw her tucked inside before walking around to the driver's side. Once settled in behind the wheel, Henry did feel a bit drunk, but it may have been because he was remembering what had transpired right before he pulled to a stop at the curb when they'd arrived. A blush heated his cheeks as he put the key in the ignition. He checked a glance at Claudia, and his heart paused its beating. "You still want to come to my place?"

"Yes."

The absence of hesitation in Claudia's voice started Henry's heart beating again. "Okay," he said, trying to come off nonchalant as he fired up the engine. His voice said he didn't care either way. His heart begged to differ. And his cock? *Down, boy.*

He released the clutch, punched the gas, and they shot off up the steep hill. Most of the houses they passed were dark, the residents already in bed. It was where Henry wanted to take Claudia, but not for sleeping. Nope. Sleeping wasn't written into the plan.

He turned right at the end of the street, and they climbed higher up on the ridge, right to the very top where one-hundred-eighty-degree views of Diamond Head, the Pacific Ocean, and Koko Crater stretched far and wide to the south and east. To the west, lush valleys anchored plunging cliffs. Long ago, the valleys had been farmland, but now they stood empty, owned by one old family who was hanging onto their land by a thread. Henry imagined that in twenty years, the family would be forced to sell and houses would crowd the views, but for now, the valley unfolded in a spotless green blanket.

Henry's house stood atop the ridge, tucked away from the road by a wooded lot. The house was nothing more than a glorified cabin. It was tiny, with one bedroom, one bathroom, and an all-in-one living and dining room. The kitchen was nothing but a thin galley with bare necessities, but that didn't matter because Henry wasn't much for cooking.

The house wasn't much to look at, and the comforts it provided were barely a step up from camping, but the view was priceless. The lot was large and wooded, and someday, when he had a wife and family, he planned to raze the house and start over.

Suddenly, Henry felt nervous to show Claudia his place. He was thankful it was dark and she couldn't see how truly shabby the little brown house was. "This is it. Not much to look at, I'm afraid."

Claudia stared out the window. "It looks cozy," she said.

Henry laughed heartily. "It's cozy all right. One bedroom, one bathroom, not much of a kitchen. But the lanai is impressive." And he couldn't wait to show her the sunrise.

Claudia reached for her bag, but Henry grabbed it before she could. He still couldn't believe she was staying the night. He'd thought last night in her hotel room was a one-off, something special that would never happen again, but it looked like he just might be the luckiest man alive, because it hadn't been.

They were at his place, where he was steps away from ravishing her again. All night long.

Henry's house wasn't much, but at least it was clean. He'd taken time to tidy up, and he'd definitely gotten rid of the magazine with Claudia on the cover. Still, his furniture was second-hand, and the curtains had been left behind by the previous owner. It wasn't up to movie star standards.

None of that mattered when Claudia touched her lips to his and asked, "Where's the bedroom?"

Henry chuckled. "Do you want a drink? I have tequila." He'd even stocked up on ice and lemons. "Or beer."

She shook her head, wrapping her arms around his neck. "Just take me to bed, Henry."

His cock liked the sound of that. It stirred to life, pressing against the seam of his jeans. Henry resisted throwing Claudia over his shoulder and hauling her to the bedroom. Instead, he lowered his head and kissed her with a patience he hadn't known he possessed.

He knew enough after last night to know the way Claudia liked to be kissed, slowly and thoroughly. He took his time kissing her, ignoring the steely erection in his jeans that throbbed with need.

Last night, they had been in a frenzy. Lust had come fast and hard. But tonight was different. Tonight was more relaxed, almost languid, like the midday heat at Waikiki.

They took their time with each other, their touches less urgent, their strokes more sure. They helped each other with their clothes, leaving little piles in the hallway on the way to the bedroom. Henry's shirt. Claudia's dress. Her shoes. His hat.

His bedroom was so tiny, there was barely room for the double bed and a dresser. A window overlooked the sloping trail that led straight to a private stretch of beaches. He'd left it open, and a cool breeze lapped up the heat in the room.

Claudia sat on the mattress, and Henry stood looking down at her for a long moment, still not quite believing his luck. She was in her bra and panties, a matching set of pale-pink silk and lace that probably cost more than Henry's entire wardrobe. She was the prettiest thing he'd ever laid eyes on. Her hair was long and loose around her shoulders, like a soft shimmering cloud. Her skin was flawless. Not a freckle dared to mar the even tone of her golden tan.

He reached down and hooked his thumbs in the sides of her pretty pink panties. Claudia peered up at him from dark, hooded eyes, her full lips slightly parted.

"Lift up," he said.

She lifted her hips, allowing Henry to peel off her panties and toss them to the floor. Her bra was next. She arched her back and unclasped it. The straps fell from her shoulders and then her perfect tits spilled free, heavy and full with rosy peaks that made his mouth water. They were perfect juicy pears that he wanted to take a bite of.

He hadn't thought his dick could get any harder, but it did. Each pulse of his heart throbbed in his cock.

Claudia reached for him and unzipped his jeans with aching slowness. His stiff erection sprang free, and he sighed in relief. Then, her hand wrapped around him, and his sigh turned into a long moan. His mind fogged as if he'd been dragged under by quicksand. It was all he could do to nudge her hand away and stretch out beside her to lavish kisses along her belly and ribs.

He kissed higher, brushing the scruff of his jaw against her breasts but purposefully avoiding the pebbled buds of her nipples. He could spend days adoring the peaks and valleys of Claudia's gorgeous breasts. He truly was the luckiest man alive to have her naked in his bed.

She tangled her fingers in his hair, and he loved it. His head was sensitive, and when she ran her fingernails along his scalp, he shuddered.

Henry sucked her nipple into his mouth, and Claudia's fingers tightened in his hair, holding him there. Exactly where she wanted him. Where they both wanted him.

His heart slammed in his chest, each pulse going straight to his thick, hard cock.

She moaned his name, and the desperate need in her voice was his undoing. He needed her now.

He sat up and reached for the nightstand drawer. He kept condoms there, although he hadn't needed them for a long time. It had been over a year since a woman had been in his bed with him.

Claudia moaned in protest. "Where are you going?"

"Let me cover up, and I'll be right back."

Claudia wrapped her arms around his neck and pulled him back to her. "I have a prescription."

"I know."

"I like feeling you inside me."

Henry groaned. He liked it too. His heavy erection notched between her legs. It was so tempting to push inside her. He wanted to feel her tight sheath around him, skin to skin, but he wanted to come inside her more. And for that, he needed to cover up. Usually it was a non-negotiable for him to use a rubber. He'd only gone bare last night out of sheer desperation.

Even though it threatened to break the fragile intimacy between them, Henry couldn't give her that. He hoped she understood.

Without saying a word, she nodded. Her eyes were as soft as velvet. She got it. She got him. He couldn't risk a repeat of what had happened in college.

He opened the drawer on the nightstand and fished out a condom. Claudia plucked it from his fingers, pried it open with her teeth, and rolled it on for him, taking care of him.

"I want you," she said, reaching up to kiss him. "Any way I can get you."

He shifted over her, and she guided him closer. The broad crown of his cock nudged the tight bundle of nerves at her opening, and they both gasped.

"Damn, we're good together," he said.

"Is that so hard to believe?"

His gaze flickered down to her smiling mouth. She was Hollywood's darling. He was the stand-in. "What do you think?"

"I think you're taking too long."

One thrust and he buried himself deep inside her. It felt so good that neither of them moved for a long moment. Henry savored the feeling, trying to make it last so he could remember everything better when Claudia was gone.

Her fingers fluttered to his shoulders, then gripped, urging him to move.

He followed her direction, answering every thrust of her hips, every demand from her lips.

Kiss me. Touch me. Faster. Harder.

Henry let Claudia direct, eagerly following every command as if his life depended on it.

Because it did. Without her, he couldn't breathe. She was his air, his blood, his life. And she was going to leave and take it all away. He wouldn't think about that now. He couldn't.

In a few weeks, she'd be gone, and he was determined to give her something to remember him by.

He knew she was close. He could tell by the change in her breathing. Her short little pants came faster. The cinch of her thighs around his hips ground tighter.

Fighting for control as it spun out of reach, he drove them both over the edge of ecstasy and straight into bliss.

He took her mouth, pouring everything he couldn't say into the kiss. He hoped she heard the words in his head that he couldn't say and she knew that he fucking loved her.

30

My Sunrise is Better

"Claudia

YOU'RE BEAUTIFUL. Did I tell you that?"

Claudia frowned and touched a hand to her hair, which was in tangles. "I'm a mess."

"A beautiful mess."

She stretched out on the bed like a contented cat. She'd slept better than she had in years next to him. "Why are you up?" *And not in bed next to me?* "What time is it?"

"Early."

"Why? Do you have to be on set?"

"Nope. It's my day off." He was wearing a pair of baggy sweats and no shirt. "I want to show you something."

"Is it in those sweatpants?" Her hand trailed up his thigh.

"God, you're insatiable." He captured her hand and brushed her knuckles with a kiss. His soft mouth and prickly whiskers made her think of Aries nibbling the sugar, and she laughed. "What's funny?"

She swallowed her laugh. "Nothing."

"Come on." He stripped back the covers.

Claudia caught the sinful gleam in his eyes as their gaze roamed over her naked body. She smiled coyly. "Are you sure you don't want to come back to bed?"

He captured her hand and tugged her upright, his eyes on her breasts. "You're a tempting sight."

Her mouth was practically watering as she ran her eyes over his delectable chest and down the V of his hips. She could see the outline of his thickening cock in the flimsy pants. She'd thought the jeans were bad.

"Get moving." He pulled her to her feet and then took a step back, putting some distance between them.

The tile was cool under her toes. They'd left the windows open all night, and the morning breeze chilled the air.

"Can I brush my teeth first?"

"Hurry."

"Can I use your toothbrush?"

Henry swatted Claudia's butt and ushered her into the hall. She grabbed a shirt from the pile on the floor. It was the one she'd bought for him in the hotel boutique. She shrugged it on, smelling the fresh masculine scent that was all Henry.

He was waiting for her with a cup of coffee when she shuffled out of the bathroom. Leaning against the wall between the kitchen and living room, dressed only in the hip-hugging sweats, Henry looked positively delicious. She wasn't normally a morning person, but she was already feeling full of perky energy.

She liked that she'd been the one to put that spark in his eye. That smug smile on his face.

His grin turned sheepish as he pushed off the wall. "I didn't know… Do you drink coffee?"

She nodded; she did.

"I hope you don't need milk, because mine expired last week."

"This is just the ticket." She took the coffee and sipped. Hot and strong, just how she liked it. Everything in Hawaii tasted just a bit better than it did on the mainland.

Henry poured himself a fresh cup and opened the door to the lanai. The sky was dark, still untouched by the first light of dawn. Wisps of black clouds floated close enough to touch. The crisp breeze blew over the tops of the trees, tickling Claudia's naked thighs.

"This is the reason I paid too much for this dump," he said, leaning his elbows on the railing.

To the south, she saw the dark outline of Diamond Head Crater breaking up the endless midnight sky. To the east, there was nothing but blackish blue, sky and sea into infinity. A thin band of gold spread along the line where the sky met the sea.

Henry put his arm around her waist and drew her close. "This is a sunrise you won't forget."

She glanced away from the pinprick of light and looked at Henry instead. Her heart clenched, a hard ache in her chest. She pressed her lips to his jaw, and his hand tightened at her waist. His low laugh echoed in the silence.

"You're missing it," he scolded.

She didn't care. She grazed his jaw with her teeth and nipped the corner of his mouth.

Henry turned his face and took her mouth with his. He claimed her with a possessive kiss. Hard and punishing, it left her breathless. His tongue tasted of rich, dark coffee, earthy and full of life.

With a muffled groan, he ended the kiss and set her away from him. "Watch the damn sunrise with me, Claudia."

Apparently, Henry got angry. And Henry angry was a sexy beast. Color stained his cheeks, and his blue eyes darkened to nearly black. His skin was alabaster against the navy sky, and a muscle pulsed in his jaw.

He was shirtless and barefoot, yet he looked ready to take on any threat. His expression was so fierce, it made her wonder if perhaps he had some Viking blood in his veins.

Unable to resist touching him, she reached up and cupped his face in her hands. His eyes blazed down at her, hungrily drinking her in. She tried to read his expression but failed. There was so much more to Henry than what first met the eye. He presented the world with a good-time-Charlie act, but there was no trace his carefree smile now.

"What's buggin' you?" she asked, rubbing her thumbs along the soft scruff of his jaw.

His brow creased, and his eyes narrowed to blue chips of ice. "You're missing the fucking sunrise, Claudia."

"The sun rises every day, Henry," she countered, sliding her hands over his shoulders and down his arms to squeeze his hands.

He squeezed back. "I'm serious."

"I thought you were never serious."

He looked at her like she'd just stuck her foot out to trip him on purpose. "Listen to me, will you?" His gaze moved over her face as if he were trying to memorize her features. "When you go home and think of the sunrise in Hawaii, I want you to think of me. Not… not Keoni."

The name was like a hot poker between them. Claudia's throat tightened. "Is that what's wrong with you?" Claudia hadn't thought about Keoni once while she was with Henry. Didn't he know that? "You think I want to be with Keoni?"

When she said Keoni's name, Henry winced as if she'd slapped him. He sucked in a sharp breath and then forced a laugh. His laugh, even a forced one, was so endearing, so familiar, it made everything better.

"I'm sorry," he said. "I'm acting like a little kid. 'My sunrise is better than his,'" he said in a self-mocking voice. "I just really wanted this moment to be special. I wanted to make an impression you couldn't forget."

Henry's tentative smile cracked Claudia's heart wide open. A wave of emotion crashed over her, flooding the spaces she hadn't known were empty.

"You made an impression," she said to assure him, then turned toward the bright ball of fire gobbling up the night sky. "I'm going to watch the sunrise now."

"Thank you." Henry wrapped his arms around her waist and pulled her snug against his chest.

Claudia sank into him, allowing his strength to take her weight. She felt weak and teary, and she knew it was because Henry had made more than an impression on her. He'd invaded every one of her senses until he was all she could think about. She'd never felt like this before.

Henry tightened his arms around her waist and bent his head to nuzzle her shoulder. She tried to focus on the sunrise like he wanted, but it was impossible to think of anything but Henry and how she felt about him.

She couldn't possibly be in love with him, could she? They hadn't known each other long enough for that. And just because he had a magic tongue and lit her up with his laugh didn't mean she was in love with him, did it?

Damn, it felt so good to lean against him. Henry was as solid as a wall behind her, his heartbeat a steady thump against her back.

She filed this moment away in her Rolodex of memories, not because the fingers of light spreading through the dark sky were the most spectacular thing she'd ever seen—they were— but because of the man who held her. The man who stirred her soul with his smile and ignited her body with a single glance. The man who never demanded, only gave.

The man she loved.

A shiver went through her. She couldn't love Henry.

Could she?

She'd come to Hawaii convinced she would find the love of her life, but she'd never expected that man to be Henry.

Waves of emotion crashed over Claudia. She stared at the sunrise through teary eyes, realizing just how wrong she'd been.

"You okay?" Henry asked, his eyes sharp on hers.

He didn't miss a thing, her beloved Henry.

Claudia turned to face him and linked her arms around his neck. She sifted her fingers through his unruly waves, pushing back the persistent lock that always seemed to fall over his forehead, contributing wildly to his devil-may-care appearance.

Had she ever thought his hair was too bright? Henry's hair was spectacular. Several different hues of red and gold blended together through his thick waves. Two streaks of strawberry blond shot through the hair at his temples.

He had a speculative look in his dark-blue eyes, and Claudia realized she hadn't answered him and that the tears blurring her vision were now clinging to her lashes. She smiled brightly at Henry, not wanting to alarm him.

"I'm fine. I was just wondering about a few things," she said.

His shoulders stiffened, and he pulled in a sharp breath. There was a look in his eyes that she'd seen a few times before, but she didn't know how to interpret it. It was a reticent look, cool and composed and totally at odds with his usual carefree demeanor. "Yeah? What are you wondering?"

His voice sounded funny, as if he had to dig deeply down a rusty well to find the words.

It was on the tip of her tongue to blurt that she loved him, or at least she thought she might love him, but at the last moment, Claudia got scared.

Henry bent his head and kissed her breathless. She was just forgetting about everything except taking him back to bed when a noise from inside the house caught her attention. She lifted her head and spied a huge figure of a man walking through the house toward the lanai.

"Someone's here."

Henry turned and looked, then his shoulders sagged. "Shit."

31

Diving Lesson

Henry

HENRY HAD FORGOTTEN ALL about Bones.

"What day is it?" he asked Claudia.

"Friday."

He had a diving lesson. Son of a bitch. He'd wanted to spend the morning with Claudia, but he couldn't put Bones off, not when he'd practically begged for diving lessons.

"I forgot I was supposed to go diving with Bones today." He stepped away, heading off the lanai. "Should I get rid of him?"

"No. Don't bother. I have to be on location at nine o'clock."

"Hey." He framed her face in his hands. "Don't be sore."

Her arms came around his waist. "I'm not sore. I just wish I didn't have to work today."

He dipped his head to hers and touched her forehead with his. "Let me get rid of Bones. We still have a few hours."

"Don't. It's okay." She glanced at the shirt she was wearing. "I'm not really dressed for company," she said.

Claudia was wearing his shirt, and while he liked the way it looked on her very much, he had no interest in anyone else appreciating the view. He buttoned the top few buttons that she'd left undone. "Can I see you tonight?"

Claudia brushed her fingers through her hair, separating the tangles he'd helped put there last night. "I told Megan I would see *Planet of the Apes* with her tonight."

"I actually want to see that one."

"Do you want me to wait for you?"

His heart skipped. "You'd do that?"

The sliding glass door opened, interrupting them. Bones walked onto the lanai, quickly followed by a man Henry hadn't spoken to in years, not since he wrapped his car around a telephone pole and nearly died.

"Henry," Declan said, striding out onto the lanai with his eyes on the view. "Cool place, man." He offered Henry his hand, then stopped short when his eyes landed on Claudia. His mouth dropped open, and his eyes darted between Claudia and Henry before he recovered and pumped Henry's hand. "Good to see you." His gaze swung back to Claudia. "And you, Claudia."

"Declan Bishop!" Claudia cried, taking his offered hand and pulling him into a hug. "I didn't think you'd still be in Hawaii."

"Claudia!" Declan said, sounding baffled. "I didn't expect to see you here." He opened his arms, and Claudia went into them for a hug.

A flame of jealousy ignited in Henry's chest as he watched the warm exchange between Declan and the woman he loved. Pain throbbed in his chest when Claudia smiled up at Declan. She'd said it had all been a setup, but the kiss he'd witnessed that night at the banquet was lodged in his brain.

"Congratulations on winning," she said. "I knew you could do it."

Declan smiled. "You don't know anything about surfing," he said, laughing.

"I don't have to know anything to know you're the best."

Declan slipped his hands in his pockets and transferred his gaze back to the view. "Yeah, well, thanks," he muttered.

A dull ache pulsed behind Henry's eyes, the beginning of a monumental headache.

"Eh? We going diving, or what?" Bones asked.

"Yeah," Henry said, running a hand through his hair. He had to get dressed and figure out how to get Claudia back to her hotel. "Give me a couple of minutes, will you?"

Bones huffed and shifted his bulk toward the door. "You got anymore coffee, brah?"

"There's a fresh pot in the kitchen. Help yourselves."

Declan followed Bones into the kitchen. When they were alone again, Henry turned toward Claudia. "Must be strange seeing him here," he said.

"Not really." She looped her hands around his neck and pressed against him. "I don't care what Declan thinks. He's got his own problems. Did you see the way he shut down when I congratulated him?"

Henry had known the old Declan, the one who didn't have a problem that a shot of whiskey couldn't fix. This new version was a mystery.

"You're not jealous, are you?" She pulled him down for a kiss. "I told you it wasn't real."

Henry gathered her close, his fingers tight at her waist. "That kiss at the banquet looked pretty real."

Claudia laughed and brushed her lips across his with deliberate sweetness. "I'm a very good actress, didn't you know?"

"Hmm." His body never failed to respond to hers. Suddenly, he was drowning in desire. He wanted to pick her up and carry her straight back to his bed, the dive be damned. "I'll get rid of them," he said, sweeping his mouth along her jaw to her ear.

She laughed and pushed him away. "You're insatiable, you know that?"

He pulled her back into his arms. "Only with you."

She smiled up at him. "I have to work in a few hours. Go

have fun with your boys." Her eyes narrowed. "Not too much fun." She arched a brow. "You're not doing anything dangerous today, are you?"

He shook his head. "Don't worry."

She gazed up at him. "I don't think that's possible, not when I know what you do every day at work."

"I told you, it's mostly illusion."

She framed his face in her hands. "Be careful, okay?"

He smiled down at her. No one had worried about him in a long time. He could get used to this. He could get used to waking up with Claudia, watching sunrises, and going back to bed. "Okay," he said. "I'll be careful."

"I better go call a cab," she said, disentangling herself from his embrace.

Henry grabbed her hand. "No. It will cost a fortune to go all the way back to Waikiki. Can you drive a manual?"

She winced. "It's been a while."

Henry didn't like the sound of that, but it hardly mattered. He'd thought of a genius way to see Claudia tonight. "Take my car; then after the movie, take me to a late dinner."

"You've got it all figured out, don't you?" she asked.

Despite the teasing note in her voice, Henry could tell she was pleased. "I wish I didn't have plans today." He cinched an arm around her waist. "I could think of better things to do."

She placed her hands on his chest, her palms warm over his heart. "I still have to work."

"Hmm." His brows furrowed, and he thought again of the bet. He'd thought for sure she was going to say something about the bet earlier, but it had never come up. He wanted to keep it that way for the rest of her time in Hawaii. "Speaking of work… Let's keep this between us, okay?"

She squinted up at him, a little line forming between her brows. "You don't want anyone at work to know we're together?"

His heart felt so light, it might soar away like an untethered balloon. "Is that what we are?" He swallowed roughly. "Together?"

Claudia reached up on tiptoe and gave him a kiss that started out sweet enough, but it quickly turned scorching hot. He took it as a yes.

\#

"EH? THAT YOUR GIRL?" Bones asked as they piled into the car.

"For as long as she wants to be," Henry said.

Bones started the station wagon and backed out of Henry's driveway. "She looks familiar."

"She's Claudia Montgomery," Declan said slowly, as if speaking to a child.

"From *Jezebel*," Henry said, sliding his sunglasses into place.

"K'den?"

"Tell me you've seen it."

"Movies ain't my bag, brah," Bones said, navigating down the switchbacks with the expertise of someone who'd grown up on these roads.

Henry tuned the two men out, thinking instead about seeing Claudia later. He wanted to take her to his favorite restaurant, a little diner in Honolulu that served Portuguese fare. It was some of the best food he'd ever eaten.

"Are you even listening to me, brah?" Bones asked, eyeing Henry in the rearview mirror.

"Nope."

"Maybe you should. I remember that chick now, but it ain't from the movies."

Henry's focus returned with sharp clarity. "What are you talking about?"

"I knew she looked familiar," Bones said. "She was that chick who turned Keoni against tourists. She really fucked him up. Man, it took years to get over her. She's one looker, but—"

Henry sucked in a sharp breath. He wanted to ram his fist straight into Bones's mouth. "Don't talk about Claudia."

"I just thought you should know, yeah? Your call if you want to get messed up with some chick who doesn't give a shit about whose heart she breaks."

Henry snorted. "You're one to talk."

"What the fuck, man?" Bones glared at Henry. "You got some chick pussy-whippin' you, and you think you know everything about women? You don't know shit!"

Declan intervened before Henry could lose his temper and do something stupid, like choke the man who was driving the car.

"Knock it off, guys," Declan said. He glared first at Henry, then at Bones. "We need to be a team on this dive today."

Henry sucked in a few breaths, trying to regulate his heart. Declan was right. It wasn't smart to go into a dive disgruntled.

"Don't say anything else about Claudia, and we'll be fine," Henry said, staring out the window.

Bones growled. "Don't fucking talk about my business when you don't understand shit, man."

Henry's eyes widened at the strangled quality of Bones's voice. Maybe he cared about Penny more than he wanted to admit.

"All right," Henry said in agreement.

"K'den," Bones grumbled.

"And you don't know Claudia," Declan said to Bones. "She's not bad. She's a really sweet girl under that facade. I know you're just looking out for Keoni, but I'm sure he's long over her by now. He's a big boy."

Henry wasn't sure how to feel about Declan's defense of Claudia. First of all, he wouldn't agree that Claudia had a facade. If she did, it wasn't much of one, considering Henry had managed to peel it back in about five minutes. Second, Keoni might be over Claudia for now, but it didn't mean he would never be interested again. Lastly—and most importantly—was the question of whether Claudia was over Keoni. Henry didn't like to think about that. He shoved the horrible thought down, sealed the lid on the box, and stored it for another time, when he wasn't about to dive fifty feet under water with two men who were currently on his shit list.

32

The Prize

Claudia

AFTER HENRY LEFT with Bones and Declan, Claudia helped herself to another cup of coffee and wandered around the house. It was roughly the size of her pool house at home, and the furnishings were mostly hideous, but it wasn't all that bad. She puttered around the kitchen, snooping shamelessly. She found a copy of *Tattler* magazine with her picture on the cover in Henry's junk drawer and discovered that his refrigerator was empty except for a case of beer, a few lemons, and a block of questionable-looking cheese.

She sipped her coffee and went into the living room, where the only personal touches were a few framed pictures and some paperback books. Claudia flipped through the books and studied the pictures, concluding that Henry had a thing for mysteries and looked exactly his father, minus the red hair.

There was a lightness in her heart and a spring in her step as she tidied the kitchen and made the bed.

She made use of Henry's shower and dressed in the shorts and T-shirt she'd brought with her.

The lanai was the perfect spot to smoke a cigarette and indulge in a final cup of coffee before she went to the studio. She really didn't want to leave this heavenly spot. Ever.

Her breath caught when she entertained a wild thought. What if she didn't leave? What if she found a way to stay? What if she moved in right here in this little cabin? She'd have to replace those hideous curtains right away, and of course that lumpy, plaid-upholstered sofa would have to go, but what if she made Hawaii and Henry her permanent home?

A Long Road Home wasn't the only television show filmed on their set. There was also a series about a private investigator, which was promising, and another filmed on the North Shore about a talking dolphin.

She'd put some feelers out with her agent. Her thoughts spun out of control as she thought of the possibilities. Then the brakes slammed. She was getting so far ahead of herself that she felt dizzy. She hadn't even told Henry how she felt. She didn't know if he loved her back or if he smiled at every woman like she was the most glorious being on the planet. She had a sneaking suspicion that he loved her too, but she'd been wrong before.

He *had* just been kissing a woman in the hallway of The SurfRider a few nights ago.

And she had come to Hawaii to find another man.

Things weren't always as they seemed.

AFTER A FEW FALSE starts and grinds of the clutch, Claudia remembered how to drive a straight shift. It was a blast once she got the hang of it.

Another wild thought skittered through her mind: she would buy her own car when she moved to Hawaii.

She would enjoy driving along the curving highway that bordered the turquoise ocean. She hadn't realized how much she missed driving until she'd come to Hawaii.

Henry only lived a few miles from the studio. It was a good thing she was early because she would need the extra time in the makeup chair. There wasn't time to wash and dry her hair before she'd left, and dark circles camped out beneath her eyes.

A secret smile took over her lips as she whipped into the parking lot at the studio. Henry was to blame for the tangles in her hair, the bags under her eyes, and the glow in her heart.

Henry…

Claudia sighed. She had it bad for Henry. When had that happened? Maybe when she saw him pull off his helmet for the first time? No. Maybe it was when he'd peeled off his shirt for their naked swim?

A car pulling into the spot next to her snapped her out of her reverie. It was Stan Beatty, and his jaw dropped open when he saw Claudia.

"Having car trouble?"

"No." She grabbed her purse and started off toward Margie's chair.

Stan hurried after her. "Isn't that Champ's car?"

"Yes." She really didn't have time to chat. Margie was going to lose her mind when she saw the state of Claudia's tangled hair.

Stan grabbed her wrist, stopping her mid-stride. "What are you doing with Champ's car?"

She shook him off. "What do you care?"

Stan's mouth dropped open. "You're fucking him."

Claudia's lips tightened into a thin line. She wanted to slap him, but she restrained herself. Why did men think it was okay to comment on her sex life?

She turned and strode off toward makeup. Stan followed. She tried to ignore him, but he persisted, buzzing around like a fly.

"I can't believe it," Stan said. "That sly dog."

Claudia dropped into the makeup chair and glared at Stan in the mirror. "Take a hike, Stan," she said.

Stan didn't move. He hovered behind the chair, his face slowly turning an unbecoming shade of red. "How'd he get you to do it?" Beneath his flaming cheeks, Stan looked truly puzzled. "Did he trick you?"

Irritation turned to outrage. "Fuck off, Stan."

He crossed his arms over his chest and looked down his nose at her. "Who would have thought ole Champ would win? I thought Koa had it in the bag when he moved your trailer."

"What the hell are you talking about?"

A thin smile spread across Stan's mouth. "You should ask Champ," he said.

Margie came up behind Claudia's chair and shooed Stan away. "I can't work with you hanging around." She picked up a stray lock of Claudia's hair and tutted. "What happened to this?"

Claudia rolled her eyes. "Can you fix it?"

Margie plucked a comb from a drawer. "I can try."

Stan gave her one last leering smile in the mirror and strode away.

When he was gone, she eyed Margie in the mirror. "What the hell was he talking about?"

Margie blanched and shook her head. "I don't know."

Claudia turned and looked at Margie, who refused to meet her eye. "You do know," she stated. A knot of frustration formed in her chest when the makeup artist's eyes met hers briefly before skittering away again. Claudia reached out and snagged Margie's wrist, then squeezed. "Tell me."

Margie's eyes went wide, and two spots of color stained her cheeks. "All right," she said with a deep sigh. "But you're not going to like it."

"Just tell me, dammit."

Margie pulled her hand free from Claudia's clutches and reached for a cigarette. She shook one out and pinched it between her lips, then offered one to Claudia, who gritted her teeth and shook her head.

"Get on with it," Claudia said, her voice surprisingly calm. Inside, she felt a spiral of emotions crashing through her. Bile rose in her throat, forcing its way through the thick dust that had gathered there when Stan gave her that smug smile. Whatever Margie was going to tell her couldn't be good. She knew it in her bones. The woman was looking at Claudia as if she were as fragile as an orchid blossom.

"There was a bet," Margie said.

Claudia's stomach tightened, and a sound like distant thunder roared between her ears. "What kind of bet?" Her words felt thick, bogged down by confusion.

"It was… the boys…"

The thunderous noise in her head grew louder, gaining momentum and drowning out Margie's stumbling explanation. Claudia wished she would have taken the offered cigarette now. It would have given her something to do with her hands, something to focus on. Dread coiled in her belly like a snake ready to strike.

She cut Margie off mid-sentence. "This bet, it had something to do with me?"

Margie's eyes sprang to meet Claudia's, sympathy oozing from behind her cat-eye-shaped glasses. "The bet *was* you." Her voice was quiet, as if it would soften the blow.

Claudia's vision blurred. "What do you mean?"

"They bet on—" Margie cleared her throat and lowered her voice. "Who could be the first to take you to bed."

A thin red line shot behind Claudia's eyes and grew fatter until all she could see was blood. She shivered, suddenly cold even though a thick blanket of humidity already hung in the island air.

Visions clouded her mind of Stan offering her coffee, Koa moving her trailer, and Jake giving her a carton of her favorite cigarettes. The assholes were trying to woo her.

Her chin jerked up. "And what was the prize?"

Margie shook her head, her eyes brimming with something

that must be pity. "I don't know," she admitted, then ventured a guess. "You?"

Humiliation swelled like a hive of bees inside her until she was filled to the brim with a buzz that blocked all rational thought.

"I don't know what got into Champ," Margie said. "He's usually not like this. He's a good kid."

Claudia's whirling thoughts slammed to a halt. Her heart stopped beating.

Henry had wooed her. He'd danced with her, hiked with her, and taken her to a luau. He'd also charmed her, used her, and penetrated her heart with his lies.

It was happening again. It was Rick all over again. Claudia should have seen it coming. After all these years in the industry, she should have been able to spot a liar.

Despite starring in a movie that raked in over thirty million dollars at the box office, Claudia was still a woman, which meant men thought they could treat her like a sex object. A prize to be won. A stepping-stone for their own achievements.

Claudia reached for the cigarettes and lit one with a surprisingly steady hand. After taking a long drag, she held the smoke in her lungs and met Margie's eyes in the mirror.

"You okay?" Margie asked.

Claudia nodded curtly and blew out an elegant stream of smoke. "I'm fine." She smiled a little too brightly. "Better get on with it." She pointed in the general vicinity of her hair. "This might take a while to fix, and the show must go on."

Margie put out her cigarette and went to work on Claudia's tangled hair.

Claudia felt strangely tender all over, as if her body was one giant bruise. She closed her eyes, mostly to avoid her own gaze in the mirror. She was exhausted, angry, and fragile—but not the kind of fragile that would blow away in a strong breeze, more like the kind that would explode as if someone had pulled the pin.

33

Pivot and Flip

Henry

HENRY'S CAR was already in the driveway when Bones and Declan dropped him off.

Claudia.

Her name crashed through his mind, not that she'd been far from his thoughts all day. They didn't have much time together before she had to go back to the mainland, and Henry was going to make the most of every moment.

He'd have to steer clear of her on set so no one found out about their relationship, but that shouldn't be a problem. After they filmed the fight scene they'd been practicing for, they weren't scheduled to work together for the final two weeks of the season.

Henry jumped out of Bones's car as soon as it pulled to a stop. If his Mustang was here, then maybe Claudia had decided to skip the movie with Megan tonight in favor of coming straight over.

He didn't mind. Not a bit.

He could hardly wait to see her. All day, she'd been on his

mind. As he'd learned how to use the equipment, he'd thought of her smile, the way it started out closed before blooming into a full-blown grin. Claudia didn't just smile. She dazzled. She sparkled.

The house was quiet when he let himself in, and no lights blazed.

"Claudia?" He flipped on the lights and glanced around, taking in all of his living space in a single glance.

It was empty.

His keys and a note sat on the coffee table. Henry had never seen Claudia's handwriting before, but he wasn't surprised to find it bold and confident, just like her. The letters leaned off the page in a sweep of rounded curves.

\#

Henry,
I hope it was worth it.
Claudia

\#

Henry read the words three times, his mind tripping over the letters.

An enormous weight settled on his chest, and he felt like he had earlier that day while he was fifty feet under water. Pressure pushed against him from all sides.

The letter probably didn't mean anything. He was reading too much into it, being paranoid.

An entire day spent under the ocean with limited air was messing with him. He and Claudia had been fine when he'd left.

Henry hurried to the kitchen and grabbed the phone. He flipped through the yellow pages until he found The SurfRider and punched in the numbers on the phone.

"Claudia Montgomery's room, please."

There was a pause and then the clerk said, "We don't have anyone by that name."

Henry ran a hand through his hair, his fingers trembling. "I mean Janice." What had she said? "Steele," he said. "Janice Steele?"

"One moment."

The line clicked and then ringing filled his ear. He leaned against the wall, waiting with bated breath for Claudia to answer.

The phone rang and rang until Henry got tired of hearing it and hung up.

He told himself it was no big deal. She'd gone to the movies with Megan like they'd planned. He'd call later, after he'd had a long, hot shower and a shave.

When he did, Megan answered the phone and said she'd put Claudia to bed with a headache.

Henry scooped his keys off the peg where he'd hung them. "I'll come over."

"No," Megan said, insisting. "I'm staying with her."

Henry gripped the phone tighter. "Are you sure?"

"I'm sure. She'll be fine."

Tomorrow was the big fight scene. He knew Claudia was worried over it.

"Tell her to get better." He swallowed roughly, wishing he could tell her himself. "Tell her not to worry. She's gonna do great tomorrow. Tell her…" *He loved her.* "Can I talk to her?"

"She's in bed. She doesn't want to talk to anyone."

Henry's heart jerked hard. He didn't like the sound of that. He forced himself to think with his head, not his heart. It wasn't personal.

But Claudia was sick, and he desperately wanted to be there for her. It didn't seem right for it to be Megan who rubbed her feet or put a cool towel on her head, or whatever a person did for another person with a headache. Henry wanted to do it, but in the end, he let it go.

\#

The next day, Henry hustled from the stables to the studio. He'd spent a sleepless night worrying about Claudia, then a long morning training with the horses. There was no time for anything but a quick stop at wardrobe to change into his costume and wig before he had to be on set to film the fight scene.

When he got to the saloon set, his eyes tracked Claudia immediately. She was wearing a modified costume for the fight scene. Even Albert had conceded that she couldn't fight in her Melanie costume and had allowed a few changes. The neckline of her dress was higher cut but no less sexy. Claudia could make a paper bag look sexy.

"Hey." Henry clasped his hands to keep from touching her. "How you feeling?"

Claudia shook her head, not looking at him.

"Your headache better?" he asked.

"It was," she said in an icy tone. "It's back now."

He shifted an inch closer. "You okay?"

She nodded.

He didn't like the set of her shoulders. They were too tense. He balled his fists to keep from massaging the stress from her neck. "You're gonna do great."

Benji strode onto set and called for places.

Henry couldn't resist reaching for Claudia's hand and giving it a squeeze. "Break a leg," he whispered.

Claudia pulled her hand from his grasp. She was all business as she strode across the set to take her place near the saloon door.

"Action!"

Claudia burst into the saloon. Henry straightened his wig and donned his cowboy hat. A moment later, Albert signaled him.

His heart raced as he ran through the crowded room. Throwing punches and dodging blows came naturally to Henry, but he was concerned about Claudia. He hoped they could get this in one take. Elaborate scenes like this were painstaking to clean up and recreate.

If there was one mess-up, they would have to start over. These days on set could be grueling or they could be magical. Henry had seen them go both ways.

Finally, it was time for their characters to meet. Henry came up behind Claudia and grabbed her waist. She felt so small and fragile in his arms. The last thing he wanted to do was manhandle her, but hopefully he had prepared her well.

He slid his arm around her neck and silently repeated the instructions he'd taught her.

Tuck your chin.

She tucked with expert timing.

Grab my arms.

Her fingers gripped his forearms, clutching as if her life depended on it.

Next she was supposed to pivot and flip him. If all went well, the scene would be coming to a close as Henry collapsed on his back. Five more seconds and the scene would be over.

Then the unthinkable happened. Claudia stomped his boot hard enough to make him wince. She was so focused, she must have forgotten she didn't need to use full force.

Claudia turned in his arms and looked at him with murder in her eyes. Her fist lashed out before he could react and caught him right in the eye. Pain flashed, throwing him off balance.

Luckily, Henry was on a first-name basis with agony.

He'd been run over by a horse, pushed out of a three-story window, and flung from a car crash. All in a week's work.

He caught Claudia's eye and gave her a tiny shake of his head in hopes she would tone it down.

She ignored him and lashed out again, swinging a loaded jab that had him ducking instinctively. He put up his hands when he saw another punch coming. But instead of throwing her fist, she kneed him in the crotch. Hard.

He grunted and went to his knees as a constellation of stars exploded behind his eyes.

34

Carried Away

Claudia

"CUT!" Benji shouted. "That's a martini!"

Claudia stood over Henry, who was curled up in a ball, clutching his crotch.

Served him right. The bastard. Tears sparkled behind her eyes, but she held them back. She wouldn't dare cry and give anyone that satisfaction. Head held high, she marched off the set and strode straight for her trailer.

Albert called her name, but she pretended not to hear. She couldn't get away fast enough. She made a beeline to the grove of trees where Koa had so kindly moved her trailer when he'd been hoping to sleep with her and win the ridiculous bet.

Claudia had been a fool to think the cast and crew was kinder in Hawaii. Nope. They'd just been out to exploit her. A chill ran through her as she thought of Rick representing California in the senate. She'd never thought anything like that could happen again, but this was worse. She'd been in love with Henry. Rick had been a handsome distraction.

When she got to her trailer, she headed straight for the

liquor cabinet. Tequila was necessary in moments like these, when one had just kneed the man one loved in the balls. She poured herself a healthy shot and swallowed it down like medicine.

The doorknob rattled, and Claudia realized too late that she hadn't locked the door.

She blinked back tears and pressed her hands to her cheeks. "Give me a minute," she called, not wanting Megan to see her so upset.

The door burst open, and Henry barged inside. "What the hell was that?"

His voice lashed out like a whip, stirring the storm of her anger. Her body vibrated with fury. She clung to the emotion like a lifeline. The last thing she needed was to feel anything else as far as Henry was concerned. Her traitorous heart still loved him, even though her head knew better.

She slammed her glass on the counter and reached for a cigarette. "I was just doing my job." She lit a match, avoiding Henry's piercing stare.

"The hell…" He tore off his hat, then ripped off the blond wig. His left eye was already swelling where she'd landed a solid punch. The color drained from his face, and he winced in pain when he took a step.

Guilt churned in Claudia's gut. She may have done some real damage to Henry. To his manhood. An evil voice in her head congratulated her, but she couldn't feel happy about it.

"You wanna tell me what just happened out there?"

"I got a little carried away," she said, exhaling a stream of smoke. "Sorry about that. I guess my teacher was a little too thorough."

He narrowed his eyes at her. She could see the wheels turning in his head as he tried to figure out what was going on.

His russet brow arched. "How's your headache?"

"It's still here," she said, glaring at him.

Henry's eyes filled with concern. "What can I do?"

Claudia took a long drag off her cigarette. "You can leave."

"You need to lie down?" He moved toward her, lines of concern etched on his face.

"I just need you to leave." She pressed her fingers onto her temples, refusing to look at him. "And send in Megan if you can find her."

The trailer seemed to shrink as Henry shifted closer. The air between them pulsed with tension. Every muscle in Claudia's body tightened as Henry's hand came up to cup her cheek.

"What's gotten into you?" His voice was soft, a lover's caress that broke something inside her.

The leash on her anger snapped. "You," she said, exhaling a stream of smoke in his direction. "You've gotten into me. So congratulations, apparently you're the winner."

Henry's face went from greenish-pale to scarlet. His eyebrows shot upward on his forehead. "What?"

"Don't play dumb. You know exactly what I'm talking about. You've been lying to me all along." She laughed bitterly, remembering his string of lies. "Even about Janice."

"I didn't lie."

"No?"

"I didn't know who you were," he said. "I swear."

"But you bet on me." She stabbed out her cigarette, grinding the filter into the tray with more force than necessary. "You're not denying that part."

"I didn't want anything to do with that." He took one step forward but abruptly stopped when she raked her icy glare over him. "I tried to tell you."

"You didn't try very hard."

"Claudia."

"Don't worry." She reached for another cigarette, needing something to do with her hands. "I was using you too."

"What?"

"I just needed a stand-in until I found Keoni."

Henry's face turned so red, it was almost purple. "You don't mean that," he said.

Relying on her acting skills, she swallowed her emotions. "You should go. I'll see you on set."

"I'm not leaving until we settle this." His voice was a low growl that sent shivers up her spine.

"It's settled." She reached for her matches, but Henry grabbed them before she could.

"The hell it is." He flung the matches across the room and reached for her. "I'm sorry. I should have told you. I swear I tried a dozen times. I just couldn't hurt you like that."

Her heart softened at his words, and his touch felt so gentle, so soothing, and so right. His eyes were like twin pools of deep, calm water. She could get lost in those eyes.

But she wouldn't.

She clutched her outrage close, hanging on with all her might in hopes it would save her from despair. "I knew about your silly bet the whole time."

Henry's blue eyes narrowed, his gaze laser sharp. "What?"

Her heart squeezed, and her knees felt weak. "You've got some real acting chops. Coulda been leading man if only you were better looking."

Henry's eyes glittered like blue diamonds, cutting straight through her. His throat bobbed when he swallowed. With a jerky movement, he grabbed his hat and stuffed it on his head.

Torn between satisfaction that she'd gotten the last word and curiosity, Claudia watched him slowly move toward the door.

Curiosity won out. "What did you win?" she asked.

Memories of seeing her picture in the paper next to filthy accusations blurred her vision. Rick had gained publicity by linking their names together. Henry must have done this for a reason. And it wasn't money. He didn't give a shit about money.

Henry's shoulders slumped as he reached for the door. "If I lost you, it doesn't matter what I won."

Grief crashed through her, stripping away the last of her

control. "It matters to me!" she yelled. "Tell me, Henry. Don't you think you owe me that?"

He hung his head, and a lock of hair fell over his eyes. Claudia smothered the urge to push it back from his forehead. Anguish trembled in the space between them. Claudia wanted to throw herself at Henry, to shake the truth from him.

When his eyes met hers, she knew he wasn't going to tell her. She lifted her chin and stared straight through him. Tears welled in her eyes, but she forced them back. She wouldn't let him see her cry. "Just go," she said.

Henry opened the door and left, closing it with a quiet click. When he was gone, Claudia abandoned her show of strength and sank to the floor. She clutched her hair in her hands, tugging hard in hopes that physical pain would upstage her heartache.

Her hopes of finding joy in Hawaii lay shattered around her like broken glass.

A knock sounded on the door. "It's Megan. Can I come in?"

Claudia was tempted to tell her to leave, but she needed help getting out of her damned costume. It wasn't as bad as the one she usually stuffed herself into, but it was still impossible to get out of on her own. "Come in," she called.

Megan opened the door and floated in, all smiles. "You were amazing," she said. When she saw Claudia crumpled on the floor, her mouth dropped open. "Oh, no. Is your headache back?"

Claudia pushed to her feet and turned her back so Megan could unhook her costume. The empty space where Henry had stood a moment ago quivered, mocking her.

"No," she said. "I think it's gone for good."

35

Two Sunrises

Herny

HENRY TRIED to forget about Claudia. In a few weeks, she would be gone. Her role as Melanie was almost over, then she would go back to the mainland. He might not ever see her again anyway, so it was best to forget her.

But he couldn't. She occupied his every thought. Every time he turned on the radio, "Brown Eyed Girl" was playing. Every time he turned into his neighborhood, he thought about her unzipping his jeans. His bed was full of her ghost. And two sunrises without her were enough.

He had to see her again.

After a long day with the horses, he dropped by the studio. Claudia was already gone, so Henry went straight to Albert's office. He hadn't spoken with the stunt director or anyone else involved with the bet since officially winning. Anger mounted in his chest as he stalked across the studio toward the small building of rooms toward Albert's office. He was angry at everyone involved, but mostly at himself. He should have refused to participate. He should have insisted Albert take the money and let him out of the bet. He should have told Claudia.

But he couldn't go back in time; all he could do was move forward. The first step was telling Albert to go to hell.

He rapped on Albert's door and then let himself in without waiting for an invitation.

Albert was sitting behind his desk with his feet propped up, talking on the phone. He signaled Henry to have a seat in one of the folding chairs. The office was small and cluttered. Just being in the tight space with Albert and his mess made Henry's skin crawl.

He pushed aside some takeout boxes and sat in the folding chair, waiting with barely contained fury while Albert finished his call.

Finally, Albert hung up the phone and stood to offer Henry a handshake. Henry didn't move. He shifted his glare to Albert, staring holes through the man.

"Eh? Don't be sore," Albert said. "You won. I won." He raised his eyebrows in a crude gesture. "Claudia won, yeah?"

Henry balled his fists in his lap, restraining himself. "You know I didn't want this."

Albert lit a cigarette and tossed his lighter on the desk. "Too fucking bad for you. I'm richer than I was yesterday, and you, my friend, are going to get a shot at directing. I've heard some very important opportunities are in the works." He blew a stream of smoke into the air, glaring hard at Henry. "What part of that didn't you want, eh?"

Fury built inside Henry until he felt his head would shoot off like a cannon. He was so hot, it was a wonder smoke wasn't billowing from his ears. "You know it's not what I wanted. Not at all." He shot up from the chair and stalked across the floor to Albert's desk, then slammed his hand so hard on the surface, the stacks of papers jumped. "Who told her? How did she find out?"

Albert stood his ground. Like Henry, he'd started out as a

stuntman. He wasn't backing down from a physical fight. He pushed himself into Henry's space, his expression fierce. "What do you care?" Albert was so upset, he dropped his affected Hawaiian accent. "You won. Congratulations."

Henry stared at Albert for a long moment before being the first to back away. This wasn't on Albert. It was on Henry.

It was up to him to fix it.

He went home and showered, shaved, and dressed in the blue button-down Aloha shirt Claudia had given him. If she couldn't stand the sight of him and told him to get lost, he would understand. But he wouldn't give up. As long as Claudia stayed in Hawaii, Henry would apologize. He could stand her not loving him anymore, but he couldn't stand her hating him.

He was nervous as he pulled up to The SurfRider and tossed his keys to the valet. If Claudia wouldn't forgive him, he planned to grovel and beg. Get down on his knees if that was what it took.

As Henry took the elevator to her floor, he considered the possibility that he might never hold Claudia again. He may never kiss her or tangle his fingers in her hair. In a few weeks, he may never see her again.

He stepped out of the elevator and stopped short when he saw a familiar figure down the hall in front of Claudia's door.

Stan Beatty glanced up and saw him. Their eyes locked, and then Stan's skittered away.

"What are you doing here?" Henry asked.

Stan shrugged. "Since you blew it with her, I figured I'd give it a shot."

Henry closed the gap between them in two strides, fury rising off him like steam. "You did, huh? What makes you think Claudia wants anything to do with you?"

"Chill out, pal." Stan took a step back.

Realization dawned as Henry stared at Stan. "You're the one who told her, aren't you?"

"She was bound to find out eventually."

Henry grabbed Stan by the shirt and growled. "Give me one reason I shouldn't break your face."

Stan reached up and tried to dislodge Henry's grip on his shirt. "What's your problem? You won. You got a sweet piece of tail and—"

Henry cocked his fist and slammed it into Stan's face. The crunch of bones breaking echoed down the quiet hall. Blood spurted from Stan's nose, and he tried to get his hands up to cover his face, but it was too late. Henry had lost all sense of reason. He wasn't going to stop until Stan was an unrecognizable pulp.

Doors flew open down the hall, and people hurried out of their rooms to see what was happening. Henry threw himself at Stan, his fists flying with rage. He landed an uppercut that sent Stan sprawling to the carpet.

"Stop!" Claudia grabbed Henry's arm. "Stop it!"

"I'm not finished with him yet."

"You've done enough." Claudia's voice pleaded. "Look around," she said. "You're making a scene."

Henry glanced around at the shocked faces in the hall, and his heart sank. This was not how he'd planned on apologizing to Claudia.

She smiled at the crowd of onlookers. "Nothing to see here, guys. The boys are just rehearsing for a scene. Go back to your rooms. Everything is fine."

When everyone had gone back to their rooms, Stan pushed to his feet. Blood spilled from his nose, soaking his shirt.

"You're done, Champ," he spat. "You'll never work again!"

Henry grabbed Stan by the throat. "Come near Claudia again, and I'll kill you."

Claudia hooked an arm around Henry and pulled him back. "Let him go," she said.

Henry shoved Stan in the direction of the elevator, wishing he could punch him a few more times. His adrenaline was still pumping so hard, he couldn't see straight.

"You're finished," Stan said from behind the hand he clutched over his face in an attempt to stop the blood. "You'll never get a chance to direct now."

When Stan was gone, Claudia dragged Henry to her room. She slammed the door behind him and disappeared into the bathroom. A moment later, she was back with a wet washcloth.

"Sit." She nodded at the sofa in her living room suite.

Henry sat. He swiped a hand through his hair and then dragged it down his face. His breathing was still ragged, and a red veil of rage doubled his vision.

Claudia sat next to him and tugged his hands down. She frowned down at Henry's bruised hands, swiping the cloth over his bruised knuckles with a shake of her head. "I thought you were going to kill him."

She pressed the washcloth to a deep cut on his knuckle, and he winced. "If he even looks at you again…"

Henry pulled his hand away and flexed his fist, trying to calm his racing thoughts. He took deep breaths, filling his lungs with Claudia's scent. He wanted to wrap his arms around her and bury his face in her neck, but when he reached for her, she pushed him away.

"Directing?" she asked. Her voice was a quiet ghost walking over a grave. "Is that what you won?"

Shame twisted Henry's gut. He looked up at Claudia, and his excuses died on his lips. He couldn't excuse away what he'd done. No matter how many times he said he was sorry, it would never be enough. The pain he'd caused Claudia could never be erased.

At the moment, the woman across from him didn't look anything like a famous movie star. Her face was scrubbed clean of makeup, and dark circles smudged her cheekbones under her eyes. She looked smaller and younger, more vulnerable than he'd ever seen her before. This wasn't the woman who commanded every room she entered, dominated every stage—

this was a young girl in pain. Henry wanted to punch himself for being the one to cause it.

"Directing?" she asked again, her quiet voice ripping him open even worse than if she'd screamed at him. "That was your prize?"

Henry dragged his hands through his hair and hung his head.

Claudia laughed, and the sound scraped over him, giving him chills. "I feel sorry for you, Henry. I really do." She crossed the room and took a cigarette out of her silver case. She reached for her lighter, but as always Henry got there before her. "You couldn't get what you wanted on your own." She touched the tip of her cigarette to the flame he held toward her and inhaled deeply. "You had to use a woman to get it." She exhaled a stream of smoke. "I thought you were different, Henry. But you're just like the rest of them, every man who's ever used me to get what he wanted." Her gaze raked over him, dismissing him. "It's very sad."

Henry felt like he'd run out of air at a safety stop. His heart drummed in his chest, a beat that drove him out of his mind. She was right. Of course she was right. He had what he'd always wanted, thanks to her. The problem was, now there was something he wanted more: her.

He rose and crossed the room. Unable to stop himself from making a giant fool of himself, he got down on his knee and took her hand. "I'm the biggest idiot in the world," he said, clutching her hand in both of his. "I don't blame you for hating me, but you have to know that I'm hopelessly in love with you. And how you feel about me doesn't change that. I love you, Claudia."

Claudia stared down at him, her eyes flashing. "Now what?" she asked, taking a drag off her cigarette and blowing smoke into the air between them. "I'm supposed to forgive you because you said the magic words?"

Henry tugged her closer. "This wasn't supposed to happen like this."

"Of course it wasn't supposed to happen," she snapped, pulling her hand away. "We were friends. I trusted you. And just so you know…" She stabbed her cigarette out in the ashtray and glared at him. "I love you too."

His chest swelled at hearing those words. A smile tugged at his lips, and he got to his feet. "Claudia…"

She crossed her arms over her chest and shook her head at him. "Just because I love you doesn't mean I want to look at your face right now. And it sure as hell doesn't mean I forgive you."

Hope rose in his chest, bursting like a bubble of much-needed oxygen. He suppressed a smile. Hearing that Claudia loved him renewed his spirit, even if she was spitting mad while she'd said the words. It was a step in the right direction. He had to play it smart. He didn't want to say anything to ruin the moment, so he grabbed her hand and spun her into his arms. His mouth came down on hers possessively. He poured his heart into the kiss, trying to convey the bottomless depths of his feelings for her.

Her fingers fluttered against his chest and then she grabbed him and pulled him closer. Her mouth responded to his demands. Her tongue was hot, thrusting into his mouth to tangle with his.

He'd never known a kiss could scorch every nerve in his body. He'd never known a kiss could be a drug. A fantasy. An awakening. Kissing Claudia was an addiction. He couldn't stop if the room were on fire.

Claudia broke the kiss and pulled away. "You need to go, Henry."

Her words penetrated his fog of lust. "What?"

"Get out of here, Henry." She pointed at the door. "Just because I love you doesn't mean I don't hate you."

A laugh exploded from his chest. "Okay." He raised his

hands in the air. He wasn't going to push his luck. He'd gotten further than he'd hoped with Claudia, and it wasn't the time to force anything. "I'm leaving."

Wanting one last kiss before he left, just in case it was the last, Henry framed Claudia's face in his hands and brushed his lips across hers. Her breath hitched, and he knew she wanted him just as badly as he wanted her, but she needed time. He could give her that.

36

Too Many Memories

Claudia

"CLAUDIA," Benji called. "I need you in Albert's office, now."

It had been a rough day on set. Stan had called in sick, and they'd had to scramble. Benji had been yelling at them all day, and Claudia had an ear-splitting headache.

She was exhausted from lying awake the whole night before. Henry was to blame for her sleepless night. She couldn't stop thinking about him. His face floated to mind even now. The way he'd looked when she'd told him she loved him, it was as if he were the luckiest man on Earth. She hadn't known it was possible to love someone and hate them at the same time.

It would be much easier just to hate Henry. Then it wouldn't hurt so badly to say good-bye.

"What's going on, Benji?" Claudia asked as the director led her across the set toward Albert's office.

"I'll wait until we get there to tell you. No need to say it twice."

Worry coiled in her stomach, spreading out foggy tentacles of fear. Was she being fired? Hadn't Albert liked the stunts she'd learned? The stunt director hadn't said more than a few words to her after the fight scene. Was he disappointed in her performance? Another part of her worried that this might have something to do with the bet. Was Benji in on it? Was Albert?

At this point, Claudia assumed that she and Megan were the only ones who hadn't known about it. She told herself she was used to it. That it didn't bother her. That she was too strong to let what others said about her penetrate her tough exterior.

Benji opened the door to Albert's office, and Claudia saw Henry sitting at one of the only chairs across from Albert's desk. She smiled before she remembered she was mad at him. He looked so cute sitting there with his cowboy hat in his hands, his hair a mess of reddish-gold waves. His left eye was bruised, and Claudia winced, remembering she'd been the one to make the mark.

Albert settled in the only other chair and crossed his ankle over his knee. "Fix us a drink, will you, doll?"

Henry stood. "I'll fix them." He offered Claudia his seat and turned toward the bar. "All you have is whiskey?" he asked Benji.

"I've got ice."

"Whiskey's fine," Benji said.

Claudia took the chair and folded her hands in her lap. She heard the clink of glasses as Henry moved behind her. He'd been with the horses again. His scent filled her nose. It was a comforting scent of hay, leather, and sunshine. The combination sent a surge of warmth straight to her heart. She could never be around horses again without thinking of Henry.

He handed out the drinks and leaned against the wall near the door. Claudia could sense every move he made, feel his eyes on her. The tension in the room was suffocating.

Finally, Benji turned to look at her. "Congratulations," he said. He raised his glass first to her, then to Henry. "To both of you."

Henry cleared his throat. "What did we do?"

"The sponsors dug Melanie so much, they want to do a spin-off." Benji tapped his glass to Claudia's. "You're getting your own show."

Claudia's heart jumped into her throat. The phrase "her own show" was one she'd dreamed of hearing her entire life. Her vision blurred, and she couldn't breathe. This was everything she'd always wanted.

"And, Champ, you're going to be in charge of the stunts, yeah?" Albert said.

Claudia turned to look at Henry. His smile faded, and the color drained from his face.

A ringing noise sounded in Claudia's head, and it dawned on her that this was Henry's prize for screwing her first. He was going to be the stunt director because of her. Because of the bet.

A wave of dizziness washed over her, and she blinked back tears. She leaned forward and plucked a cigarette from the carousel on Albert's desk, not caring if they weren't her brand.

Henry was there with a light before she could reach for matches. How he always had a light when he didn't smoke was baffling. She never had to light her own cigarette when he was around, or fix her own drinks, or rub her feet.

They locked eyes as he bent down to light her cigarette. For once, Henry wasn't smiling. His eyes were tight in the corners, and his jaw was set. His gaze probed hers, and Claudia felt a chill all the way to her soul.

Henry gave her a small smile and straightened. "Congratulations," he said. "You deserve it."

Claudia didn't have to be a mind reader to know what Henry was thinking. *She* deserved it. *He* did not. She'd told him as much.

Shame was etched in the lines on his face. Claudia reached for his hand, but he didn't notice and moved away to lean against the wall.

"Welcome to Hawaii," Benji said. "You're one of us now. An official transplant."

Claudia had gotten so stuck, hearing she was getting her own show, that she hadn't thought it through yet. Of course it would be filmed here, sharing a set with *A Long Road Home*. The sets were in place, and the location was perfect. Getting her own show meant moving to Hawaii. It meant packing up her life in California, saying good-bye to the Dunlap scandal for good, and it meant Henry.

She turned in her chair to look at him. He'd placed his hat back on his hair, and the brim shaded his eyes. She couldn't read his expression.

"There's a party at Diamond Head Lighthouse tomorrow," Benji said. "Everyone who's anyone on the island will be at the party. I need both of you there."

An invitation to a lighthouse party.

It was something else Henry had coveted. She tried to meet his eyes, but he refused to look at her.

He looked at Benji instead. "I haven't accepted yet," he said.

Claudia coughed as she exhaled a cloud of smoke.

"Eh? What? This is everything you always wanted, man."

Henry nodded. His eyes finally blazed toward Claudia's. They glittered brightly under the brim of his hat. "It used to be."

Claudia leaned forward and crushed her cigarette in the ashtray. "I need to consult with my agent too, of course."

"Of course." Benji took a swallow from his drink, his eyes tracking back and forth between Henry and Claudia. "I know Ari will get you the best deal possible."

Claudia crossed her legs, adjusted the skirt around her knees. "Oh, it isn't that," she said. "It has more to do with my schedule. I may have another film in the works."

"Ari didn't mention anything."

Claudia's brow lifted. "You've spoken with him already?"

"I wouldn't have offered it to you if you had a conflict. Ari said you were good to go."

Claudia rolled her eyes. "Ari doesn't have the final word. I do."

"What's to think about? Eh?" Albert asked. "You get a starring role on your own show, and you get to join us here in paradise, yeah?"

Claudia stifled a scream. She was tired of Albert's fake Hawaiian accent. Just because he sprinkled *yeahs* at the end of sentences didn't make him a native. Suddenly the office seemed incredibly too small. She stabbed out her cigarette and pushed back her chair.

"I'll be in touch, okay?" Her eyes darted away from Albert and landed on Henry.

He reached for the door and opened it without looking at her. "Me too."

And then he was gone, leaving the room in a single stride and shutting the door firmly behind him.

Claudia stared at the door. Henry had left without even looking at her.

"Champ is the best there is," Benji said. "You don't have to worry about working with him."

"This isn't about that silly bet. Eh?"

Claudia's heart skipped. So everyone did know about the bet, just as she'd feared. Would she ever get past the humiliation?

She lifted her chin and sliced her gaze to Albert. "Of course not. I knew about it all along."

Albert chuckled. "Why'd you pick Champ?"

Claudia got to her feet and went to the door. "Everyone loves a good underdog," she said.

The men snorted with laughter as Claudia let herself out of the office.

"See you at the party tonight," Benji said. "Wear something sexy."

Claudia ignored him and pulled the door shut behind her. She was surprised to see Henry waiting just outside the hall.

He took off his hat and held it to his chest. "Underdog?"

The raw hurt in Henry's voice was like a dagger to her heart.

"I didn't—"

He smiled brightly, shaking his head for her to stop. "It's okay. I'm used to being the stand-in."

"Henry." Her voice was a soft whisper. "I didn't—"

"You didn't mean for me to hear that?"

"No." She squeezed her fists at her side. She wanted so badly to push that lock of hair off his forehead, to skim her fingers along the bruise on his eye. "Don't turn this around on me. You know I didn't mean that."

Henry shoved his hat on his head and started to walk away. "I know. It's okay."

"Wait." She went after him. "You should take the job. You wanted it so much."

"No. I can't take it, knowing what it cost us. You asked me in that note if it was worth it." He turned and walked away. "It's not."

"I might not take the job anyway," Claudia called to his retreating back. "I might not want to stay in Hawaii."

There were too many memories in Hawaii. Too much pain. That joy she'd thought she'd find was lost forever.

37

Desperate Men

Henry

DAYS OFF WERE THE WORST. Henry woke up early, watched the sunrise alone, and drank a whole pot of coffee on his porch.

He always kept so busy with work or friends, it was rare for Henry to have a whole day ahead of him with nothing to do.

He couldn't stop thinking about Claudia. What he'd done to her. What she'd said about him. Had they hurt each other too much to find a way back to happiness?

The whole thing had been like a stunt gone wrong, like she'd fallen and he hadn't been in the right place to catch her.

Henry hoped giving up the job as stunt director was enough to win Claudia back, but he thought it was too little too late. She'd said she didn't know if she'd take the job. He wouldn't beg her. It needed to be her decision.

If he didn't take the job, he'd be giving up the chance of a lifetime, but he didn't care. He wanted Claudia more than he wanted to direct. If he backed off, surely she would come around. She'd stay. He could get her to love him again.

Hope filled his chest, lifted his spirits. Henry wasn't the kind of person who stayed down for long. He was the kind of person who found solutions. He made sacrifices. His career would be dead, but there was so much to gain.

His thoughts spun as he made his plan.

"You stay livin' out here now, cuz?"

The deep voice sliced through Henry's thoughts. He turned and saw Bones standing in the doorway.

Henry tried to remember if they had plans to dive again today. He'd been so preoccupied with Claudia that he'd forgotten everything else.

Bones walked onto the lanai and looked around at the view with an appreciative nod. "Lucky we live in Hawaii, yeah?"

Henry watched the big man move to the railing. "Are we supposed to dive today?"

Bones's massive shoulders raised an inch, then dropped. "If you want, I can get the boat, but…"

Henry's mind buzzed. He'd over-caffeinated this morning, and he couldn't think straight. If they weren't supposed to dive, then why was Bones here so early on a Saturday morning?

"You want some coffee?" Henry didn't need any more, but Bones looked like he could use a cup.

Bones leaned against the railing and let out a long sigh. "Sure. I'll take a cup."

Henry went into the kitchen and poured Bones a cup. He had no idea how the man liked his coffee. He left it black, poured himself another cup, and went back to the lanai.

Bones sat at the table, looking uncomfortable in the flimsy lawn chair. A smile curved Henry's mouth as he handed Bones the mug of steaming coffee.

"You ever break a chair before?"

In response, Bones grunted and took a swallow of the coffee.

Henry took a load off in one of the other chairs, and they drank their coffee in silence. It wasn't an easy silence like the ones Henry experienced with Claudia. Every sip added to the tension in the air.

Finally, Henry couldn't stand it any longer. He set his half-empty cup on the table and leaned back in the lawn chair. "You gonna tell me why you're here, man?"

Bones glanced up at him, his dark gaze spewing fire. His fierce brows pulled together, and his lips thinned. He looked exactly like what he was: a man descended from merciless warriors.

Henry wasn't scared. He knew Bones hadn't come here to kick his ass. If he had, he wouldn't have bothered with coffee first.

Now that Henry thought about it, Bones had been showing up a lot lately, mostly unannounced and unwanted.

"Why you always coming around?" Henry asked.

Bones sighed and dropped his head into his hands, refusing to answer.

Henry was concerned for his chair, which strained under Bones's girth. He wondered if the legs would give out first or the arms.

"Have you heard from her?" Bones asked, raising his head from his hands.

Henry's heart ached. "Not since yesterday. But I'll see her tonight." And he had a plan. Sort of. He had the start of a plan. If Bones would get out of his house, he may have a chance to think through the rest of it.

"Whatsamattah you?" Bones shot up from the chair so fast, it fell to the wooden floor. "She's here? Where?"

Henry's thoughts froze. He blinked rapidly, trying to keep up. "She's at The SurfRider," he said. "What do you care?"

Bones's chest puffed up. A cord stood out on his neck. "Ain't she staying witch you?"

A tight ball formed in Henry's stomach, and he dropped his head to the table. "I messed up," he mumbled downward.

Bones jerked Henry up by the back of his neck and tossed him across the deck. Henry landed on his feet, immediately dropping into a fighter's stance. Fists raised and feet planted, he was ready for battle.

Bones was instantly in Henry's face. "Why didn't you tell me she was here?"

Bones reminded Henry of Aries in a temper. His lips were pulled back to bare his teeth. His nostrils flared. If he'd been a horse, Bones's ears would have been pinned back to his head.

The cloud of confusion in Henry's brain lifted. Bones would not be this upset over Claudia.

"You're talking about Penny?" Henry asked, lowering his fists.

Bones's brow creased. He dragged a hand through his hair, his fingers tugging. His eyes squeezed shut, and he pulled in a sharp breath.

Henry had been friends with Bones Keaukalani for three years. He'd seen Bones laughing at parties. He'd seen him serious on practice dives. He'd seen him turn on the charm for the ladies. He'd never seen him like this. The hulk of a man was almost in tears.

"How is she? I know she don't wanna see me, but—"

"She's not here." Henry put Bones out of his misery. "When I talked to her last week, she said she was moving to New York City. She's gonna try modeling."

Bones's giant shoulders sagged. "New York City?"

"Sorry, man." Henry reached out and placed a hand on Bones's shoulder. He patted gently as if he were touching a porcupine.

Bones shrugged and walked to the railing, giving Henry his back.

"I thought you and Penny were just having a good time."

Bones turned and gave him a startled look. "You don't know shit, cuz."

Henry hadn't thought Bones had any loyalties when it came to women. He had a different girl every week. Sometimes every day. Henry had assumed Bones was the type of guy who was incapable of having a steady girl, or caring about anyone. But the man standing on his deck right now was definitely broken. Henry knew the signs well. The bags under his eyes. The creases of misery around his mouth. The haggard gaze.

"You love her?"

The color drained from Bones's face, and he nodded. "I guess I do."

Henry started to laugh. He wasn't the only desperate man in love with a woman he couldn't have. "We should be drinking liquor instead of coffee."

"Eh? It's not funny." Bones winced and reached up to rub the back of his neck as if he could massage away his discomfort.

"I didn't realize you two were really serious," Henry said.

"Me either."

Henry's cousin Penny had been a talented ballerina when she was in her teens. When her career had been cut short by an accident, she'd moved back home to Seattle to teach dance. Penny had what Henry considered an artist's temperament. She was passionate and dramatic. Unlike Bones, who didn't seem capable of falling in love, Penny fell in love every other week. Henry couldn't count the number of times she'd been engaged.

"You're better off without her."

A strange noise came from the big man's throat, and Henry realized Bones was holding back tears. "Yeah," he said. "You're probably right, cuz."

Guilt stabbed Henry's gut as he said good-bye to Bones. Here he was telling Bones to give up on Penny when all he could think about was Claudia.

It was different though.

Claudia was right here on the island; Penny was a thousand miles away.

Henry still had a chance.

38

Lighthouse Party

Claudia

THE PARTY at the Diamond Head Lighthouse was fancier than Claudia had thought it would be. It reminded her of a party in Los Angeles. A-list guests mingled in cocktail attire, and the food was catered, not homemade.

Claudia made her way to the lawn, speaking with a few people she knew, turning on the charm like Benji had asked her to do. She still hadn't decided if she was going to do the show. After talking to her agent, Claudia knew taking the part was the best thing for her career. She just wasn't sure it was the best thing for her heart.

Her thoughts drifted to Henry, and as if she'd conjured him, she spotted him in the crowd. She hadn't expected to see him tonight considering he had given up his job as stunt director. Had he changed his mind, or was he at the party to see her?

She wanted to find out.

She wished she could hate him, but it was too damn hard. One look at him brought up a flood of memories. She felt his hot gaze on her beneath the dark lenses of his aviator-style sunglasses.

The coil of stress in her belly loosened, and she felt the lick of desire. She knew what he had on under those jeans —nothing.

Claudia longed to stride across the lawn and rip off his sunglasses. Expose his hot blue gaze. Make him look her in the eye. Kiss him breathless.

The moment pulsed between them.

His lips slowly curved in a smile, and a tremor of joy spread through her. Henry wasn't Rick. He hadn't used her and betrayed her. He'd even given up the job he coveted for her. He'd proved his love. Now she just had to reach out and take it.

"Claudia?"

She froze. Her stomach clenched. Her heart skipped, then raced, and she felt like she was flying above herself, looking down. She knew that deep melodic voice that made her name sound like a rare flower. She hadn't heard it in six years, but she would never forget it.

She turned and saw Keoni. He was even better looking than he'd been six years ago. Same dark hair, a little longer than before. Same caramel eyes, plus a few fine lines around them. Same smile, charming the panties off women everywhere.

She'd forgotten he was so tall. And had his shoulders always been so broad?

"Say something so I know you're real," he said.

"Keoni."

A slow grin curved his mouth, then bloomed into a full-fledged smile. His white teeth flashed. A dimple in his cheek winked.

He stepped closer and then his arms were around her. She melted into his embrace, breathing in the salty ocean smell of him that took her back in time. In his arms, Claudia was a young girl again, happy and carefree.

"I never thought I'd see you again," he said, releasing her. "What are you doing here?"

"Looking for you," she admitted. It had started out that way, but then something along the way had changed. Claudia lifted her head to look at Henry. He was gone, swallowed by the crowd.

"Everyone's staring at us," Keoni said under his breath. "Let's get out of the spotlight."

Claudia glanced around and saw that every eye was glued to them. She searched the crowd again for Henry, but there was no sign of him.

Keoni took her hand and led her up the path toward the lighthouse.

She'd anticipated this moment for weeks. Years. But it didn't feel like she'd thought it would. Tears welled in her eyes as the truth slammed down on her. She loved Henry. He made her feel alive. He'd used her, and lied to her, and made a fool of her, but Claudia didn't care. She looked forward to him making it up to her for a very long time. Him and his magic tongue.

"I never thought I'd see you again," Keoni said.

She'd dreamed of hearing his deep rumbling voice again, of gazing up at his handsome face, of smelling the ocean in his hair. Now, all she could think of were the tiny freckles across the bridge of Henry's nose.

"You're a big star now," Keoni said. "Is it everything you always wanted?"

Claudia's chest tightened. "Almost."

"I still can't believe it's you." He sat on the stone wall enclosing the path and stared at her as if she were an angel who'd dropped from the sky.

"What are you doing here?" Claudia asked, still not quite believing it was him either. She'd tried so hard to find him. *And now he appears?* The timing couldn't have been worse.

Keoni swallowed and looked down at his clasped hands. "The mayor invited me," he said.

Claudia's eyebrows rose. "The mayor? Why?"

Keoni lifted his shoulders. He glanced up at her, and she saw he was blushing. "I saved a little baby from drowning, and they're giving me an award or something."

Claudia's heart slammed in her chest as she remembered the day Keoni had saved her from nearly drowning. "You're a hero," she said, her voice breaking.

"Nah." He shook his head, eyes smiling. "I was just in the right place at the right time."

"You seem to have a knack for that." Except he wasn't home when she called or dropped by. Looking back, she realized maybe that had been a good thing. If Keoni would have been there, Claudia would have never fallen in love with Henry.

"I was mad at you for a long time," he said, looking out over the ocean.

"I'm sorry." The words she'd prepared started coming back to her. She'd planned all along to start with an apology. "I should have come to meet you that morning. I should have told you good-bye."

Keoni's eyes slid from the view toward her face. "No." He took her hands in his. "You did everything right. You left so you could become you. I stayed so I could become me."

And now, there they were together. Years later, the two of them finally face-to-face. Keoni had changed. In 1962, he'd been guarded, but the 1968 version was an open book.

"I spent years loving you," she said, feeling tears prick the back of her eyes. She planned on telling him she loved him, present tense, not past. It felt like her heart was ripping in two. She looked into his eyes and saw the glimmer of a smile.

"I hated you," he said.

She nodded. She'd been expecting that. She'd thought she would have had to convince him to change his mind, but she no longer cared how Keoni felt about her.

"I came here for you." Her tears began to flow.

He pressed a napkin into her hand. "We were just kids."

She tried to find the right words to tell him how she felt. "I know. We were silly kids. Teenagers. But whenever my heart was hurting, I thought of you. I thought you could save me." She sniffed back tears. "You were so good at it."

Keoni's cheeks turned pink. She'd never known he could blush before. "I can't save you. You have to do that for yourself. You have to be brave on your own."

Claudia dabbed at the tears filling her eyes. "I know." And she did. She had to be brave enough to forgive. "I'm sorry."

"Nah, it's okay." He shrugged. "You taught me I could love a tourist."

Claudia raised her brows. "Are we really that bad?"

Keoni looked at something in the distance. Both his eyes and his mind were somewhere else. "No. Not all of you."

"I wanted to win you back more than anything," Claudia said.

"K'den?" he asked. "What happened?"

Claudia shook her head. "I don't know." But she did know. Henry had happened. He'd made her fall for him. He'd done something she thought no man could ever do: he'd made her stop wanting Keoni. Tears burned behind her eyes. "Everything is ruined," she said softly.

Keoni chuckled knowingly. "What did he do?"

"He lied to me." Claudia's chest tightened at thought of the unfortunate bet that had poisoned everything.

"Lies aren't always bad," Keoni said mysteriously.

"When is a lie good?"

Keoni took Claudia's arm and steered her along the path. "Have you heard the story of Hiiaka?"

Keoni's stories were one of the things Claudia remembered about him most. He was full of Hawaiian tales and myths. He had one for everything.

She laughed softly. "You haven't changed a bit."

Keoni smiled and launched into his story. "Long ago, there were two sisters who were goddesses. Hiiaka, goddess of lightning, and Pele, the volcano goddess. They were equal in rank, but Pele enjoyed giving her sister orders. Hiiaka obeyed the orders because she felt she owed Pele for taking care of her."

They walked along the stone path that wound around the lighthouse and stopped to take in the breathtaking view. Below, the turquoise Pacific gently washed against a pristine white beach. Above, the sky glowed magenta with the last rays of sunlight. Beside her, Keoni leaned his elbows against the metal railing that overlooked the beach. A soft wind rippled his hair. His majestic beauty embodied the best of the island's treasures. He was everything she'd always remembered, but he was no longer what she wanted.

Keoni continued his story of the goddess sisters, but Claudia was no longer listening. Years ago, she would have hung on his every word, but now all she could think of was Henry.

The easy rumble of his laugh. The gentleness in his touch. He was patient and kind and made her laugh when she least expected to.

She imagined how he'd been roped into that bet by men who didn't care about anyone else's feelings but their own. Henry wasn't Rick. He hadn't seduced her with an eye on the prize. There had been no artifice in him. He'd been genuine and sweet, even going so far as to help her find Keoni.

It must have killed Henry to see Claudia go off with Keoni. He must be imagining the worst. Where was he now? In conversation with some important person? Soaking in the prestige of being invited to a party at the lighthouse?

No, she didn't think so. He was probably miserable, waiting for Claudia to decide their fates.

She pushed away the railing, cutting Keoni off midsentence. "I've got to go."

He stopped talking and grinned at her. "You goin' to get your man?"

Claudia winced. "I don't think I can call him that. Not yet."

She pressed her fingertips to her temples. "I'm not sure of anything."

"You'll know when you find him," Keoni said. "Go."

Claudia turned and hurried down the path back to the party.

39

Every Single Day

Henry

HENRY COULDN'T GO HOME, but he couldn't stay at the party. He got in his car and he drove, figuring he would keep driving until he felt better—until he could forget how Claudia had gone straight into Keoni's arms and looked like she belonged there.

He drove and drove.

He didn't feel better.

Going home meant sitting by himself all night, staring at the walls and going crazy imagining what Claudia and Keoni were doing.

Henry kept driving. He didn't realize where he was headed until he recognized the dirt road that led to the stables.

The horses always made him feel better. Being with the animals calmed his soul. He hoped their soothing presence would make his heart stop breaking, but it was a lot to hope.

He couldn't stop thinking about the way Keoni had folded Claudia into his embrace, or the look on Claudia's face when she'd seen Keoni.

He gripped the steering wheel so hard, his hands shook. The way they had looked together broke his heart.

He sped past the caretaker's house without slowing down. Normally he would stop to say hello, but his mood was too sour. His company was only fit for the horses. He passed the empty pastures and stopped at the side of the barn.

For a moment, he sat in his car, staring at the faded sign on the side of the barn. Each breath he took felt more difficult than the last. His thoughts whirled until his head ached. He pictured Claudia lying beside next to him in his bed. He heard her the echo of her laughter.

He wanted to slam his fist into something. Someone.

Didn't Keoni have enough women in his life? Did he have to take Claudia too?

Would Henry never have a woman who belonged to him? His thoughts spiraled down into a black hole of despair as he thought of the little girl he would never know. She would be ten years old this year.

Did she have his red hair?

Did she like to ride horses?

Henry didn't even know his daughter's name. Henry's mother was Violet, called Vi by everyone. He'd always thought Violet was a pretty name. But he hadn't gotten a choice in naming his daughter. He hadn't even gotten a choice in meeting her.

Henry sat in his car for a long time, listening to the radio at low volume, soaking in the sounds of the night. Usually, just being at the stables calmed him, but tonight was different. The grove of trees that had always transported him back to his family farm now reminded him of training with Claudia.

He couldn't get the image of her and Keoni out of his mind. Would he ever be able to banish that image?

The first bars of "Brown Eyed Girl" sounded over the radio, and Henry couldn't move fast enough to turn the dial. He never wanted to hear that song again.

He got out of the car and went into the barn, where the only noises were the familiar sounds of the horses settling in for the night. The comforting smells of leather and sandalwood began to work their magic as soon as he stepped into the barn.

He stopped to grab six sugar cubes from the jar in the office and made his way down the aisle to greet each horse.

There were six horses, each in individual stalls. They were all male, all trained to perform and remain calm in the midst of chaos. The horses were the reason he was in the business. If it weren't for his job in the stables on *Turner and Ditz*, he would have never started doing stunts.

He had the horses to thank for his career. When he became a stunt director someday, he would make sure the horses under his care were never mistreated or made to do anything dangerous.

"Hello, boy." Henry offered a sugar cube to each of the horses, saving his favorite, the big chestnut called Rusty, for last. "How you feeling?" Henry smiled as Rusty nuzzled his palm for the sugar cube. "Sorry, no carrots tonight."

He took a brush from the hook next to the stall and showed it to Rusty, who responded with a snort. Rusty loved being groomed more than any horse Henry had ever known.

Henry let himself into the stall and began to brush the horse's broad back. He checked Rusty's foot, making sure the hoof wall he'd broken off a few weeks ago was growing back in properly. It looked fine, and Rusty hardly noticed anything was wrong, but Henry had made sure Rusty was getting proper rest until he was healed.

"Just think of it as a few days off," he told the horse who had a stronger work ethic than any man Henry knew. "You'll be back on the job in no time."

Rusty neighed as if he understood Henry, and maybe he did. The two of them had a special bond. Henry liked Rusty more than he did some people.

He'd take Rusty over Stan any day.

His grip tightened on the brush at the thought of Stan. It was easy to blame Stan for what had gone wrong with Claudia, but it wasn't right. Henry knew he'd blown it with her. It was his own fault.

He hoped giving up the job as stunt director would be enough to show her how much he loved her. The only reason he'd been at the party at the lighthouse was to see her. Now, he wished he had stayed home. He couldn't scrub the image of Claudia and Keoni from his mind.

If she ended up taking the job in Hawaii—and why wouldn't she now that she had reunited with Keoni?—Henry would be forced to see her all the time. His heart would break every single day.

A loud bang broke the silence of the barn. Henry went still, listening.

"Hello?" he called. There hadn't been anyone else in the barn when he came in. He would have seen them.

The noise sounded again and then again, a rhythmic pounding of steel against wood. After a moment, Henry recognized the sound as hooves striking the stable wall.

Aries was at it again. The ex-racehorse had been stall-striking for weeks. Everyone was worried he would break his legs or kick through the walls. Aries hadn't settled into life as a stunt horse as well as everyone had hoped.

The horse had been a handful from the beginning. Big and black, with elegant features and a high-stepping gait that looked excellent on film, Aries was as difficult to work with as a prima donna celebrity.

Henry had been the only one to penetrate Aries's prickly exterior, and the two of them had formed an uneasy truce. Aries permitted Henry to ride him, but none of the other stuntmen could get close. The crew was getting tired of catering to Aries, and Henry feared the horse's days as a cast member were numbered.

He left Rusty's stall and locked it behind him. Keeping his voice at a low murmur, Henry began to talk to Aries. He made soothing clucking noises as he approached the stall where Aries stomped and snorted, tossing his black mane.

"Hey, boy."

Aries pinned back his ears and reared slightly.

Henry approached the stall cautiously. "What's your problem, eh?" He dug in his pocket, but he was out of sugar cubes. "Easy, there. It's just me. Your old friend, Champ. You like me. Remember?"

Aries snorted and tossed his head, but his ears relaxed, and he stopped rearing.

"Attaboy," Henry cooed. "You just wanted to steal the show, didn't you? You can't stand someone else getting a turn. You're like someone else I know." Henry grimaced, his heart hammering as he remembered Keoni's big hands wrapping around Claudia's waist. "You like to hog all the attention? Well, you got it now." Henry laughed at himself. He'd been such a fool to fall in love with a woman like Claudia, who wasn't suited for him at all. "How did this happen?" he asked Aries. "I never fall in love. I didn't think I could do it." He smiled at Aries as if they were sharing a joke. "How did I wind up with a broken heart?"

Henry didn't expect an answer, but it felt good to talk, even if it was with a horse. No matter if she moved back to the mainland or not, Claudia was going to haunt Henry forever.

He would see her face on television, in magazines, at the movie theater…

A sob caught in his throat, and he swallowed it down, careful not to show his distress to the agitated horse. Aries was extremely intuitive and influenced by emotional cues.

Aries pawed the ground and flipped his mane. His ears pinned back to his head, and he reared back on his hind legs. Henry didn't have time to move before Aries lashed out with his front legs. His hooves struck Henry in the chest and sent him flying.

The last thing Henry saw before he hit the ground was Claudia's face—the glimmer in her chocolate-colored eyes, the curve of her smile—and then darkness.

270

40

Digging Deep

Claudia

NO LIGHTS BLAZED from Henry's house, and his driveway was empty. Claudia parked her car and stared at the quiet house, debating what to do. She could go back to her room. Maybe he'd gone there, or he could be at the bar in the hotel. She gripped the steering wheel in frustration.

If he wasn't home, she would just wait. He had to come home at some point, and when he did, she would be there waiting for him.

The front door was unlocked. Remembering how Bones had let himself into Henry's house the other day, she guessed Henry was used to people letting themselves into his house. She went inside and flipped on the light.

Henry's house was a typical bachelor pad. It needed a woman's touch. Her touch. The first thing she'd get rid of was the hideous beast of a sofa, and the curtains had to go. They looked like someone's grandmother had chosen them.

Claudia went completely still as the realization that she'd made up her mind hit home. She wanted to wake up every day to the view off Henry's lanai. She wanted to smell his neck in the morning and stretch out next to him at night. Claudia walked to the sliding glass doors and looked out at the view of the twinkling lights down the mountain.

That was a view she could get used to seeing every day. It was easy to picture herself living right here in this house on this island with this man.

Where was that man? She paced the living room, feeling jittery with nerves.

She picked up a framed photograph of Henry and two women. They were all smiling broadly, as if someone—probably Henry—had just said something funny.

A flash of jealousy sparked to life in Claudia's chest. She didn't like seeing Henry with his arms around other women.

Claudia placed the offending photograph back on the table and paced across the room. She picked up another framed photo of Henry sitting astride a dark horse. He held the reins loosely in his big square hands, his chest bent toward the horse as if he were telling him a secret.

The horse's head was thrown back toward Henry, and he looked to be smiling. His mane flew, and his dark eyes danced.

In his Western-cut shirt with pearl buttons, cowboy hat, and jeans, Henry looked rugged and confident. Very sexy.

A tingle of awareness shot down Claudia's spine as she stared at the photograph of the smiling horse. She knew exactly where Henry had gone.

She grabbed her purse and raced out of the house to her car. For a moment, she panicked, thinking she might not remember how to get to the stables. She knew they were near the studio, so she headed in that direction. She drove on instinct, making a few wrong turns before she finally found the long dirt road that led to the pastures.

Claudia gripped the steering wheel as she bumped down the dirt road. Her stomach rolled, and her hands trembled. She had a terrible feeling that Henry was going to tell her to go to hell, that he wanted nothing to do with her. He'd seen her go off with Keoni. He couldn't be happy about that.

She chewed her lip, eating off the remains of her lipstick.

Dread balled in her stomach as she drew nearer to the barn. The rolling green pastures were lit with moonlight. The grove of trees reminded her of the time they had trained for her fight scene. Had it only been a few weeks ago? It seemed like years to Claudia.

So much had changed since that day. She'd fallen in love. She'd had her heart broken. She'd found the man she was looking for and realized the one she wanted was right there all along.

The coil of tension in Claudia's stomach tightened when she spotted Henry's car in front of the barn. She flipped down the visor and checked her reflection in the mirror, wishing she would have taken the time to touch up her makeup and change her clothes.

But it was too late for a wardrobe change, and her ankle-length crocheted dress would have to do.

She reached for a cigarette and then changed her mind. She was too nervous to smoke.

After another minute of stalling and preparing what she'd say to Henry, Claudia was finally ready to get out of the car.

As soon as she entered the cozy space of the barn, she knew something was wrong.

The well-lit space was eerily quiet, except for Rusty, who snorted from his stall.

"Hello?" she called. "Henry?"

She passed the small office at the entrance and continued down the aisle toward Rusty's stall.

"Sorry, boy," she said. "I didn't bring you any treats."

"Hello?" Claudia's wooden sandals rang out on the concrete floor. "Henry?"

A chill ran through Claudia's veins when she noticed an odd scent in the air. The barn smelled of leather and hay and something else she couldn't quite name. It was sharp and coppery.

Claudia stopped abruptly as she recognized it.

Blood.

A wave of dizziness crashed over her, and she wobbled on her feet.

"Henry!"

At the end of the aisle, she noticed something odd. A pair of boots stuck out from behind a bale of hay, and attached to the boots were denim-clad legs. She knew those boots. She knew those legs.

A scream was trapped in her throat as she ran down the aisle. She halted in front of the bale of hay, and her entire body clenched when she looked at Henry lying facedown on the concrete floor.

Her heart jackhammered in her chest as she bent to the concrete floor. She pressed her fingers to his pulse and sagged with relief when she felt it beat. She ran her hands down his body, searching for injuries, and gently turned him onto his side.

"Henry!" She touched his shoulder gently, afraid to do any more damage. "Wake up. Please wake up."

Her throat closed when she saw the odd angle of his arm trapped beneath his body. White bone showed through his skin. The acrid smell of blood hit her nose, and she gagged.

When he didn't respond, Claudia ran back to the office. She grabbed the phone off the desk and dialed zero. Her heart beat so hard, she could hear it pounding between her ears like a wave crashing over and over inside her head. Chills sprang out along her skin while she waited for the operator to pick up. The only sound in the barn was her raging heart and the noise of Rusty stomping and pacing in his stall.

Finally, the operator answered, and Claudia got control of her voice.

"I need the fire station nearest Waimanalo."

It took forever to get connected to the fire station. While she waited for someone to answer, Claudia dragged the phone out of the room as far as the cord would allow and stared at Henry's immobile boots. Every moment they'd shared flashed before her eyes. She remembered seeing him for the first time behind the bar at The SurfRider, watching him crash his car on set, and dancing to their song at the luau.

The fire station finally answered and assured her they would have a rescue squad to the barn as soon as possible. They told her to stay with him and not to move him.

"Try to stop the blood if you can," the fireman advised her over the sound of screaming sirens.

Fighting off a wave of nausea, Claudia hung up the phone and ran back to Henry's side. She glared up at Aries, who was calmly surveying her from behind the door of his stall.

"What happened?" she demanded of Aries, not caring that she was yelling at a horse. "What did you do?"

Unsurprisingly, he had no answer for her. She grabbed a blanket and draped it over Henry's body, then tried to do something about his arm.

Claudia had no medical training, but she'd visited her uncle's farm back home enough to see a few accidents. She pressed the long hem of her dress to Henry's arm and wiped away the worst of the blood. She almost fainted at the sight of his fractured bone breaking the surface of his pale skin, but she dug deeply and breathed through the nausea.

"You're lucky I love you, you damn fool. This is one of my favorite dresses your blood just ruined."

She choked on a sob, taking a small amount of comfort in the fact that help was on the way. Rusty continued to make plenty of noise from a few stalls down, and she knew she wasn't the only one who loved Henry. It felt good not to be alone, even if Rusty was a horse.

"Help's coming, Rusty," she said. "And I'm not going anywhere."

41

Full Speed Toward a Crash

Henry

HENRY COULDN'T FEEL the right side of his face. His head throbbed. His chest ached. His head felt like someone had smashed it with a sledgehammer.

Just another day at work, he thought, struggling to open his eyes.

Pain knifed through him, and the old mantras he used on a daily basis weren't cutting it.

This too shall pass.

Pain doesn't last.

What doesn't kill you makes you stronger.

The pain was too much, and he drifted off again, dreaming that he was diving deep in the ocean. The warm water surrounded him, pushing him deeper into the abyss. He let go, sinking under the glassy surface of the waves. The sea pulsed with life. Exotic sea creatures darted through the colorful reefs. The whoosh of water filled his ears, and he lost track of his place in the world.

Claudia swam beside him, a sexy siren of the sea. She was

naked from the waist up and had a shimmering mermaid tail below. The ribbons of her hair brushed his arms, and the soft tinkle of her laugh echoed along the waves. She turned to smile at him, and Henry was instantly under her spell. Her brown eyes twinkled mischievously, and the pout of her mouth invited his kiss.

The dream was so real, Henry swore he heard the soft whisper of her voice. Insulting him.

"You idiot," she said. "You stupid goddamned fool. You selfish bastard."

Henry opened his eyes and blinked slowly to clear his vision. A bright light shined down on him, scalding his eyes. Just before he squeezed them shut again, he saw Claudia with her head bent over his chest. She clutched his hand, and her golden hair spilled over his chest.

He tried to lift his free hand to touch her hair, but his arm was too heavy. He tried to speak, but his tongue felt too thick in his mouth.

"What did I do?" he asked, his voice coming out gruff and raspy as if he hadn't spoken in days.

Claudia moved quickly, jarring Henry's chest. A riot of pain exploded behind his eyes, and he sank back toward uncon-sciousness.

"Don't you dare!" Claudia cried. "If you die, I'm going to kill you."

He swallowed painfully and cleared his throat. He hurt too much to be dying. "I'm not dying," he said, cracking open his eyes. "Am I?"

Claudia pinned him with an intense gaze. "You better not be."

He lifted his good hand to rub the tears from her cheek. "Don't cry."

Claudia smiled, her eyes shining with fresh tears. He curved his hand around her neck and pulled her close. Her soft lips landed gently on his, and his body responded instantly. His pulse raced. His skin tingled. His cock went stiff. Thank God everything down there was still in working order. He wasn't dying.

Henry's thoughts were sluggish. He didn't know what was real. His head was in Claudia's lap, but she didn't seem to have a mermaid tail. He still felt like he was dreaming, and the light hurt his eyes.

He glanced around and recognized the smooth wooden walls, the bales of hay, the saddles draped over horse blankets.

Henry shut his eyes against the blinding lights. The last thing he remembered was hugging Rusty's neck. No... he'd been checking on Aries, the anxious quarter horse. Aries had reared. Henry had been kicked.

His eyes snapped open, and he craned his neck to look at Aries's stall. "Aries? Is he okay?"

Claudia gently pushed him back to the comfort of her lap. "The damn horse is fine." Claudia's eyes sparked with temper. "He tried to kill you, but he's carrying on like nothing happened. It's Rusty who's going nuts. Listen to him."

Henry heard the unmistakable sounds of a horse in distress. "Rusty," he called. He winced as more pain rocketed through his head. "It's okay, boy. I'm okay."

"You better be," Claudia murmured, smoothing his hair back from his face. "Help is on the way. I called the rescue squad."

Confusion warred in Henry's mind. The last time he'd seen Claudia, she'd been in Keoni's arms. "What are you doing here?"

"Waiting for you to wake up. What else?" Her fingers fluttered over his cheek, where pain throbbed.

He noticed she was still wearing the dress from the party. Her hair was messy. Her makeup was smeared.

He ran his tongue along his teeth to make sure they were all there. His arm hurt so much, he wanted to pass out, but he forced himself to stay awake. "What happened?"

"I told you." Claudia's brows drew together. "There was an accident—"

"No, I meant at the party." He swallowed what felt like rusty nails in his throat. "With Keoni."

Claudia narrowed her eyes at him. "If you would have gone home instead of going to the stables, you would already know the answer."

Henry's eyebrows rose. "What?"

"I left the party and went straight to your house." A sob caught in her throat. "When you weren't there, I came to the stables. I knew you'd be here." She closed her eyes and pulled in a slow breath. "God, I need a smoke."

Henry reached up with his good hand and wiped her tears. God, he couldn't stand to see her cry.

She glared down at him. "You could have died."

"Nah. I don't think so."

"Henry, it's not funny."

"Who's laughing?" He frowned. "It hurts too much to laugh."

"I almost lost you." She leaned closer to his face. Her hair fell over her shoulder and tickled his arm.

"What about Keoni?" He didn't want to ask, but he had to.

Claudia shook her head. "We don't need to talk about that now."

"We do."

Claudia swiped the tears from her cheeks with the back of her hand. "I don't love him."

Despite all the pain in his body, Henry felt elated. "Why?"

"You're as dumb as a box of rocks." Claudia blew out a frustrated breath. "I love you. That's why."

A lock of hair fell across her face, and Henry reached up to tuck it behind her ear. "Say it again?" His voice was thick with need, but he didn't care. "Please."

"I love you." She lifted his hand and presses kisses to his

palm, punctuating each kiss with the most beautiful words he'd ever heard. "I love you. I love you. I love…"

"If I'm still dreaming, don't wake me up."

"You," she said, finishing on a laugh.

A roar filled Henry's ears. He felt like he was driving full speed toward a crash. He curved his good hand around her neck and pulled her face close. "I love you too." Pain shot through his chest, stabbing his heart. "I want to explain. I don't know how I got pulled into that bet, but I should—"

"Shhh." Claudia put a hand on his cheek. "You don't have to explain."

"Yes, I do." But he couldn't speak anymore. It hurt too much. His eyes drifted closed. "Later. I promise. I'll make it up to you."

A siren blared in the distance.

"Yes, you will."

Henry wanted to laugh, but it hurt too much. He wanted to kiss her again, but he couldn't do that either. He sighed in frustration. "I can't kiss you like I want to," he said.

"Let me do the kissing." She pressed soft kisses, wet with tears, to his forehead, his brow, and his cheeks.

Henry sank back into the softness of her lap as joy spread through the aches in his body. "You missed a spot," he said.

Epilogue

Six months later

Henry

HENRY BALANCED two mugs in one hand and stuffed the envelope in his mouth so he could use his free hand to slide open the glass door.

"You're missing it," Claudia called, beckoning him with an impatient wave.

The sky was at the bursting point right before sunrise, when the atmosphere shivered between darkness and light. It was Henry's favorite moment of the day. He'd always been an early riser, but having Claudia to share the sunrise with was a welcome addition to his daily routine.

He took the envelope from his mouth and shoved it in his back pocket, then walked across the lanai to join Claudia at the wrought-iron table and chairs.

They were new. A gift from Claudia. And a nice improvement from the heavy plastic table and metal lawn chairs he used to have. He placed her mug in front of her on the table and took a swallow of his own coffee.

"Thanks." She took a small sip of hers, then reached for her cigarettes.

Henry picked up the matches and lit it for her. He never mentioned that he didn't like her smoking, but he noticed she was doing it less and less. A pack would last a week these days, when it used to barely last a day.

Claudia made a noise of frustration, then stabbed out her cigarette in the ashtray. "I think they changed something in my brand," she said, reaching for her coffee. "They taste different."

Henry eyed the ashtray of barely smoked cigarettes. They tasted terrible. Maybe it was starting to sink in.

He shrugged and set his mug on the table. "Maybe you're outgrowing them."

Claudia narrowed her eyes at him. "What's the matter?"

"Nothing." He raised his eyebrows. "Why do you ask?"

She eyed him for a long moment. "You've been acting funny for days."

"I always act funny." He scooped Claudia up from her chair and sat down with her in his lap, then nuzzled her neck until she laughed. He ignored the envelope burning a hole in his back pocket. "Be still and watch the sunrise," he said sternly.

She looped her arms around his neck and rested her head on top of his. "What's in the envelope?" she asked.

Henry's blood ran cold. "What?"

"I saw you stick it in your pocket. Is it the electric bill? I know I've been staying here almost every night. I can contribute…"

He cinched his arm around her waist and nipped her neck. "Hush. We don't have to talk about that ever again."

"Okay." She settled in his lap again. "Why don't we talk about what's in your pants?"

He grinned against her neck. "Again?"

"Not that." She swatted his shoulder. "The envelope in your pocket."

Henry's heart raced. He always felt like he was in a speeding car heading for a crash when he was with Claudia.

Being with Claudia wasn't easy. His senses were always on high alert. His skin felt stretched too tightly, and his heart ached. But when he wasn't with her, it was worse. When he wasn't with her, he felt half alive.

He shifted her in his lap so he could fish the envelope out. "Here."

Claudia took it and slid her finger under the flap. She tugged the card out and reached for her coffee. She took a small sip, and Henry felt her body tense as she scanned the words.

His heart thundered, and his thoughts whirled as he waited with what felt like the patience of a saint for her to finish reading.

Finally, Claudia set her mug on the table and stood from his lap. The card slipped from her fingers. The color drained from her face, and her eyes filled with tears. Before he could say anything, she ran into the house.

He'd known the invitation was going to spark a reaction, maybe even a fight, but he hadn't been able to predict Claudia would get so upset she had to run away.

He grabbed the invitation and paced to the railing. His chest tightened painfully as he reread the words.

Please join us for a celebration of the wedding of Mary Lou Hunter and Keoni Kealoha Makai…

Henry's vision blurred, and he shoved the invitation back in his pocket. If the thought of Keoni marrying another woman made Claudia run away, then she must still be in love with him. His shoulders sagged, and he leaned against the railing, feeling more miserable than he'd thought possible. He wished he hadn't shown her the invitation.

It was clear from her reaction that she was still looking for something from Keoni. His name hadn't been spoken in months, but now it was time to dredge it up again, time to face her and talk this out.

Henry strode into the house, giving himself a little pep talk as he headed down the hall toward the bathroom. If Claudia didn't want him, well, he would just beg. He would grovel. He would throw himself at her feet.

First, he would knock.

"Claudia?" He rapped on the closed door. "You okay in there, babe?"

He heard the flush of the toilet. Pressing his ear to the door, he thought he heard a muffled sob. The door flew open so fast, he almost fell into the room.

Claudia stood in the doorway, holding a wet washcloth to her throat. Her eyes were glassy, and her face was tinted green. She reached out and grabbed his hand, then yanked him into the bathroom. Her arms circled his neck, and she buried her face against his chest. Her tears wet the front of his shirt.

Henry clutched her tightly, taking most of her weight. "Are you still in love with him?"

The words wedged between them, and she shifted back to glare up at him. "Sit down." She pointed at the only seat in the bathroom: the toilet. Her brows were drawn together, but some color was returning to her pale face. "Look at me."

Henry sat on the lid of the toilet and looked at her. God, she was beautiful. Her hair was a glorious mess as usual, a wild mane tumbling down her shoulders. He'd done that, with his hands in her hair last night. Her lips were pink and swollen. He'd done that too.

"I'm looking."

"Do you notice anything different about me?"

Henry wasn't sure where he was supposed to be looking at. She was breathing hard, and it made her chest rise and fall rapidly. His gaze slid down her body. She wore one of his old Tshirts, and he could see her gorgeous tits clearly. Her nipples were hard little pebbles under the thin fabric. He dragged his eyes back toward her face.

"Umm… no?"

Claudia grabbed both his hands and placed them on her breasts. She forced him to cup their weight. He wasn't complaining. His dick stood up and noticed how amazing she felt in his hands, but his mind swirled with confusion.

"You feel that?" she demanded.

He squeezed, and her eyes glazed over. He recognized the blaze of lust that shot color into her cheeks. She bit her bottom lip and leaned closer. He filled his hands with her, kneading her soft flesh. Come to think of it, she felt different. Fuller. Heavier. He rolled her nipple between his thumb and finger, and she pushed him back, straddling him on the toilet.

Henry's eyebrows shot up as she ground against him. He'd done it in a lot of strange places, but the toilet wasn't one of them.

Claudia threaded her fingers in his hair and laid a hot kiss on his mouth. Their tongues tangled. She tasted like minty mouthwash.

"God, Henry." She slid her mouth along his jaw. "I can't get enough of you. You smell so good. Why do you always smell so good?" Her mouth trailed back to his, and she kissed him deeply.

Henry was so confused that his mind checked out. He gripped her hips and pulled her closer, right up against his heavy erection.

Claudia pulled back and lifted her shirt over her head. Henry didn't mind the view one bit, especially when Claudia cupped her generous breasts in her hands and offered them to him.

"See?" she demanded.

His dick strained against his pants. "Yeah."

"Look at me."

He couldn't be paid a million dollars to tear his eyes away.

Claudia took his chin in her hand and tilted his face up until their eyes met. "My breasts are swollen and tender. All I want to do is crawl into bed with you. I can't stand the taste of my cigarettes. One sip of coffee and I almost threw up." Her eyes filled with tears. "Don't you see?"

Henry's skin heated, but his thoughts froze. He searched Claudia's soft brown eyes, trying to understand. "I thought you were upset about the wedding invitation."

Claudia exhaled forcefully. "What?" She pinched his chin, jerking his face up to hers. "No. I'm upset because I'm pregnant."

Tension coiled tightly in his chest. His vision blurred, and he felt light-headed. "That's impossible."

"You do know how it works, right?"

Claudia ground against his erection as if to prove her point. His dick reacted by swelling to meet her, and Henry grabbed her hips to stop her movement.

"We've been so careful. We've done everything right."

Claudia's eyes filled with tears. "I know."

Henry's chest ached at the sight of her tears. "Don't cry. Please."

"I didn't mean for this to happen."

Claudia tried to stand, but he pulled her back onto his lap. He cupped her jaw and pulled her face down to his. His heart was beating so hard, he thought his chest would burst. He kissed Claudia's trembling bottom lip. "I love kids," he said. "I love you."

"You do? I mean… This wasn't supposed to happen, not like this."

He curled his hand around the back of her neck and kissed her, sliding his tongue along the seam of her lips until she opened for him. He claimed her mouth with a possessiveness he hadn't known he could feel. He had so many emotions swirling inside his mind. One thought tangled in with another. All he knew was how good she felt. How right.

"What about your career? I don't want you to give up anything."

"I don't have to," she said. "It's not the 1950s anymore. I can be a mother and an actress. I can have it all." She kissed his mouth. "As long as I have you."

Henry tightened his grip around her hips and laughed. It seemed very wrong to propose to the love of his life on the toilet, but he couldn't stop himself.

"Will you marry me?"

Claudia shook her head. "You don't have to marry me. We can work things out."

"Are you sure?"

He watched the light die from her eyes. "I'm sure. We can arrange to share responsibility."

He lifted a finger to her mouth, silencing her. "Are you sure you're pregnant?"

Claudia smiled and nodded. "Pretty sure. I have this feeling."

Henry smiled back. He had a feeling too. "I want this," he said. He cupped a hand against her flat stomach. "I want you. I want this baby. I want us." His throat worked as he swallowed. "Will you be my wife?"

Claudia threw back her head and laughed. "Only you would propose on the toilet."

Henry grinned and stood with her in his arms. He carried her from the bathroom. "If you want me to ask again, I'll do it from the bedroom. Just say yes." He swallowed roughly. "Please."

"Yes." Claudia wrapped her arms around him and held on tight.

"And remember, I like chocolate chip."

"What?" Claudia's fingers tightened in his hair.

He deposited her on the bed and leaned over her, grinning from ear to ear. "You're going to make me cookies, right?"

She laughed and pulled him on top of her. "Nope. You're going to be making the cookies." She rolled over and straddled him, pinning him to the bed. "And I like peanut butter."

Keep reading in the Aloha Series

Try Over

Acknowledgments

Thank you to all my readers who waited patiently for this book to be written.

Thank you to all the underdogs who inspire victory.

Thanks to my family, my beta readers, and my editors for their guidance and patience.

My editors are amazing! Thank you for saving me from all the embarrassing mistakes and for teaching me how to be a better writer!

About the Author

Jill Brashear is a hopeless romantic and author of swoon-worthy contemporary romances that will leave you breathless. With a pen in her hand and a heart full of love, Jill weaves tales of passion, longing, and happily-ever-afters that will make your heart skip a beat.

Also by Jill Brashear

Aloha Series

Try Easy

Try Me

Try Over

Blue Ridge Book Club Series

Love, Lacey Donovan

XOXO, Valentina

Blue Collar Crush

Sincerely, Thatcher Hayes

Standalones

Win, Lose, or Love

www.ingramcontent.com/pod-product-compliance
Lightning Source LLC
Chambersburg PA
CBHW061016120726
47910CB00006B/1967